INSPECTOR GHOTE GOES BY TRAIN

INSPECTOR GHOTE GOES BY TRAIN

H. R. F. Keating

CHIVERS
THORNDIKE

This Large Print book is published by BBC Audiobooks Ltd, Bath, England and by Thorndike Press®, Waterville, Maine, USA.

Published in 2005 in the U.K. by arrangement with the author.

Published in 2005 in the U.S. by arrangement with The Peters Fraser & Dunlop Group Ltd.

U.K. Hardcover ISBN 1–4056–3291–7 (Chivers Large Print)
U.K. Softcover ISBN 1–4056–3292–5 (Camden Large Print)
U.S. Softcover ISBN 0–7862–7609–6 (British Favorites)

The text of this Large Print edition is unabridged.
Other aspects of the book may vary from the original edition.

Set in 16 pt. New Times Roman.

Printed in Great Britain on acid-free paper.

British Library Cataloguing in Publication Data available

Library of Congress Cataloging-in-Publication Data

Keating , H. R. F. (Henry Reymond Fitzwalter), 1926–
    Inspector Ghote goes by train / by H.R.F. Keating.
       p.   cm.
    "Thorndike Press large print British favorites."—T.p. verso.
    ISBN 0–7862–7609–6 (lg. print : sc : alk. paper)
    1. Ghote, Ganesh (Fictitious character)—Fiction. 2. Police—India—Bombay—Fiction. 3. Bombay (India)—Fiction. 4. Large type books. I. Title.
    PR6061.E26I393 2005
    823'.914—dc22   2005003432

BEFORE

The two of them were both reading the same item in *The Times of India* at much the same time. But a distance of something like three miles separated the carefully locked and bolted luxury flat in the big, new, yellow-coloured block up on Cumballa Hill from the stuffy, dust-smelling, little cubby-hole of an office in Bombay CID Headquarters where Inspector Ganesh Ghote sat.

The small down-column item in the paper spread out in front of him on the scratched and ink-blotted surface of his old wooden-topped desk was to have considerably more effect on his future than he realised. It was, equally, to affect the future of the other reader. But at this moment it seemed to Ghote to be simply, but wonderfully, a landmark passed. His picture in the paper. In *The Times of India.*

Admittedly, it was not a very good picture. A grey featureless face stared straight forward above the open collar of a white shirt, a small whitish blob indicated the tip of the nose, a dark set line the mouth. But it was an achievement. It was public recognition.

Wild, totally unexpected notions suddenly entered his head and swept about there as if it was their familiar display-ground. This would

1

be only a beginning. Detectives in other countries were famous people. They were respectfully greeted in the public streets. In Europe—he had read this—they were like film stars. Ordinary people would go out of their way just to have darshan of them, to receive the influence coming from their persons. And in America there were books, whole books, about the careers of famous detectives.

He looked down at the black print in front of him, hardly seeing it but snuffing up its delightful savour.

BHATTACHARYA TO BE BROUGHT BACK
'A detective of the Bombay police is to bring A. K. Bhattacharya, alleged to have committed antiques frauds totalling Rs. 72.85 lakhs, from Calcutta where he was arrested yesterday. The officer, Inspector G. V. Ghote, of the Detection of Crime Branch, Bombay CID, leaves by the Calcutta Mail tonight.'

The actual words of the report, when they penetrated, brought him sharply down to earth.

Very well, he thought, perhaps this task is not as difficult as all that. All right, he had not made the actual arrest, and he had not had anything to do with the investigation itself. Well, it may have been just the chance effect of the work-roster that had dropped this duty

2

into his lap. But it was still an important matter. The Bhattacharya affair was, after all, the biggest fraud case Bombay CID had ever uncovered. It was being personally supervised by the Commissioner himself also. It was no job for just anybody to fetch that man back to stand trial. And the picture in the paper was of him. That proved it.

Although, he conceded with a further descent to reality, it would have been rather more use if they had printed not his own grey and smudgy photograph but a good clear one of A. K. Bhattacharya. That might have brought forward useful witnesses. But the legendary Bhattacharya, it was notorious from office talk, had always avoided the camera. No matter how much he had mingled with the rich Americans and Europeans who had been the victims of his gigantic swindles, bewitching them with his knowledge of India's past, the keen-witted Bengali had always avoided being photographed with them. No matter how western he had been with his Paris-made silk suits, his London-made shoes, his neckties specially bought for him in New York, he had never let himself be recorded on film.

But he had been very much part of that high-society scene. He had mingled with the wealthy art-lovers. He had made his contacts with the representatives of the big dealers and museums of the west. And he had sold them, under conditions of the most stringent secrecy, all those ingeniously faked temple statues, those 'two-thousand-year-old' images, those 'antique' stone friezes, supposedly abstracted from their sites and all ready to be smuggled out of India. He had done it magnificently. And he had done it for years.

But in the end—Ghote recalled the stories his colleagues on the case had told endlessly in the last few days, those still confidential details that would form the evidence at the trial—in the end the great Bhattacharya had been caught. He had met his match in an American who had turned out to be much more astutely tough than the legendary confidence-trickster's usual victims.

A. K. Bhattacharya had been caught, simply enough, with a cigar-lighter. It made a good tale. Of how the arch-trickster had fabricated one of his customary wax statues and had applied to it his special process that made it look and feel stony to the touch. The American, a Professor Frankenheimer, had been in the usual way shown the statue ready for crating in some dark backroom. But he had been more suspicious than he had allowed himself to appear. At some stage in the negotiations he had helped himself to a cigar. Just as he was about to light it he had held the flame from his big cigar-lighter right up close to the statue. And the age-old stone had sagged.

But A. K. Bhattacharya had run for it and

4

had, largely thanks to his care never to get photographed, very nearly got away. Only his description, meticulously given by Professor Frankenheimer, and relayed to the police all over India, had been recognised in Calcutta and an arrest had been made. Now, once Professor Frankenheimer, who was shortly due to pass through Calcutta, had formally confirmed the identification, it was simply a question of making sure A. K. Bhattacharya was brought safely back to Bombay and trial. Of course, with someone as sharp as the Bengali and with access, no doubt, to much illicitly-got money, the trial was by no means certain to be the end of the business. But that would be someone else's worry.

In the meantime his own concern was simple: to do his duty and bring back A. K. Bhattacharya.

He stopped here, a little awkwardly. His duty? Was he really doing it by going to Calcutta by train? He ought to have gone by air. His Deputy Superintendent, in giving him his orders, had taken it for granted that this would be the way he would travel. And when, thinking with yearning of the long, long cocooned train-journey, as well as just a little of the taut-stomached feeling the thought of flying brought on, he had asked if he could go instead by rail, D.S.P. Samant had not been exactly pleased. But after an agreement to sacrifice a day's leave to make up the working-

5

hours lost the D.S.P. had reluctantly agreed.

'If you want to be so generous with your own time, Inspector, it is not me who is going to stop you.'

And then, just as Ghote was leaving the office, he had thrown out a last warning.

'But do not think you can charge air-fare in expenses.'

'Oh, no, D.S.P. Certainly not, sir.'

So by the Calcutta Mail, leaving that evening, it was to be. He almost hugged himself with joy at the thought.

*   *   *

In the locked flat up on Cumballa Hill at about that moment the other reader of the down-column item in *The Times of India* was looking at Inspector Ghote's pale grey photograph with a tiny, irrepressible smile of amusement beginning to curl the corners of a wide, thin-lipped mouth. He fanned long fingers through his sweep of dramatic white hair and frowned thoughtfully for a moment.

Then A. K. Bhattacharya flashed a wide, white-teethed grin out in the direction of the big window of the flat's drawing-room looking over the wide and free expanse of the limitless sea and rose to his feet.

He called sharply to the one raggedly-dressed boy who was for the time being his only servant.

When the boy came in, A. K. Bhattacharya pulled a well-filled wallet from an inner pocket and selected two big hundred-rupee notes. He held them out towards the mop-headed brat.

'There are some things I want you to buy,' he said. 'First, some hair-dye. A bottle of the best you can get. And then sun-glasses, a good pair of sun-glasses. You are not to buy any bazaar trash, mind. Get Polaroid. Polaroid. You understand that?'

The boy stuffed the two broad notes carefully away inside his grubby khaki shorts while his employer stood contemplating himself in a full-length plate-glass mirror that formed the back of an alcove in the drawing-room. He saw a tall distinguished figure in a well-cut silk suit, which the flat's air-conditioning allowed him to wear despite the 90 degree temperature outside. The wide necktie was flamboyant, but still tasteful. The black shoes were of fine leather and elegantly pointed.

'And I shall need some clothes,' he said. 'A dhoti, a good one. White, of course. And a kurta—no, three kurtas. Now be careful not to go getting any European shirts. Good Indian kurtas are what I want. So off you go.'

And then, just as he was drawing back the heavy bolts on the flat's outer door, he added one more item.

'Sandals,' he said. 'I must also have sandals, the best you can buy.'

On time to the half-second that evening, the Calcutta Mail began pulling out of Victoria Terminus with Inspector Ghote ensconced in his seat in a four-berthed air-conditioned compartment. It was the start of what was to prove an altogether different journey from the one he had looked forward to that morning. At times it was to seem to him indeed like a malevolent waking nightmare. But it was also ultimately to vindicate the cast of mind he had preserved in himself all his life, the engrained outlook which, oddly, had been responsible in the first place for his choice of this mode of transport, a choice that more than once he was to curse himself for.

As the great train began slowly to move, Ghote leant back from the heavy faintly blued double glass of the window that had reduced to a murmur all the clamour of the busy station. He wriggled his shoulders into the comfortable back of his seat. For the next forty hours till they pulled into Howrah Station at Calcutta he would be detached from all responsibilities. Sitting here, cut off from all everyday cares, doing nothing beyond living out the railway life, he would nevertheless be proceeding with the task that had been assigned to him. He would be fetching back A. K. Bhattacharya from Calcutta, and all he had to do on the way was just travel.

Opposite him, as he turned from the window, the only other person in the compartment, an intense-looking kurta and dhoti-clad individual with sweeping black hair and dark-tinted glasses, who had entered a few moments after himself, leant abruptly forward.

'So,' he said, speaking noticeably English-style English, 'so we are to be travelling companions, my dear sir.'

CHAPTER ONE

THERE

Inspector Ghote sharply sized up the man who had addressed him so eagerly at the very start of his two-day journey. He had spoken in good English, probably polished up in the UK itself. So, coupled with the deep coffee, sepia colour of his skin and a certain fleshiness of face, it was pretty likely he was a Bengali travelling back to his own part of India.

And Bengali, Ghote thought with a sudden sinking, means talker among talkers.

He accepted a gritty lump of disappointment. It was not that he had expected on a train journey not to be talked to. He had been quite prepared to answer as often as necessary the customary questions about himself, his wife,

9

his children—a little struggle over admitting to having only one child at his age—and one or two matters more. But he had counted on not having to spend long as subject of such interrogations. He had counted on many happy hours, with the train huffily eating up the miles, during which he could meditate about himself and the responsibilities of his position, about his Protima and his little Ved, about his hopes and his actual tangible assets.

And now he was faced with a Bengali. Faced it was, precisely. The fellow had taken one of the three vacant seats that was exactly opposite him. True, the seat diagonally across had above it a white reservation-card marked out in elaborate very black handwriting as being kept for a 'Passenger Jabalpur-Calcutta' and Jabalpur was six hundred long miles away. But it was additionally upsetting that the stranger should be where he would fall under his gaze every time he chanced to look up.

Swiftly he completed the mental indexing that his profession caused him to make of any person he was confronted with. Age: sixty. No. Less, with all that luxuriant black hair. Caste: probably Brahmin, though he could catch no glimpse of black sacred thread under the fine white muslin kurta. Status: wealthy enough, despite the simple dhoti and kurta, otherwise he would not be travelling 'air-conditioned' class or have that look of assurance about him. Eyes: those sunglasses—wealthy man's

10

Polaroid again—unfortunately prevented a proper look at this tell-tale feature, but opportunity would come. Forehead: high. Nose: powerful and fleshy. Teeth: good, white and even, with perhaps a glint of gold at the back on the left-hand side.

'Yes,' he answered the poised, inquisitive face still leaning towards him. 'It would look as if we are to be travelling companions. Is it all the way to Calcutta you are going?'

'It is, it is,' the Bengali replied with relish. 'To Calcutta, that magnificent city, that appalling city. Is it not so, my dear sir, is it not so?'

'I do not know Calcutta,' Ghote replied shortly, hoping at least to stem some pouring-out of Bengali patriotism.

'My dear chap, you do not know Calcutta? Then it will be my great pleasure, to tell you something of that city. Did I say "tell you something"? No, my dear fellow, to tell you— though I suspect you are already stiffening yourself up against an outburst of Bengali patriotism—to tell you a very great deal about that appalling, and yet magnificent, and yet so magnificent, city.'

The long train crept at hardly more than trotting pace out of Bombay. Slowly it gathered speed as it moved on to the centre tracks past the frequent suburban stations, Masjid, Sandhurst Road High Level, Dockyard Road, Reay Road, Cotton Green. And all the while Ghote listened, endeavouring to display enthusiasm, to the complex hymn the Bengali produced to the virtues and vices (which were in a way virtues) of Calcutta, the city in which he himself would in two days' time spend a few brief hours while Professor Frankenheimer, that astute American, formally identified A. K. Bhattacharya and whence he would return with the legendary Bhattacharya firmly under his charge.

They ground past the old P and O Dockyard at Mazagaon. They passed, at a gathering tempo, the grain depot and the cotton depot, rows upon rows of tall, gaunt godowns and jutting, rusty cranes. And, with the wheels under them beginning now to click sharply over the rail joins, they went through the big blank of Sewri Cemetery—strange to put dead bodies in the earth like that, somehow making too much of them, insisting too much—and before very long they were up on Sion Causeway, running for miles above dark swampland. And then they were among the close cultivation and rich earth of Salsette Island.

'But enough of me,' said the white-teeth-grinning Bengali, though for the half-hour and more that he had been talking he had not once mentioned himself. 'Enough of me. Let us turn to you, my dear sir.'

At once Ghote realised he was going to be awkwardly caught. The questions this man

12

would ask would go far deeper, he knew by now, than mere natural curiosity about a fellow human-being. A person as sheerly overwhelming as this highly educated, forceful and quick Bengali would not be content with hearing just that his travelling companion was a police officer. He would want to know exactly what it was he was doing now, at this instant, in this train beginning to rattle and rock with self-importance as it moved quickly past the cotton mills of Kuria.

And any question about his actual mission would be difficult to answer. To say straight out that he was the Inspector G. V. Ghote whose photograph had been printed in that morning's *Times of India* as the man entrusted with the task of fetching back to Bombay the notorious A. K. Bhattacharya, daring confidence-trickster due to face charges to the extraordinary amount of Rs. 72.85 lakhs, this would be claiming for himself an importance that the simple facts of his journey did not justify. And, once the nature of his journey was admitted, the probing man opposite would want to know a hundred and one details that it was a matter of plain duty not to reveal. What precise charges the police hoped to bring, the exact nature of the evidence they had, how precisely the great confidence-trickster had been caught at last—all these were things he knew and had to keep secret. Yet give the incessantly talkative Bengali half an

13

opportunity and the nature of his profession would be bound to come out and then all those secrets would be at stake. No, he must try not to give anything away.

'But you,' he broke in quickly. 'You, sir, have not told about yourself. Why, I do not know your name even.'

'I, my dear sir? I am a totally unimportant person. But you. Do you know, I sense that you are not altogether an unimportant person. I see you, I do not quite know why, as a man on a mission. An important mission. Tell me, my dear sir, what is your name?'

Ghote knew himself: he knew that he lacked simply the bold cheek to ignore such a question in the way that the Bengali had ignored his question when he had put it to him. So he snatched at the first way out that entered his head and swung away to the blued glass of the window.

'Excuse me,' he said, 'is that embankment we are able to see now Vehar Lake?'

'It is,' the Bengali replied, giving a cursory glance across some jungly terrain to the distant line of the long reservoir bank. 'Vehar Lake, haunt of the notorious crocodiles.'

He dropped back his head, with its fan of black hair that looked somehow a little too young for his face, against the seat and let his eyelids droop behind his Polaroid sun-glasses.

Ghote breathed a sigh of relief. One crisis appeared to be past. He must, though, think quickly of some new subject of conversation so as to forestall any more questioning.

The slightly fleshy face opposite him jerked abruptly forward and the half-hidden eyes clicked fully open.

'But I am surprised, my dear sir, that you did not know the famous Vehar Lake. Can I be right in supposing you have never left Bombay by rail on this line?'

Ghote for a moment contemplated brazening out the lie, although from the days when he had been at police college this had been a route he had quite frequently travelled by. As quickly, he rejected the lie. That way lay a mounting heap of falsehoods and an inevitable betraying descent into reality.

'Oh yes,' he answered. 'I have been out this way ever since I was at— I have often really been out this way, but not recently. I was not quite certain whether that was Vehar Lake.'

'You may rest assured it was,' the Bengali replied, with a great flash of long teeth.

He regarded Ghote closely for a few instants.

'And it is a sight, you tell me, that you have not seen for some time. Now, this begins to give me a clue about yourself, my dear sir.'

He raised a long-fingered, deprecating Bengali hand.

'I beg you one thing now. Tell me nothing, absolutely nothing about who you are or what it is you do.'

He seemed to be seeking a definite assurance on the point. After a short silence Ghote stifled his misgivings.

'Yes,' he said. 'If you want, I would say nothing at all of myself.'

The Bengali rubbed his hands together with dry-rustling eagerness.

'Excellent. Excellent. This is excellent. Now we shall have some sport.'

He glanced at the expensive watch worn on the soft inner side of his left wrist.

'Let me see. In just fifteen minutes we should cross the creek at Thana. I venture to wager, my dear sir, that by that time I shall have guessed your exact occupation. How about that? Is it a bet? Yes or no?'

Ghote made no reply.

'Come, my dear fellow, a sporting wager between gentlemen. I guess by Thana Creek, or I cease to plague you with that talkativeness we Bengalis are so ridiculed for. Is it a bet, yes or no?'

Unable to see how he could refuse, though prey to undefined doubts, Ghote cautiously assented.

The Bengali clasped his hands together in front of himself in a positive ecstasy of enjoyment. His body swayed slightly from side to side with a little rocking motion from the hips as if he was a wrestler searching for a vantage. Then he pounced.

'A job that keeps a man in the city,' he said.

'Keeps him there day after day, week after week, month after month. Not then a very pleasant job?'

An inclination of the head conveyed the question.

Ghote sat stock still.

'Ah ha,' said the Bengali delightedly. 'You are not going to be an easy man to crack. Something of the poker player there. I would say you were a professional gambler—only, no, I can tell at once you are altogether a more serious person than that.'

Ghote could not help feeling a small upswelling of pleasure at this last remark. Sharply he forced away the smile he feared had lifted the corners of his mouth.

The Bengali leant back in his seat.

'Well, of course, in a big city like Bombay there are thousands and thousands of different jobs that keep a man from travelling about. There are mill workers, there are clerks, there are . . .'

He paused searching.

'There are postmen?'

Ghote kept his face utterly impassive. The Bengali smiled again with wide, white, flashing teeth.

'But, of course, that is ridiculous,' he said. 'A postman could never travel air-conditioned class. Not even if his fare were paid out of public funds.'

Furiously Ghote wondered whether he had

17

by some small flick of the eyes given something away there. And shamefacedly he admitted to himself that he probably had.

'Yes,' said the Bengali, confirming at once his fears, 'let us assume for the sake of argument that you are travelling, my dear sir, at the public expense. So what to do?'

He paused a long moment, apparently deeply puzzled. Then light came.

'Ah, I have it. We must add that this travelling is something you do not find yourself doing very regularly. No, you have in principle a job that ties you down to the city. But now you are travelling. That is the line we must pursue.'

Sitting bolt-upright, trying to preserve a front of the utmost immobility, Ghote found that, behind rigid face muscles, his own mind had begun to work busily. And it was working in sympathy with the Bengali. He was every bit as busy as the latter trying to solve his own riddle.

He brought himself down to earth with a sharp jerk.

He was Ganesh Ghote, and doing no more than going to Calcutta to bring back a prisoner, one A. K. Bhattacharya, whom he was determined not to discuss. So it was his simple duty to sit there and keep his mouth shut. Let the man rant.

And, as the train clicked and clacked past the deserted, sun-baked fields over which before long night would fall, drawing towards Thane, rant the man did. He suggested innumerable jobs that Ghote might hold, all of them well wide of the mark. For a good long time Ghote let the performance go on. But then he noticed an element of the ridiculous creeping into the suggested occupations which the Bengali was pouring out with a fluency that despite everything captured his unwilling admiration.

At the start this fancifulness simply was amusing, though Ghote determined not to let himself be seen to be amused. But, after all, there was something pleasingly comical in the concept of his being employed as 'a cricket and part-time racing commentator'. Then, as the suggested vocations became more and more absurd, Ghote found they were no longer quite so amusing. Did the fellow really think he could be 'a court pornographer to a maharajah off to obtain the latest information from that sink of iniquity, Calcutta'?

He frowned sharply, and at once the Bengali pounced.

'But, my dear sir, I fear I have offended you. And, to tell you the truth, I fear I have been allowing my mind to wander somewhat from the strict path of my objective.'

He glanced out of the window through which the outskirts of Thana town, just beyond which lay the creek, were now visible.

'And we are nearly at our finishing-post

already,' he said. 'Dear me, it looks as if I have lost my wager and will have to go the whole length of the journey without allowing myself to put to you all those questions I feel pressing up within me.'

He sighed heavily and appeared, indeed, to be totally dejected by his lack of success. His head sank back on to the seat and he ceased completely to talk. The train passed, without stopping, through Thana Station, its long cement platform almost deserted, the trucks in its goods yard empty and silent. The bridge over the creek loomed ahead. Ghote, against his better judgment, began to hope.

'Got it,' said the Bengali, without moving his flung-back head with its great halo of over-black hair.

'Yes?' said Ghote, feeling already a rushing back of misery.

He turned quickly to the window to check whether they had arrived at the bridge. The Bengali spoke with slow dreaminess.

'A job that keeps a man in the city year in, year out. And which yet allows him suddenly to make a long journey by train, air-conditioned class, at the public expense. Only one answer.'

Were they fully on the bridge? It was not easy to decide. On the whole, not.

'A police officer. A police officer. Have I got it, my dear sir?'

'You have,' said Ghote.

20

     *   *   *

Victory however seemed to satiate the Bengali. He did not pursue, as Ghote had feared, all the implications of what a police officer sitting here at this time in the Calcutta Mail must be doing. Instead he took from a suitcase, oldish but of first-quality leather, in the rack above him a large and heavy-looking book. Giving Ghote a quick, teeth-flashing smile of apology he plunged into its pages. Ghote wondered what the volume's title might be, but it was impossible to see. He found too that he was irritated by the way his companion did not take off his expensive-looking Polaroid sunglasses. Surely they must make seeing the words on those creamy pages very difficult? What a ridiculous parade.

He fumed with irritation over it all the way to the junction at Kalyan where the train began the steep haul up the Western Ghats, its powerful diesel locomotive seeming to growl ever more fiercely with the effort of the climb.

Ghote tried peering out of the window here to catch glimpses of the dramatic landscape he knew from the times he had made this journey on his way to and from the police college at Nasik. But the lid of darkness had already rapidly fallen, and all that he could see in the window was the straining reflection of his own face. It looked worried.

Hardly, he reflected, the carefree figure he had envisaged making this holiday-like journey in so much greater comfort than when he used to travel to Nasik. His thoughts turned sharply to the Bengali again.

What would such a man be reading? And who was he also?

The fellow had guessed his own occupation, and might very well have guessed what his task was too. It was quite possible he had seen *The Times of India* and would put two and two together.

An uneasy thought sprang up. Could his questioner have actually remembered the photograph all along and have been playing with him over this business of guessing his job? He put the notion out of his mind. The photograph had not been so striking after all, and in any case why should a perfectly innocent traveller want to play such a game?

But what was the man reading? He slowly tilted himself forward to see if he could make out the thick book's title which appeared to be printed in tiny capitals across the head of every left-hand page.

Without looking up, the Bengali quietly placed a long finger over the tantalising little capitals.

He had delib—

Crossly Ghote shook himself. He was allowing the man to get on his nerves, causing himself to indulge in all sorts of ridiculous fantasies. After all the fellow was no more than a chance encounter in a railway train.

They wound their way laboriously on up the mountains, swaying across viaduct after viaduct, just visible in the light of the train's own windows, and plunging into the blacker darkness of frequent tunnels. The Bengali sat all the while quietly absorbed in his heavy tome and with that long finger always remorselessly blotting out the titles. And Ghote sat, back straight against his seat, and stared in front of him.

At last they came to Igatpuri at the head of the pass where their diesel engine was due to be replaced by the steam locomotive that would take them almost all the way across the enormous breadth of India to within a short distance of Calcutta and its electric rail network. There was a great deal of loud clanging and distant shouts in the night when they came to a halt. Ghote pressed his nose against the cool glass of the window and peered hopefully out.

'All the same,' a voice said behind him, speaking that infuriating English-style English, 'I wonder you do not go by air when you are travelling at the public expense.'

Ghote felt as if the muzzle of a pistol had been placed firmly and quietly in the small of his back. He did not take his face away from the glass of the window.

'It happens to be the case that I am going by

train,' he said.

'Well, you know, my dear chap, I find that rather extraordinary. Here you are, a police officer on a mission of public importance, and you have got time to travel in this ridiculously old-fashioned way. Do you know how quick it is to go from Bombay to Calcutta by air?'

Ghote reluctantly flopped back in his seat so that he was again facing his tormentor. A glint of anger flared up in him.

'But you also,' he exploded, 'why are you not flying?'

'And not only is the air journey so much quicker,' the Bengali said, taking no notice whatsoever of the interruption, 'but it also leaves one feeling a great deal fresher on arrival. Surely, my dear chap, you must know that two long nights in a train, even air-conditioned, is not exactly a recipe for making you feel alert at the end of the journey?'

'But air travel also has its disadvantages,' Ghote countered. 'Frequently air passengers are sick.'

The Bengali let the thrust glance off his armoured hide.

'Yes and you will need all your wits about you when you arrive in Calcutta,' he said. 'You are going to fetch that terrible fellow A. K. Bhattacharya, are you not?'

Ghote moved his head in sad confirmation. Now, he thought, the real probing will begin.

'I read about the arrest and the case,' the

Bengali went on happily. 'Most commendable. But let me tell you, from all that I know of your Bhattacharya, he is not going to be an easy bird to cage. Dear me, no. So a tired and travel-worn police inspector . . .'

The Bengali wagged his head sadly. Ghote was about to ask pretty sharply how exactly he knew that he himself was of inspector rank—could the fellow have recognised that photograph?—when the Bengali smiled his white-teethed smile again.

'I take it you are an inspector of police, my dear sir? I have hit on the right rank, I hope. It would seem appropriate to the task you have.'

'Yes,' said Ghote. 'I am inspector.'

'Good, good. And now this question of flying. It cannot be, of course, that you are frightened of entering an aeroplane? I do not question our policemen are more redoubtable than that.'

'It is a matter of preferring train only,' Ghote said.

'Preferring it? I almost think an unadventurous policeman is worse than one who is scared.'

'No, no. Not at all. It is nothing like that.'

Ghote knew he was stammering. He pulled himself together.

'I will tell you what it is,' he said with some force. 'It is this business of rushing everywhere at top speed. That is wrong.'

'Wrong? My dear fellow, what nonsense.

25

What nonsense, if you will forgive the blunt and terse speech of an older man. To get from place to place in this great country of ours that extends from the Arabian Sea in the west to the Bay of Bengal in the east, from the lofty Himalayas in the north to the boundless Indian Ocean in the south, to be able to go from place to place in all this immensity within a matter of hours. How can you say that that is wrong?'

Ghote felt unhappy. He knew within himself that there was something wrong about air travel. After all had he not sacrificed a whole day of free time to travel by train because of this feeling? Had he not sacrificed too a certain real excitement at the prospect of flying, a real excitement despite that stomach-tautening at the thought? But for the life of him he could not exactly put this feeling that something was wrong into words.

And another thing worried him a little too. The Bengali had spoken of himself authoritatively as an older man, but he did not appear to be all that much more than his own age. How did it come about that the fellow successfully assumed such airs?

But this was a puzzle to be postponed. Getting clear his feelings about flying was what had to be done here and now.

'In many cases,' he offered tentatively, 'it is not at all necessary to accomplish a journey in such a short time.'

The Bengali waved this away with a generously sweeping gesture of his long-fingered right hand.

'Perhaps, perhaps . . . But, my dear sir, consider this. To fly is an adventure. It is to defy the elements. But to go by train is to plod. I tell you, my dear fellow, there is really only one place to be on a train.'

He leant forward, poised, teasing Ghote to guess where.

'Where is that?' Ghote asked, seeing no decent way of avoiding the question.

'In the cab, my dear sir. In the engine-driver's cab.'

'Well,' said Ghote, after a moment's reflection, 'we cannot all be travelling there.'

'No, my dear sir, we cannot,' said the unabashed Bengali. 'But what we can do is better than that: we can fly. Fly, my dear sir, think of that. Conquer gravity. Assert our independence. Look down from above. My dear sir, I have said that our country is immense. But, you know, we poor mortals can now truly experience that whole immensity. By seeing it from a vast height. By climbing higher than Kanchenjunga itself. By the marvellous power of the aeroplane.'

He paused, both hands held high, fingers spread, in a pose of dramatic praise. Ghote longed to jab sharply out at him the words 'But why are you in train now?' But too quickly the Bengali brought both hands crashing down on

27

to his knees and shot out a query of his own.

'All that, and you wish to creep along by train. My dear sir, why?'

And it stung.

'No, no,' Ghote retorted. 'That is what is wrong. I tell you it is wrong. Wrong to go so high, wrong to like to see so much, wrong to feel it is important to go so quickly. Wrong, wrong.'

His voice had risen excessively, far louder than necessary to speak above the sounds of the now slowly re-starting train. He knew it had. But he had been unable to stop himself.

'My dear fellow,' the Bengali said, stretching himself back luxuriously in his seat, 'you cannot be meaning to tell me that you equate the simple act of travelling by air with the presumption of Icarus?'

Ghote did not know who this Icarus was, or why he had shown presumption. He glared at the Bengali mutinously.

And in the very act of doing so he realised something about the man that had nagged obscurely at him ever since the first moment the fellow had leant forward and spoken to him. His hair. Of course it was somehow too young for that face. It had been dyed.

CHAPTER TWO

Of course, Ghote said to himself, as he in his turn leant back against the cool comfort of his seat, of course hair-dye manufacture is a considerable industry. But nevertheless this fellow is not really one of those people you would expect to conceal the marks of age. He appears altogether too confident. But undoubtedly his hair is dyed. And that accounts most certainly for the way he called himself 'an older man'. So, after all, the fellow is not what he seems.

Into his mind there came then one of the many pithy remarks he had stored away from that talismanic work of reference which stood always on top of its bamboo set of shelves in his little office in Bombay CID Headquarters, Dr Hans Gross's *Criminal Investigation.* 'Everything which appears unnatural,' the good doctor had written many years ago, 'should be considered as suspicious and unauthentic.' Well, that hair certainly appeared unnatural.

Yet, Ghote was constrained to admit, although to think of the Bengali as unauthentic was correct enough, there was really no reason to label him suspicious. He was, after all, just a traveller to Calcutta. No more than that.

Still he did have dyed hair. Ghote allowed himself a small smile of triumph.

'Well, sir,' he said, 'I can see that this question of flying is a matter we shall have to differ.'

His new-found spurt of strength was to escape for some time being put to the test of the Bengali's powerful personality. The compartment door was noisily drawn back at that moment and an attendant presented himself in the doorway with a fat, white bundle of bedding clasped in his arms. In all the following bother of folding down bunks and making up beds—and the attendant doggedly prepared places for four sleeping passengers in spite of the fact that one seat in the compartment was allocated to the unknown 'Passenger Jabalpur-Calcutta' and that Jabalpur would not be reached till after midday tomorrow—Ghote was able to retain his sense of quiet superiority.

Only in one thing was he defeated. There came a moment when he thought he was going to be able to see the title on the cover of the Bengali's book. It had been lying face down with its spine pointing away, and the attendant picked it up respectfully intending to place it on a little net shelf which a thoughtful railway company provided for just such a purpose. As he did so Ghote craned forward to get a better look. And the Bengali's long-fingered hand swooped, took the thick volume out of the attendant's grasp and replaced it in his fine-leather suitcase on the rack above him.

It might have been chance, Ghote told himself. It was really most likely that it was chance.

As soon as the beds are ready, he thought, I will get into mine even though I am not at all sleepy and then at last I shall be able to enjoy my journey as I should.

The attendant gave a final pat to the Bengali's flattish pillow, salaamed to them both and left.

'They always make up the beds too damnably early in these trains,' the Bengali said as the door thumped closed. 'A man does not want to crawl between the sheets before midnight like a schoolboy.'

'No,' Ghote agreed.

At once he wished he had not. But the truth had simply come out, and had in one unreflecting syllable condemned him to heavily one-sided conversation at least until the train made its first proper stop, at Manmad some time around a quarter to one.

Abruptly he determined to make a fight for it. After all, there were other things a man could do at the end of the day than just sit gossiping. If the Bengali had a book, so had he. One he had bought for himself, with a secret tickling of pleasure at the small unwarranted expenditure, at a secondhand bookstall near V.T. Station. It was not exactly a heavy tome of the sort the Bengali was reading, but it was a book and he had a right to enjoy it.

He produced it, with a certain amount of contrived display *The D.A. Breaks An Egg* by Erle Stanley Gardner. Well, when he had the chance, and it was not very often, he liked to read something about crime in which he could be sure the forces of law and order would come out shining clear on top. Mr Stanley Gardner's D.A. and his Perry Mason had been favourites of his when he was a young man: it was years since he had had the chance of reading one of their cases.

He sat on the made-up lower bunk and bent his head to the task.

'You know,' said the Bengali, leaning forward and shamelessly peering at the book, 'I find that sort of literature infinitely depressing. Crime, murder. Why should anybody want to spend time reading about such sordid things?'

Ghote felt he could hardly tell the fellow that for him an Erle Stanley Gardner book was not at all sordid, that it was on the contrary a world away from the slimed-over affairs he had to deal with as his daily duty, the beatings-up, the extortion, the protection rackets, the deaths. Instead he launched into another attack.

'But what is it you yourself read instead?' he asked.

'Yes,' said the Bengali, 'I know you are a policeman, my dear sir, my dear Inspector. But nevertheless I feel bound to tell you, as a friend, that I find your occupation unpleasant.'

'Unpleasant perhaps,' Ghote bridled. 'But necessary.'

The shot appeared to have gone home.

'As to that, my dear sir,' the Bengali began, a little hesitatingly.

And then something seemed to catch his eye. He looked out beyond Ghote at the night. Ghote swivelled round and looked through the window in his turn. The train had slowed and they were passing cautiously through a town. Its railway station was even now sliding past them, occasional dim lamps making it plain in the darkness.

He wondered where it was. And then one of the station name-boards, well lit by a lamp, swum momentarily into his full view. GHOTI. He knew the place well. The similarity to his own name had been the subject of jokes with his fellow-trainees at Nasik.

But why had the Bengali seemed so transfixed by the sight of the station? Could it be, after all, that he had even known his own name from the start? The fellow had admitted, more or less, to knowing that A. K. Bhattacharya was to be fetched from Calcutta. Had he in fact read that newspaper story with care and concentration?

Ghote, still appearing to be looking

33

innocently out of the window, contrived a sideways flick of a glance across the compartment.

The fellow did seem to be looking at him with an air of amusement. Damn him. Damn him.

He bounced round in his seat ready to resort to some plain speaking. And it appeared he had disconcerted the Bengali. Because, altogether too abruptly, the fellow rose from the lower bunk and pretended to be groping among his possessions for something he wanted. Eventually he swung down the old suitcase into which he had plunged his mysterious book, dropped it on to the bunk beside him and made as though he were rummaging among its contents.

Ghote sat still, determined to wait till the fellow had to turn round and then to ask some sharp questions.

And that would not be long now. Slowly the Bengali was closing the case—he had got out the book again, its title still not visible— and slowly he was straightening up. In a moment—

But then Ghote saw something that quite sent his determination spinning from his mind. On the case, faintly stamped in the old fine-quality leather, was a set of black-printed initials. They had almost faded away altogether with time. But, with that last careless movement the Bengali had put the case where the light fell sharply on the letters. And they were precisely the initials that had been in and out of Ghote's thoughts ever since he had been given this particular mission. They were the letters A.K.B.

Ghote felt as if a great split had opened in the middle of his head. Was this Bengali A. K. Bhattacharya? He could not be: A. K. Bhattacharya was in Dum-Dum Gaol, Calcutta, awaiting transfer under his custody to Bombay.

The man opposite—Who was he? He had not even yet given him his name—sat down comfortably again on the made-up bunk beside his old but good-quality suitcase. He was holding the heavy book, still with its title obscured.

'Well, my dear sir,' he said, 'what was it we were talking about? You know, I can remember it as being a most interesting conversation, and then suddenly I was distracted. To tell you the truth, my eye caught the name of the station we have just passed through, and it brought back such vivid memories to me that I quite lost track of what I was saying.'

'Vivid memories?'

All Ghote could do was stupidly to put that query.

'Vivid, did I say? My dear sir, in truth my memories of that little place we have just passed through are the very opposite of vivid. I

35

found myself there once, some time ago now. I had business in the neighbourhood, you know—my business takes me to some very out-of-the-way spots at times—and I had to spend several days there. My dear sir, those were the dullest days I think I have ever spent in my life.'

Ghote, by now, had begun to get his mind into order. Plainly the whole business of the initials was some trick of an over-active fancy. But he was still a good deal too upset to take a very rational part in the conversation. All that he could rise to was an automatic opposition to whatever this fellow was saying to him.

'Life in small towns is not dull,' he stated. 'In small towns and in villages life is lived as it ought to be.'

'My dear fellow, let me assure you that small-town life is dull. I was bored almost to death in Ghoti. What a terrible fate. Imagine it. Worse, far, than being trampled to death by elephants as criminals were in the good old days. Oh, impossible. Impossible. Small towns, my dear Inspector.'

'I was born in a small town, perhaps much like that place,' Ghote said, declining to pronounce the syllables.

'You were? And you have taken my passing remarks as a personal attack? My dear chap, I cannot too sufficiently apologise. And then to you, with your name, Ghote and Ghoti, will have felt it as an added insult. It was careless of me, damnably careless. Once again I apologise, unreservedly.'

So the fellow had all along known his name. Ghote was unable to tell because of the never-removed dark glasses whether the genuine-sounding apology he was being offered was sincere or not. But he felt that hardly mattered. What counted was that this man had recognised him from the very start and had played on him a trick that he had spun out and out for a whole long evening. He was more now than a mere talkative fellow-traveller, not too concerned if he made himself look cleverer than a chance acquaintance: he was now a person capable of spite.

Ghote noted it. And the man was still going on. He paid him sharp attention.

'My dear fellow, I repeat I can well appreciate how you must feel. One's name is a very personal thing. I know that. I feel it acutely myself. My own name happens to be Banerjee, an abnormally common name in Bengal, as you must know, my dear Inspector. An abnormally common name. And yet every Banerjee who gets into trouble seems to hit at me. To hit at me here, in the heart.'

His clenched right fist smote his breast with a dramatic gesture.

'How was it that you knew my name?' Ghote broke in, tipping a cold clear bucketful of dousing water on all the fervid intensity that Mr Banerjee—so that was his name—had created. 'How did you know?'

The tall Bengali sat hastily back in his seat on the bunk opposite. But he recovered swiftly enough.

'Ah, your name? How did I happen to know that? My dear Inspector, ridiculously simple. Ridiculously. It was in the paper. Did you not know? You see, you have become somewhat of a figure of fame. The start only of a brilliant career, I have no doubt. But there it was this morning for all to read in *The Times of India*, your name. How could I not know it, especially as it was accompanied by a photograph? Not, I feel bound to say, a very flattering photograph, but recognisable, recognisable.'

'It would have been better if there had been a picture of the criminal I am going to fetch,' Ghote declared, unmoved. 'But the fellow successfully avoided the camera during his whole career of crime.'

'Indeed? Indeed? Now that really is most interesting,' Mr Banerjee said, removing his Polaroid spectacles and waving them in the air to emphasise his point. 'A little piece of what they call inside information. My dear Inspector, I am most grateful, really.'

He folded the precision-made Polaroid glasses with a neat little click and attempted to slip them into a pocket on the front of his kurta in about the position where the breast-pocket of a suit would come. Finding, after an unseeing rub or two, that there was in fact nowhere to put the spectacles, he looked round for a moment and then dabbed them carelessly down on the thick white counterpane of the bunk beside him.

Ghote went back to the adventures of the D.A. This was his time for enjoying himself, his forty hours marvellously lifted out of the banging routine of life, and he was going to enjoy himself. Why shouldn't he spend his time reading about such people as the D.A. or Perry Mason and his Della Street, blonde, cool and untarnishable?

But all too soon his eyes ceased even to attempt to trace their way along the smudgily printed lines. His gaze, which had flicked obsessively three, four and five times across to that old but excellent-quality suitcase lying carelessly on the white bunk opposite and had seen each time, as if carved in fire, the almost obliterated letters 'A.K.B.' finally came frankly to rest upon them.

They were there. There could be no doubt about that. They were a fact. Something you could get hold of, not any airy-fairy imaginings.

Of course the fellow had said, eventually, that his name was Banerjee. So the 'B' was properly accounted for. Yet A.K.B. was precisely the combination of letters that had been a sort of heading in his own mind for his task. Could it be—but the combination of forenames beginning with A and K must, after all be pretty common.

'. . . of forenames beginning with A and K is, after all, pretty common in Bengal.'

He look up, startled. The Bengali, Mr Banerjee, was talking to him again.

'You do not agree, my dear sir?'

Ghote blinked.

'That the initials . . .' he offered tentatively.

'That the initials A.K.B. are an extremely common combination, as it happens, in Bengal. But I agree it is odd nevertheless that they should be mine as well as those of the person with whose fate you have become so inextricably tangled.'

'Not at all,' Ghote answered sharply, coming planing back to reality like a settling bird. 'My fate has not, as you say, become tangled with that of A. K. Bhattacharya. Such is a most extremely fanciful way of talking. I am taking him back to Bombay only.'

'Oh, yes, my dear chap, I forgot. You are taking A. K. Bhattacharya back to Bombay only. You must forgive me if I allowed my imagination to run away with me. I am afraid it is somewhat of a failing among us Bengalis.'

Ghote did not want to hear any more about the failings, which were always virtues, of Bengalis. He held up *The D.A. Breaks An Egg* smack in front of his face and began reading again. It was not quite where he had left off, but he would not trust himself if he had to look for the exact works he had last read. Those light-catching black initials on the worn leather case had not really been exorcised.

A period of silence followed. But it did not last long.

'I see we are coming into Nasik Road Station.'

Ghote looked up and out of the window. It was difficult to make out much in the darkness, just a few dim lights in irregular patterns.

It was a long time since he had been at Nasik itself, five miles away along a rackety tramway. His training days, when everything had been in the future and hopes of he knew not what had filled him like great bright balloons, seemed far, far away now. His life today was so real in comparison with that time that it might have been two different people experiencing the two periods. There were no bright balloons now, none.

He thought for a few seconds sombrely about the fading of once-bannered ideals. Perhaps they had to go, but it seemed wrong.

Then he pulled himself together: the few tiny pebbles in his horizon that did have colour today were infinitely more worth cherishing for being hard and real than all the balloons of the past. And this was so even though at times such pebbles were almost hidden by the dozens of real and hard, dull and cutting-edged stones surrounding them.

Suddenly he recognised out in the darkness the curious shape of the motor-ramp at the station, and for an instant he was once again the old self he had been, the tensely keen youngster, almost trembling perpetually in his determination to do the right thing. What would that young man have said about the figure sitting, in such comfort, such luxury, here, the man who had more than once slipped off a little from the exacting demands of the right thing?

'I used to know Nasik well when I was a little younger,' Mr Banerjee said suddenly.

'Yes?' Ghote answered, forgetting to keep his gaze turned well away from the talkative Bengali.

'Yes, indeed, I have spent many happy hours here. Both then, and indeed more recently.'

'The golf-course is highly recommended,' Ghote said, fishing blatantly.

Mr Banerjee raised both hands in mock horror, with the long fingers outspread like stars.

'My dear sir, I hope you do not think I am the sort of person who indulges in that wretched game. I'm not one of your "Ye maun have a heid" men.'

'Excuse me?' said Ghote.

'Your "Ye maun have a heid" men. You are unacquainted with the story?'

'Yes,' said Ghote.

'Well, this was said by a caddy at St Andrews, or some such place, to a professor at the university to whom he was teaching the game. "As lang as ye are learning lads at college it's easy warrk, but when ye come to play golf ye maun have a heid".'

Ghote laughed. He had not really meant to. But he found the story funny. And besides he was pleased with himself for following the Scottish accent.

'It is not so very amusing,' Mr Banerjee said crossly. 'I was saying golf is a much over-rated pastime.'

Ghote sobered himself up a little.

'So what was your reason for being at Nasik?' he asked with a new touch of authority.

Mr Banerjee did not reply for a moment. And when he did speak it was with a bravado that he had not shown before.

'I was interested in the antiquities of the area,' he said.

And after that for a long time he was silent. They left the few lights of Nasik Road Station behind them and ploughed on in the darkness, climbing still, steadily upwards though mounting by no means as quickly as when they had ascended the Ghats between Kalyan and Igatpuri. There were picturesque ruined hill-forts to be seen hereabouts, Ghote knew, but nothing was visible outside the windows of the great, snorting, lighted train. Perhaps these ruins were the antiquities Mr Banerjee had been interested in. Only why did he have to have as a hobby precisely the same interest that had formed the necessary groundwork of that other A.K.B.'s profession? Damn him.

He tried to involve himself again in Erle Stanley Gardner. Only from time to time did he slip the most cautious of flicked glances across at Mr Banerjee, who had taken up his own book—so weighty and learned-looking in contrast to the paperback—and was reading it with an air of calm efficiency. One long finger still blotted out totally the little capital letters spelling the title across the top of each left-hand page.

And at last, when it had well gone midnight and they were due quite shortly to make their first proper stop at Manmad, Ghote did manage really to get absorbed in the puzzle the D.A. was coping with so crisply. Ah, to be a man to whom life never presented problems that could not be pretty soon dealt with by the use of a little easy authority.

Mr Banerjee's long fingers descended abruptly on Erle Stanley Garter's open page and tapped it imperiously. Startled, Ghote looked up. The tall Bengali had put down his own book, outside titles still invisible, and was looking at him with a slight smile.

'We were talking of the antiquities of Nasik,' he said. 'There are, of course, some notably fine things there, as indeed there must be in a city that has been a holy place since before recorded history. With so many temples, and many of them of great age, you would expect to find works of considerable interest by the hundred.'

And, as he continued ladling out archaeological history, Ghote found to his growing consternation that, as far as he could recollect from talk he had heard and half-heard in the office and in the canteen, every single one of the antiquities Mr Banerjee spoke of also featured in the charges which those working on the A. K. Bhattacharya case were striving, with considerable difficulty, to formulate. How could it happen that this A.K.B. too had been connected with precisely those places where A. K. Bhattacharya must have spent long periods acquiring detailed knowledge of the antiquities he was later to forge? Were there two master tricksters? No, that was nonsense.

Almost as fantastic as saying that A. K. Bhattacharya was not lodged in Dum-Dum Gaol at all but was sitting here at this moment in what seemed to be a solid railway-carriage compartment.

'But, of course,' Mr Banerjee was saying, his flashing smile back in full flaunt now, 'of course one must not forget that Nasik has other places of interest in these modern times. There is a police training-college there, I believe.'

'I attended that institution,' Ghote declared.

'Did you, indeed, my dear Inspector? And no doubt you were most excellently taught

45

there. Sharpness of apprehension, the inability to be deceived, unfailing observation. All those qualities instilled into you. Never afterwards lost. I envy you. By God, how I envy you.'

'I have always found the instruction I received most helpful,' Ghote answered.

'You know I wish I had had the pleasure of receiving such instruction myself,' Mr Banerjee said. 'A really well-trained faculty of observation would have been of the utmost use to me.'

He left the thought dangling. And Ghote, knowing it would be better to leave it to hang, asked the question Mr Banerjee so clearly wanted.

'And why would training in observation be of particular use to you, sir?'

'Oh, it is just a small hobby I have. I very much enjoy going about the country when I can and finding for myself works of sculpture that have hitherto not been appreciated. In all this great country of ours with its thousands and thousands of temples, some huge, some tiny, there are many, many objects of the utmost beauty and rarity which have never yet been recorded. It is my pleasure—and I feel it even my duty—to find such of these as I can and to record them as meticulously as possible.'

'Oh, yes,' said Ghote.

'Yes. My pleasure and my duty. Of course the camera does a lot of my work for me. But, as you will appreciate, my dear Inspector, some of the places where I discover rarities are by no means well-lit. And one cannot always import lighting equipment into sacred edifices, while of course often they are extremely remotely situated, far from any source of electric power. It is there that I could wish I had your trained faculty of observation.'

'I can see that such training would be most useful in the circumstances,' Ghote replied.

He found his mind was racing. Could the man really be saying what he seemed to be saying? It was as if he were deliberately describing the sort of procedures which that other A.K.B. must have gone through. The unrecorded temple statues that it would be so much easier to copy and sell rather than attempting to steal and sell. The remoteness of the sort of places it would be most profitable to do such work in. It all fitted.

But A. K. Bhattacharya was in Dum-Dum Gaol. And even if he had not been, it would be the wildest fantasy to think that he should be sitting here.

He felt intolerably oppressed for all the steady coolness of the expensive air-conditioning. Was all his journey going to be a nightmare like this? Was he going to find himself sitting opposite this unreal figure, uncannily knowing what he should not, all the long, long way to Calcutta?

'Well, we will be off again at any instant,'

47

Mr Banerjee remarked.

'Off again?'

'My dear chap, for the last ten minutes we have been securely resting at Manmad. Had you not noticed?'

'Oh, it is Manmad. No. No, I had not realised.'

'Yes,' said Mr Banerjee with a smile, 'I thought you seemed rather preoccupied.'

'I was thinking only,' Ghote said.

'And of what were you thinking, my dear Inspector?'

But Ghote was saved from answering this altogether unanswerable question by the most extraordinary interruption.

The door of the compartment was abruptly jerked back and into their air-conditioned calm there came one after the other three of the most unlikely people Ghote could have imagined at this instant.

The first was a young man apparently in his early twenties. He was a European with a thick mop of entwined auburn hair and a solid block of auburn moustache in the middle of his sun-reddened face. But, except for the fact that with the three strings of peasant beads he had dangling from his neck there were also two expensive-looking cameras, he had nothing about him of the European. He wore a pair of faded khaki shorts and no more. His chest, on which there was a fuzz of auburn hair beneath the beads and camera-straps, was bare. His feet were bare. He wafted out a strong odour of dried sweat.

Closely following him, there came a girl, perhaps a year or two younger, equally un-Indian in complexion and even more Indian in dress, though the happy unkemptness of her sari would have shocked all the Indian women Ghote knew, for all that the garment was worn with obvious ease. She was pretty too, young and fresh. Her hair was neatly brushed to her head and secured, Ghote saw, with a tidy rubber-band, and her eyes beneath the red tika mark carefully placed on her forehead were a bright and sparkling blue.

But, as if the appearance of these two incongruous figures were not enough, the other person who entered the compartment with them, drifting in as if attached to the boiling wake of the two young people, was that traditional figure of Indian travel, a wandering guru. He wore his orange robe with indifferent dignity. He carried a wooden begging-bowl and apparently nothing else. He peered round the compartment with mild curiosity and immediately went and hoisted himself up on the other end of the bunk where Ghote was sitting, tucking his long bare legs efficiently under him and waiting for what would come next.

CHAPTER THREE

Inspector Ghote not a quarter of an hour earlier had been fervently hoping he would not find himself alone in this compartment of the Calcutta Mail with the so dazzling Mr Banerjee all the way to Jabalpur and the possible relief of the 'Passenger Jabalpur-Calcutta'. But now he found the sudden arrival of these three newcomers was anything but a relief. Hippies. This is what the two young people were, he registered disapprovingly. Hippies.

He was aware from many a newspaper and magazine article that India was a target for hundreds of young people from the West who saw her as a land marvellously free from the clogging materialism of their home countries. He knew they swarmed aimlessly in various localities from Nepal to Goa, idling their days away, smoking hashish and opium and begging like professionals but without their excuse. Up to now, however, he had not come into any real contact with these drop-outs, though there had been a party of them he had seen in Bombay dressed in orange robes and parading the main thoroughfares chanting 'Hari Krishna, Hari Krishna' in a manner he found altogether ridiculous. But his disapproval had been only an undirected little wasp pinging

50

away somewhere in the back of his mind.

Now he was in contact with hippies and with a vengeance. Already the two of them were plainly settling down for a long stay in the compartment. The auburn-haired young man had given their fellow-travelling guru a friendly pat on his bare, emaciated thigh and then had dipped outside the compartment again to bring in a couple of quite substantial rolls of possessions. The girl had actually climbed on her bare feet, which were dirty-soled as bare feet could not fail to be in these sun-hammered dusty days, up on to the lower bunk opposite, leaving plain dark grey imprints on the thick weave of the white cotton counterpane. She was standing there now hanging on to the upper bunk and cheerfully examining the various amenities in the way of light switches and bedside gadgets that the compartment offered.

Ghote looked at her more closely.

Her feet, however dust-encrusted, were neat and shapely. Her ankles were slim yet sturdy. Above them the calves swelled with all the freshness of lusty, new-growing, rain-blessed plants till they were hidden by the cotton of that efficiently-worn but not entirely graceful sari. She was young. She was almost youth personified, resilient, confident, ignorant youth. And more than that, Western youth, for all the sari and the tika mark and for all the quest for mystic India. Western youth, youth from a new world.

'Hey, Red,' she called out eventually to the young man in the corridor. 'It's okay in here.'

American.

Ghote found it needed only this to confirm in him the feeling he had been trying to fight down ever since the two young people had bounced in: he was deep down inside afraid of them.

He was afraid of their youth. He was afraid of the certainty with which they had abandoned all the progress of the West and had plunged into hot, poverty-shackled, sharp-smelling India, picking up a wandering guru as casually and easily as they would pick a cigarette out of a thrust-forward pack. He was afraid of all that they did not know and could not. He was afraid of his own youthful self in them.

'Excuse please,' he said, abruptly and loudly. 'Are you in possession of air-conditioned-class tickets?'

The girl, dirty feet firm on the rim of the lower bunk, held the edge of the top bunk in one neat-nailed, sun-browned and well-muscled little hand and swung round to look at him.

'Air-conditioned-class tickets.' she said. 'Land's sakes.'

From the doorway, leaning restfully against the jammed-open sliding door, the young man spoke. His accent, Ghote noted with perhaps even more inward sinking, was not American. It was British, even recognisably the British of the sahibs of his own boyhood days. But his words were not those of a pukka sahib, not at all.

'Listen, friend,' he said. 'You don't have to get steamed up about things like tickets. Didn't you know that? Didn't you know tickets are only pieces of paper?'

Ghote turned to him nevertheless with some relief. He was, after all, a young man. And cheeky young men were a type he had been used to dealing with from the first day he had joined the police. Here was altogether a more easy to handle proposition than the girl still hanging carelessly from the top bunk looking at him with pure humour shining in her sky-blue eyes.

'No,' he said to the young man with fast-returning authority. 'A railway ticket is not a piece of paper only. It is a duly-issued receipt for cash handed over, being an entitlement to travel.'

The young man's auburn-moustached face moved slowly from side to side in apparent astonishment.

'Friend,' he said, 'what are you, a policeman or something?'

Directly opposite Ghote Mr Banerjee produced a look of painful straight-facedness. And then, the moment the young man dipped back again into the corridor, he added a

53

colossal wink.

Glad of this plain sign that he was not going to be sabotaged by his Bombay-originated acquaintance, Ghote went back to his task of lowering the young man a peg or two.

'If you have not got a ticket you are not entitled to travel,' he said. 'You will kindly leave.'

The young man came fully back into the compartment.

'Tickets I don't bother about,' he said. 'Nothing paper do I bother about. Do you think we've got visas to be in this marvellous country of yours, friend? No, we have not. We were given them, and we tore them up. Isn't that so, Little Cloud?'

He directed a glance from above his thick auburn moustache towards the girl hanging on the bunk. Slightly unexpectedly, she did not say anything by way of agreeing. Instead she dropped down on to the floor, reached for one of their rolls of possessions and began busying herself with unknotting the thin cord that tied it up.

Ghote firmly returned to the auburn-moustached young man.

'If you have no ticket,' he repeated, 'then you must leave.'

'An excellent idea,' said the cool voice of Mr Banerjee from his corner.

Ah, thought Ghote, he too does not like this invasion. Here was an ally he hardly

54

welcomed, but an ally always added strength.

'You will leave at once,' he said again to the young man.

He saw with satisfaction that the robust, naked-chested figure in front of him had begun to look at once uneasy and aggressive. There would be some shouting now, and then it would be done.

'Yes, leave at once,' said Mr Banerjee. 'An excellent idea, except that the train is now moving at some speed and I doubt whether the gentleman, the lady and gentleman, or rather the lady and the two gentlemen, really can leave.'

His gaze came to rest thoughtfully on the leg-tucked form of the guru, squatting peacefully at the end of his chosen bunk, rocking slightly from side to side with the motion of the train, which, Ghote acknowledged now, was indeed going at a fair pace.

He frowned sharply.

'Very well,' he said, 'they must leave at the next stop. All three of them, if they have not got tickets.'

The presence of the guru discomposed him, but he was determined not to let that affect his judgment. People who had not paid for their journey should not be allowed to travel.

'And yet, you know,' Mr Banerjee said, leaning forward and enveloping them all— Ghote, the hippy pair, the guru—in a warm, teeth-flashing smile, 'and yet is it so very, very terrible to travel without a ticket?'

'It is,' said Ghote.

Mr Banerjee ignored him. The heavily-built young hippy and his girl gave each other a quick glance of mutual satisfaction and promptly settled down on Mr Banerjee's bunk, their eyes fixed on this new-found typical representative of unexpected, mystical India.

'After all,' Mr Banerjee said, his hands spreading wide, 'are we not all, in a sense, travelling without tickets? Making our way through the thickets of the years without any authorisation of any kind? We do not know our destinations. The trains come by, and we run and jump on them when we can, and gradually make our way from point to point of our great journey. We travel, we travel . . .'

His eyes—the mask of the Polaroid spectacles removed now—shone with excitement as the metaphor took hold.

'It is not so,' Ghote interrupted. 'In life we are always paying for where we travel.'

But Mr Banerjee swept over the interruption as a river in flood sweeps over and past a frail stick-erection planted for some small private purpose in what happens to be its path.

'And how right it is that we should travel in this unpaying way,' he declaimed. 'That we should go from place to place as the spirit takes us, that the spirit of man should not let itself be cramped and confined with little bits

56

of paper saying "Go here" "Go there" "You may not proceed beyond this point" "You may not proceed beyond that."'

'Excuse me,' Ghote said, leaning sharply forwards. 'But are you also travelling without a ticket?'

Mr Banerjee did hear him this time. He could hardly have failed to do so, Ghote had spoken so determinedly. And he smiled, an enormous chuckling smile lasting seconds.

'My dear sir, a good point, an excellent point. And I will tell you something: I ought to be travelling without a ticket, I ought to be doing what these brave young people are doing. But, alas, my dear sir, I am old, I am conventional, I am a law-abiding citizen—yes, that most shabby of all things, a law-abiding citizen, is precisely what I am now—and I have got my ticket, air-conditioned class. Look. Look.'

His hand dived towards where the inside pocket on a suit would come. It stuttered along the surface of his softly-woven, collarless kurta.

'Oh, yes, of course,' he muttered.

And he dived into the generous pocket at the shirt's waist to produce a smoothly-worn crocodile-skin wallet and from this his ticket, duly stamped, clipped by the gate inspector at V.T. Station in Bombay, in the most perfect order.

'Oh, dear me, alas, yes,' he said. 'I am

equipped with a ticket.'

'I am glad to find,' Ghote said stiffly.

And it seemed that this very stiffness attracted the attention of the young, careless, blue-eyed Amazon in the grace-lacking sari, attention he had hoped to avoid until their next stop, Jalagon, at about three in the morning. He had counted on sleeping, or at worse pretending to sleep, until this awkward interlude was over. And now the girl, with a radiant smile, had turned to him.

'Gee, don't be like that,' she said. 'Hell, you're Indian, you must know half the guys on this train aren't paying a cent. It's the way people get about in this country, and it's one hundred per cent okay with me. Now don't get so uptight about it all. Just let's relax and be people together.'

Before she was half done Ghote was, in fact, perfectly willing to concede her point. It was wrong, but she was—there could be no getting away from it—delightful. Earnest, sincere, muddle-headed, pretty. But she was wrong.

'I regret,' he said, 'there are the Regulations of the railway and travelling without tickets, with intent, is illegal.'

'And, my dear sir, ought we not just once in a while to condone illegality?'

Mr Banerjee's eyes were shining again.

'No, more than that,' he went on, 'ought we not just once in a while to practise illegality? Bounds are bad things, my dear sir. Oh, I know

58

they are necessary, but they are bad. You know they are necessary. No one knows better than you.'

He leant forward and gave Ghote so meaningful a look that the very conditioned air seemed to vibrate with it.

And now, Ghote thought, he is going to tell them I am a policeman. Of course the fellow had not taken any open oath. But that enormous wink had nevertheless constituted a promise. A promise to let him deal with the situation in his own way, and without, if he wanted, invoking any official powers. Was this promise going to be broken now?

'And, my dear sir, I am asking you to acknowledge that bounds can be bad. That a restriction, even conceived with the very best motives, is nevertheless a restriction. It restricts. Human freedom is lost. My dear sir, will you concede that sometimes it is our duty to break a small law?'

And Ghote, out of a sort of gratitude that his cover had not been atrociously blown, did grunt out two acknowledging words.

'Sometimes, perhaps.'

'Excellent, excellent, my dear fellow. So we will allow these two charming young people and Guruji here to share our compartment for just a few hours? Yes?'

'Yes,' Ghote said. 'Unless a ticket-inspector should arrive. I regret I would not be party to deception.'

It was stuffy, and he knew it. But he was determined not to get involved in any web of falsehoods that Mr Banerjee might start to weave should an inspector enter their compartment. But it seemed that he need not have said a word. Young Red at once confidently intervened.

'You don't have to bother with inspectors in air-conditioned,' he said lazily. 'That's why we pick this part of a train.'

'That's so,' the girl he had called Little Cloud put in with eagerness. 'I guess anybody would want to travel third-class if they could. To go along with the real people, with that natural rhythm of living an' all. But that's just where these inspector guys love to hang out, so we're kinda forced in here.'

'Where,' commented Mr Banerjee, a sharp smile poised to fly from his wide mouth, 'it happens also to be very much more comfortable.'

The girl's eyes blazed fire.

'If you think that—'

'No, no,' Mr Banerjee said hastily. 'And in any case I promise you if a ticket-inspector should come in here I would do my best to distract him. That I promise.'

'Okay then,' the girl said casually. 'But I tell you if it wasn't for those inspectors we'd never be here. But those guys have a way of not ever checking on air-conditioned snobs, so I guess that's it.'

And then she went back to unpacking her bundles, spreading about possessively and expertly certain articles from the contents mostly of a photographic nature—rolls of film, a light-meter, a carton of flash-bulbs—but also including a large box of Kleenex.

Soon she had finished and settled comfortably on the bunk again beside the solid, auburn-moustached Red who had been sitting rolling cigarettes from the contents of a small tin she had handed him as the first duty of her unpacking.

Would the cigarettes contain hashish, Ghote asked himself. If they did, what was his duty? But to his relief even the sharp watch he felt obliged to make did not reveal the presence in the self-rolled cigarettes of anything other than tobacco. He relaxed.

And then suddenly asked himself if this lack meant simply that the two hippies preferred opium and would later, when the mood took them, produce a pipe.

Abruptly he found he very much wanted to get into bed, fall asleep and put the intruders and all the complications they had brought with them out of his mind. After all, his purpose was clear: he was here just to travel to Calcutta. That and no more. So he was entitled to sleep.

The guru certainly was squatting on his bunk. But he was well down the far end and it ought to be possible to get between the sheets and lie down, if he was careful not to stretch his legs. And, of course, there could be no question of undressing. He was not going to appear in pyjamas with that girl sitting looking across towards him with those clear blue humorous eyes.

He took off his shoes and placed them side by side just underneath the bunk. What about the socks he wore as appropriate to the importance of his task, sweaty and uncomfortable though they were and envious though they had made him of Mr Banerjee's simple sandals? No, he decided, to take them off even now would be somehow to make him too defenceless.

He swung up on to the bunk in one scurrying movement and thrust his feet into the top of the folded-down sheets. His head, when he endeavoured simultaneously to turn round and shoot his legs down, came into firm contact with the bottom of the bunk above and at the same time the sweat-sticky sock on his left foot encountered a fold in the top sheet and lodged obstinately in it. He was stuck.

'You want to strip right off when it's as hot as this,' the American girl said with puppy-dog helpfulness.

Ghote decided not to hear.

'My dear young lady,' said Mr Banerjee, leaning happily forward, 'you have a lot to learn about our country. I think you can have no conception of the state of utter prudishness in which a young man like our friend so curiously crouched on the bunk there would have been brought up.'

Slowly Ghote forced his left knee upwards until the sticky sock had got beyond the top of the sheet fold. There was hardly room to conduct the manoeuvre and a light sweat broke out on his face with the effort. But he decided he must suffer it, and Mr. Banerjee's slightly malicious teasing. After all, he had been the one to start it by so obviously trying to cut himself off from them all. He was fair game.

The knee was high enough. With a jerk of effort he straightened himself up and slid rapidly down the rest of the bunk. His suddenly released toes came into violent contact with the bony haunches of the squatting guru.

Ghote apologised to him in Hindi. The guru turned and gave him a long dreamy look from big brown eyes. He giggled a little too, but otherwise made no acknowledgment.

'It was the best piece of luck we ever had meeting him,' the thick-moustached Red said by way of comment. 'At first you think he's just a nice chap. But then when you feel the spiritual power that comes from him. Wow.'

Ghote slowly drew back his feet till he was sure there was no longer the least chance of their coming into contact with this source of spiritual power. He was unable to wriggle round enough to turn his back on everybody else, but he did turn away his face and firmly shut his eyes. At one time he had nurtured a hope of being able to squirm out of his trousers under cover of the counterpane. But now he abandoned any such ambition in favour of a simple desire to blot out everything if possible right till Calcutta.

'Now, my dear young people,' he heard Mr Banerjee's precise voice easily penetrating the thick weave of the counterpane that he had managed to pull up over his ears. 'Now, my dear young people, tell me all about yourselves. Tell me about your splendid morality-free life. Tell me all the things you have stolen. Let me share even in your illegal hashish-smoking. Or is it opium you take? Tell me how many policemen you have assaulted. For now you can speak freely. Our friend there, who, let me tell you, is none other than a fully-fledged inspector of the Bombay CID, is asleep.'

A red rage ignited in the centre of Ghote's head and bloomed like a spreading orb of annihilating fire.

That man had betrayed him. Because of feeling sure that the hippies would never know he was a police officer he had condoned their breaking railway regulations and boasting of not being in possession of visas. And now, after he had compromised himself through and through, the man had wantonly told them just who he was.

64

This was going beyond mere teasing spitefulness: this was an active malice.

All right then, let him talk on now. Let him go on the way he has been doing. Almost ever since the hippies came he has incited them to break the law. And that is not something you can do and get away with. That can be in itself breaking the law. And law-breakers can be punished.

Eyes shut, head bent under the moderate darkness of the cotton-weave counterpane, Ghote set himself to recall word by word the exact law that Mr Banerjee was on the point of infringing.

It came—this was not difficult to remember—under Section 505 of the Indian Penal Code, with the key words being 'whoever makes, publishes or circulates any statement, rumour or report' and then the appropriate sub-section would begin 'with intent to—' To what?

Like a powerful charm the vital words threaded themselves one by one on the waxed cord of his memory '. . . with intent to cause, or which is likely to cause fear or alarm to the public or any section of the public.' Well, the guru there at his feet was a section of the public and he himself was certainly alarmed by the Bengali's talk. Now the rest: '. . . whereby any person may be—' May be what? Ah, induced. '. . . may be induced to commit an offence, ter-um, ter-um, ter-um, against the public tranquillity.'

And the penalty would be three years R.I.
or a fine or both. If only that Banerjee would
come up before a magistrate who would
send him off for three years' rigorous
imprisonment. That would teach him.

But, before he had time to hear from the
Bengali's lips any statement, rumour or report
made with intent to cause alarm whereby some
person might be induced to commit an offence
against the public tranquillity, suddenly and
unexpectedly sleep visited him.

CHAPTER FOUR

Sleep, however, was not for long to remove
Inspector Ghote from the troubles which
assailed him. He stirred when the great train
slowed as it approached Jalgaon, and, when
into his half-dreamy state there penetrated the
long squeal and judder of the stop, he became
aware that an interminable, swooping, soaring
conversation was still going on between Mr
Banerjee and the two young hippies, whom the
Bengali was already calling with immense
suavity Red and Mary Jane. (So that was her
real name: Little Cloud had been too much).
But while the train was stationary he drifted
off again and in a dream at once found himself
back in Bombay. He was flying like a bat up

and down the length of the big, long grass stretch of the Maidan, skimming above the roped squares of the cricket pitches, looking down on the white shapes of night sleepers beside their little smouldering fires, swinging up into the tops of the tall, fringing palms and all the while trying and trying to get his feet down on to the ground. Below him now too someone was calling his name 'Inspector Ghote, Inspector Ghote, Inspector Ghote.'

'Inspector Ghote.'

It was his name. He sat up, blinking. A railway porter in red headcloth was standing there, peering down at him. Beyond he caught a blurred glimpse of Mr Banerjee and Red and Mary Jane pointing to him.

'Inspector Ghote?' the porter said.

'Yes, yes. I am Inspector Ghote. What is it?'

'Telegram for Inspector Ghote, passenger to Calcutta.'

Ghote took the coarse-paper envelope and began tugging it open. The porter thrust his face forward. Ghote, with difficulty, reached under the sheet, located his trouser pocket, squeezed a hand in, got hold of some coin or other and thrust it into the man's ready palm.

He managed then to swing his legs out of the constricting bedclothes and sit on the bunk edge. He felt a little sick. In a moment he got the telegram out of its envelope and peered at the thin strips of white paper pasted on to it with their lines of faint grey capitals which he felt hardly capable of making out. There were a lot of them. Was the message really for him?

Yes, there was his name. He blinked hard again and was able to read the letters at last.

'PROFESSOR FRANKENHEIMER UNABLE AWAIT YOUR ARRIVAL STOP GRAVELY DISPLEASED STOP HAS VISITED DUM DUM STOP PRISONER NOT REPEAT NOT AAA KKK BHATTACHARYA STOP NOW IDENTIFIED AAA KKK BISWAS WANTED HERE OFFENCES CARD-SHARPING ON TRAINS STOP RETURN WITH BISWAS IN CUSTODY STOP TRAVEL SECOND REPEAT SECOND CLASS SIGNED SAMANT DEPUTY SUPERINTENDENT'

Each hammer-blow that the telegram had contained which he had somehow managed to hold in suspense as he read, now seemed to strike successively on the fragile shell of his equilibrium.

A. K. Bhattacharya not in Dum-Dum Gaol. So his journey now was suddenly all piffling and pointless. His task, far from being important and at the same time pleasurable, had become ridiculous and with nothing in it to savour. His picture had been in *The Times of India* for nothing.

Professor Frankenheimer too impatient to wait for him. His insistence on travelling by the slower means of rail was all of a sudden made to look like a puffed-up form of self-indulgence.

The card-sharper A. K. Biswas to be brought back to Bombay by second-class. This was salt being rubbed into his wounded pride indeed, and it would be the beginning only of a long period of D.S.P. Samant's low esteem.

He sat holding the coarse sandy oblong of the telegram in front of him, staring unseeingly at the white lines of gummed-on paper. And then with total suddenness the rough sheet was whipped out of his fingers.

His head jerked up in astonishment.

Mr Banerjee, opposite him, was reading his message.

And at the same moment that Ghote registered this piece of unbelievable cheek he also became aware of another enormous shift in the circumstances of his journey: now it was in the realms of possibility that the somewhat mysterious Mr Banerjee could actually be A. K. Bhattacharya himself.

The thought came as yet one more hammer-swing on to his already shattered inner calm. He sat letting it whirl and rush through the already mad confusion in his head, completely deprived of the power of decision. The man was a Bengali. He had even the right

69

initials, and a clever criminal assuming a false name is always careful to choose one with his own initials to avoid accidental betrayal by something like . . . an old suitcase. And the man too had shown a wide and deep knowledge of Indian antiquities. Could it be?

Only one tiny saving thought crouched somewhere in the turmoil: there was nothing that had to be done at this instant. The train had already started again, and while they were both in it together the situation was in suspense.

And, almost invisible in his mental landscape so low was it lying, another thought was revealed as the implication of realising that the man now greedily and cheerfully reading his telegram could be A. K. Bhattacharya: if the legendary Bhattacharya was really here, in this compartment, on this train, sitting within touching distance, then he could be arrested.

Ghote would not let himself, even by as much as the thickness of a hair, speculate on the consequences of such an arrest to himself and his career. But there could be no doubt about it: A. K. Bhattacharya was perhaps the single biggest haul a thief-taker could have made in the past twenty years of the history of fraud in India. It would be the capture of captures.

If the criminal was within capturing range. And that, Ghote hastily assured himself, was in fact ridiculous. Why in the name of everything that was simple, straightforward and logical would the very man he had set out to fetch from Dum-Dum Gaol be actually sitting in the same train compartment with him, sitting right opposite him?

Fantasy must be kept for after-hours' moments. And in the meantime there was one small, important piece of business to be done.

He leant forward and pointed a bluntly accusing finger at the telegram.

'That document is police affairs only,' he said. 'You have no right—'

But with an enormous, flashing grin of white teeth Mr Banerjee interrupted him.

'So,' he said in triumph, 'it seems after all, my good Inspector, that you have not been doing what you thought you were as we travelled together across this great country of ours. There you were, so determinedly doing nothing but fetch that terrible Bhattacharya from Calcutta and trying to tell me you were not making any voyage into the great unknown. And, bless me, that, it turns out, is precisely what you were doing. My poor fellow, you should learn a lesson from it all.'

Ghote stiffened.

'What the purpose of my journey is,' he said, 'is of no concern of yours. And I remind you that you have in your possession a document in restricted circulation.'

With a courtly inclination the tall Bengali extended the telegram towards Ghote. Ghote

71

took it, folded it time and again and pushed it hard into his pocket.

'And of course,' Mr Banerjee continued, 'had you travelled by air in the first place, my dear fellow, as I recommended, then at least the Professor Frankenheimer part of this business, which I can see is devilishly unpleasant for you whatever it is, would have been avoided.'

That was true, Ghote acknowledged again. If he had not given way to that ridiculous desire to go by train then he might have been able to ensure at least Professor Frankenheimer's co-operation when they had properly caught A. K. Bhattacharya and brought him to trial. And that fullest co-operation was pretty well bound to be vital in court with the arch-trickster fighting and twisting at every turn. If he ever came to court now.

He should have gone by air. He admitted it fully. And, he added in an undertone of spite, if he had done so he would at least have avoided the company of Mr A. K. Banerjee.

Only, fantasy suddenly insisted, in that case Mr Banerjee would undoubtedly have gone by air too, in the same aircraft. And why was it, in any case, that he had not flown?

He felt altogether too dispirited to attempt to probe into that now. And realised too that the train had halted and had set off again without anything having been done about expelling the ticketless hippies. Or the presumably ticketless guru.

Pretty Mary Jane was talking about the latter now.

'We like just picked him up,' she was saying in answer to Mr Banerjee. 'Guru, we call him. And we're his chelas, I guess. We go just everywhere he goes.'

For an instant, as she looked at the skinny knees of the cross-legged guru projecting over the bunk-side opposite her, a visible conflict took place on her pink and white face. Then came a victory.

'Well,' she said, 'it's really more he goes every place with us, I suppose.'

To Ghote, sitting in a sullen hunch on the edge of his bunk, it came as a distinct disappointment that that small uprising of candour went totally without reward. But Mr Banerjee simply leant back and regarded Mary Jane with decidedly cool, even sharp amusement.

'So he is your guru,' he said, 'and you are his disciples, his chelas. And you wander all three through teeming, people-filled, colourful India. Tell me, which of you has been reading *Kim*?'

'Kim?' Mary Jane said, so plainly foxed entirely by the syllable that she looked simply comic.

'Ah, then,' said Mr Banerjee, rubbing his long-fingered hands together, 'I see that it is

the so-British Mr Redmond Travers—I beg
your pardon—it is my friend Red who is
conducting a pilgrimage in the renowned steps
of the late Rudyard Kipling.'

'Just because . . .' Red muttered and fell into
silence, sullenly fiddling with the two cameras
dangling in front of him.

Ghote, still creaky-minded with
despondency, looked at him. And as he did so
the unformed wisps of an idea began to draw
together in his brain. He paid closer attention
to the two hippies and their dealings with the
unsatisfactory Mr Banerjee. The two intruders
might, after all, be just what he needed.

'Oh, come now, my dear Red,' the Bengali
resumed, warming to his work. 'Come, do not
pretend you are not acting in the spirit, in the
very letter even, of young Kim wandering
through Imperial India as chela to his guru.
Because you so plainly are. I wonder you do
not say you are seeking a mysterious river.'

'The river. The river that will answer all.'

It was Mary Jane. And she was furious. She
rounded on young Red, eyes sparkling blue
fire.

'So you got it all out of a book,' she said. 'It
wasn't even your own rotten idea.'

And this earned her such a glare of snarling
hostility from Red that Ghote felt, to his own
surprise, distinctly upset. The pair of them
ought in their fecklessness and squalor at least
to be happy together. And plainly now they

were not to be. He decided he had been doubly right not to like Mr Banerjee from the first.

But the Bengali had not yet finished with the bullock-like Red.

'So,' he said, 'we have this picture of you, the clean upstanding young Englishman who imbibes the high ideals of the late Mr Kipling, perhaps from his father's knee. But then something changes. The young Redmond becomes plain Red, and he departs, casting aside all the values he has been taught, to plunge into wonderful, non-materialistic India. And there—'

He paused and cast on the clashing Mary Jane and Red a look of sickly sentiment.

'Well, there he meets,' he continued, 'a most charming young lady from Montana and he falls in love, I am sure, and—And perhaps certain events take place, and—'

'Hell,' said Mary Jane, 'we sleep together when we're friends, sure, we do. What's there to get in such a tangle over about that?'

Mr Banerjee was, for once, quite clearly disconcerted. Ghote felt a sudden orange jet of inward laughter lifting up from inside his depression and hardening instant by instant his secret idea about using the two hippies.

But Mr Banerjee was not the sort to be disconcerted for long and he turned resolutely back to Red.

'And our young hero,' he said, 'in India he

75

finds the wonderful blossom of love and, as much or more than that, freedom from the trammels of reality. He finds a true, happy, free, mystical existence at last.'

'All right,' Red said with grunting suspiciousness, 'so I do find that. You seem to think it's fake, just because it ties in with a book I read. But I tell you the life where nothing material counts a damn is the right life, the only life for me. And I mean to go on living it, just here.'

At this Mary Jane flashed him such a new look of fury that Ghote guessed that here was the seat of her quarrel with Red. But this was no time to moon over the two hippies as if they were hero and heroine of a film and would at any instant break into song. What was necessary now was to put into effect his plan for making use of them against the Bengali.

The Bengali, too, was not giving his attention to Mary Jane's fury. Instead he was continuing with his baiting of Red.

'So that is why,' he said, with his toothiest and most flashing of smiles, 'that is why you feel the obsessive need to record the reality of everything you encounter with not one but two cameras. My dear young sir.'

But with those words Ghote felt a positive surge of triumph. They were a sign, he felt. The enemy had dug a trap for his own feet.

He bounced up on his bunk seat.

'Ah, yes, indeed,' he said, 'our friend here is

a photographic expert. Thank you for reminding me of it, sir. I have been most desirous of seeing him exercise his art. And it seems to me, sir, that you yourself would make an excellent subject.'

He was afraid that Red, still smarting from Mary Jane's attack, would not co-operate. But he visibly brightened.

'Why not?' he said. 'Yes, why not?'

'My dear young sir,' Mr Banerjee said, raising a quick, deprecatory hand till it obscured most of his face. 'My dear Inspector, are you thinking that I am a representative Indian figure? Now that really is too much.'

But Red implacably was unfastening his cameras' shutter guards.

'No,' said Mr Banerjee. 'No. What do I, a poor tired businessman represent in great mystical India?'

'You talk a lot,' said Mary Jane, seizing this opportunity of backing down towards Red.

'Oh, my dear madam, if each one of us who opens his mouth is to be photographed, where would our country come to? Where would my beloved Bengal come to? Stop, stop, I beg.'

Ghote, listening like a parched desert sucking water, hardly knew what to think. Was this a natural reluctance, even just a pretence of reluctance? Or was it the absolute refusal to face the camera that it had been his plan to detect?

Mary Jane moved nearer the Bengali now.

'Jeeze,' she said, 'there's nothing wrong with being photographed. It's not some kind of punishment.'

'No, no, I am sure you are perfectly correct,' Mr Banerjee said. 'There is of course nothing at all wrong with being photographed. Only perhaps some of us are not really very suitable types for the art. There must be more picturesque fellows than I.'

He looked hastily and searchingly at Ghote, as if trying to see what picturesque qualities could be offered in instant illustration.

'Well,' he said, 'I am sure that when the train next stops Red will find plenty of excellent subjects.'

'No,' said Mary Jane implacably, 'I reckon you'll make a darn' fine picture, with your long nose and that. And those lines down your cheeks. Wouldn't he, Red?'

'Yes,' said Red.

His camera lenses were unshuttered now and he was busy fixing on a bright flash cube from the carton beside him.

Mr Banerjee looked from side to side, almost huntedly, Ghote thought, feeling as if some sheerly incredible event was beginning to happen before his eyes.

'But listen, my dear young people,' Mr Banerjee hurriedly expostulated. 'There is more to this matter than simply whether I am, for my sins, what I believe is called a photogenic subject. I am not a subject only,

78

please remember. I am a person also. You may wish at this moment to photograph me, but do I wish at this moment to be photographed?'

And the answer to that was plainly 'No'. But no one asks the cornered tiger if it is willing to receive the rifle bullet, and Red was now laying out a small line of flash cubes along the white coverlet of the bunk beside him, evidently ready when he had exploded the first to seize them one after the other for instant use.

Mr Banerjee looked at the advancing line of shiny cubes as if it were a cobra slithering towards him. He licked his lips with a nervous flick of the tongue.

'Mr Travers,' he said.

Red lifted up one camera. Mr Banerjee leapt to his feet.

'Mr Travers. My dear Red. Now, stop. Listen, my good young friend, have you considered the full implications of what you are about to do?'

Red made no reply. But he too got to his feet and advanced across the gently swaying carriage floor towards Mr Banerjee, his feet spread wide to give him balance, knees slightly bent, camera bobbing slowly in the region of his tufty auburn moustache.

Mr Banerjee retreated to his corner. Slowly he lowered himself down, eyes fixed on Red and the hovering camera. Ghote tensed himself for the moment when the dazzling flash would come.

Mr Banerjee put his two hands flat in front of his long fleshy face and spread the ten fingers in a wide fan.

'No,' he said.

Mary Jane swung athletically along the length of the bunk up to his side. She put a hand on his shoulder.

'Listen,' she said, 'like I told you, it isn't some terrible torture or something. It's a sign he likes you. It's a sign Red likes you. He wants to have a record of you.'

'But, my dear young lady,' Mr Banerjee said stiffly from behind his taut finger fan, 'cannot the gentleman really remember a person unless he has some desperate black-and-white memento of him?'

'Red always uses colour,' Mary Jane said.

'Then unless he has some appallingly garish coloured memento,' Mr Banerjee retorted, his fingers falling away a little with the intensity of his objection.

Red swayed to one side like a boxer seeking an opening. Mr Banerjee's guard shot up again.

Mary Jane put an efficient little tanned, muscular hand on his right wrist.

'Relax,' she said. 'It's not going to hurt you any.'

Mr Banerjee's wrist could be seen to be stringy with tenseness.

'It will hurt me,' he said. 'It will hurt me in

my pride. To be pinned down like this, to be fixed, to be labelled. It is appalling, truly appalling.'

And it seemed that this argument did at least appeal to Mary Jane. Because, though Red manoeuvred sideways here and there over the central floor of the compartment, she did at last loose her hold of the Bengali and turn away.

'Hell, Red,' she said. 'He's right in a way. There's no use taking him if he's acting up like this.'

Red darted forward, camera up.

Mr Banerjee, unsure of the protection of his frail hands from the fury of this assault, actually flung himself right round and buried his head in the back of the seat.

His abject rounded back reminded Ghote, a transfixed spectator of every detail, of nothing so much as some lean-skinned about-to-be-kicked pi-dog. But he could not find it in him to feel sympathy. After all, did not this mean, illogical and incredible though it was, that the fellow very well might be A. K. Bhattacharya himself?

Red stopped and lowered the camera slowly to waist level. He too looked at the rounded back.

'Oh, all right,' he muttered. 'We'll leave it till morning. At least I'll save a few flash bulbs.'

He turned away and morosely started

putting his array of cubes back into their box. Slowly, inch by half-inch, the Bengali began turning to face the world. Only when he was perfectly certain that Red was truly engaged in packing up his apparatus did he straighten up and look at them all with something of an air of bravado.

'Yes,' he said. 'The morning. Tomorrow. That will be the time to consummate, as it were, our friendship with the seal of the camera. Because, my dear young people—and this, you know, was the sole point of my objection to your proceedings just now— because I feel we have hardly as yet properly got to know each other.'

Perfectly certain now that Red, who was strapping the lens guards back on the cameras and stowing them for the night in one of their bundles of possessions, had abandoned his attempts, he expanded again like a closed flower greeting the sun.

'How long is it after all,' he said, 'that we have been talking together? A mere three hours or so. What can we have got to know of each other in such a little time? No, tomorrow, we will talk. Tomorrow we will talk and talk, and then, if you care to, I will with pleasure pose for photographs.'

And, standing up and giving each of the hippies in turn a small but courtly bow, he went to prepare himself for bed.

Ghote scrambled back again between his

own sheets, remembering to take care not to disturb the unmoving guru at the foot of the bunk.

As he lay flat on his back, eyes shut, hoping for sleep to come again before too long, he tried to decide what that apparent happy acceptance, after all, of the idea of being photographed had meant. If the Bengali was willing, then surely he could not be A. K. Bhattacharya. And, when you added the fact that nothing was more unlikely that he should be the legendary confidence-trickster, the situation indeed seemed to be back to its starting-point.'

His scheme, it looked, had failed.

And yet . . . And yet he was uneasy.

CHAPTER FIVE

The light of day woke Ghote at about half past six next morning. Sleep he noted, had done nothing to ease his perplexities. Dry-mouthed and loath to make any movement, he looked about him. Outside the lightly blued windows he could see the endlessly flat countryside gradually being revealed, dry and dusty, as the white light spread, the limitless miles broken only occasionally by small clumps of ghost-grey trees where a village huddled. Along the narrow, hard-beaten paths closer to the line he could see already the black silhouette forms of lanky, loinclothed men going off with hoes on their shoulders to work in the fields with the occasional softer sari-clad form of a woman, the brass water-jar on her head catching the sun's early rays.

In the compartment the others still slept, with the exception of the guru who sat impassively, not on the end of his bunk now but on the floor. At some stage of the short night, Ghote registered, he must have moved. He supposed then that he must have been more deeply asleep than he had thought that the sway and thump of the onward-hurrying train had allowed him to be.

After a little he felt capable of offering a quiet greeting in Hindi. The guru, a little surprisingly, replied with calm. But it was somehow plain that he did not wish to talk.

Neither did Ghote. Hugging a harsh but still comforting silence about him, he raised himself up a little further and made a new survey of the grey and frowsty compartment. Mr Banerjee was sleeping with completely characteristic magnificence. He lay flat on his back with his fleshy prow of a nose pointing upwards not just to the curved carriage ceiling but to the great heavens. His mouth hung a little open, allowing a glimpse of those long white teeth. Doubtless while the train progressed across the vast wheatfields of the Narbada Valley, where far from any cooling ocean the temperature was likely to go up to and beyond a hundred degrees Fahrenheit, those teeth would flash and flash in grin after grin as new flights of fancy issued from between them. From his lofty brow the long hair fanned sweepingly downwards, harshly black and unnatural from its dye.

That hair. Was it, could it be a disguise? Was this sleeping man after all A. K.—

Ghote stamped on the thought as if it were a wriggling white-banded krait that had to be killed at once. There was no point in tormenting himself with such ideas. The day would decide. If Mr Banerjee let himself be photographed he was Mr Banerjee. If not, he was—No, he might be A. K. Bhattacharya. Time would bring the answer.

He forced himself to look elsewhere. On the narrow top bunk above the tall Bangali he could just see that Mary Jane and Red were fast asleep, lying back to back. He blushed.

But they were none of his business, he told himself. They were a couple of foreigners, let them abandon the decencies like foreigners. And in any case he would be able to get into the toilet compartment before either of them.

There remained too, of course, the reservation card with on it the many-flourished words in jet black ink 'Passenger Jabalpur-Calcutta'. The new day would bring this unknown, wealthy enough to travel air-conditioned and careful enough to make a

85

proper reservation, into their midst. What changes would his presence make? After the hippies he felt any new element was somehow bound to be for the worse.

He sighed.

Perhaps a shower and a shave would make things look a little more cheerful. And a sudden, darting thought occurred to him: if Mr Banerjee was still deeply asleep when he returned he might get an opportunity to have a quiet look at the title of that book of his. To sit knowing that all day when the long fingers of the Bengali were deliberately hiding it would make up for a lot.

His small spurt of energy and determination met almost at once with fizzling setback: when he came to the point of shaving he found that he had left his shaving-cream back in Bombay.

It had been a new brand, too. He had decided he had better have a fresh supply for the journey and had yielded to certain advertisements which had been tempting a corner of his mind for months. And now he was not to experience the rich, penetrating lather of Lakmé for Men. He could see the tube as he stood there in front of the stainless-steel basin, legs wide apart against the rocking of the steadily progressing train. It was gaily striped and promised brisk and yet underneath sensuous starts to the days. The tube would be waiting wherever he had left it in the unaccustomed flurry of packing. But the joy of it would be removed. In the grim bustle of everyday life there would be no time to let its rich and penetrating delights curl up like secret temple incense into his head.

So he shaved with what feeble suds he could work up from the piece of soap he had. And, what with the basic difficulties arising anyhow from the sway and swing of the train, it was not a success.

Patchy-bristled, he returned to his berth, openly expecting every sort of adversity from a day that had begun so badly. Young Red, in a typically hippy way, would forget all about photographing Mr Banerjee and take instead to smoking opium, so that, far from cunningly having used the Westerners to deal with his problem, he would find himself faced instead with all the business of having to enforce the law they were flouting. Or, Mr Banerjee having persisted with his refusal to be photographed, thereby making it likely in spite of its total unlikeliness that he was A. K. Bhattacharya, he would then contrive to get away at the next halt. Or Mr Banerjee having at last agreed to be photographed, would then definitely be established as being himself and would be there to plague the whole of the rest of the journey.

Blackly at odds with everything, Ghote slumped down in his seat.

And Mr Banerjee contrived to be, it felt, even more irritating than either forecast of his behaviour had predicted. He simply stayed asleep.

He lay there, still on his back, still with that fan of dyed hair spreading downwards from his brow, still with that proud and fleshy nose pointing upwards, and he snored. Ghote watched him. The two hippies had been awake when he had returned from the toilet compartment, and soon they had gone to wash themselves. But even their clambering down from the bunk above had not disturbed the Bengali.

He must be very tired, Ghote thought. But then the fellow had talked abominably late into the night.

Suddenly he wondered if he really was asleep. Say he was A. K. Bhattacharya. This would be a fine way of avoiding being photographed till they had reached Piparya at about ten o'clock, and then, alerted to the possibility that he had been detected, he would contrive to escape.

While the hippies were still absent, and ignoring the distantly spiritual presence of the guru, he rose from his seat and bent over the sleeping form. The eyelids lay relaxed on the eyes that had been for much of the journey concealed behind those expensive Polaroid sunglasses. Had those been a measure of disguise too, abandoned when their owner felt safe? The jaw that had moved so incessantly in talk the day before hung slackly now. The faint bubble of repetitive snoring lurked somewhere in the heaven-pointing prow of a nose.

It looked as if he really was asleep. But, there was no way of being certain.

And he was lying on the book. Despite its heavy thickness it was well tucked under his sleeping form. Ghote leant right under the top bunk and twisted his head round as far as it would go. But the title of the tome remained impregnably buried.

At the sound of the hippies returning he darted back to his own seat.

Mary Jane looked at the profoundly sleeping man on the lower bunk, turned to Ghote, briefly mimed the taking of photographs and then gave him a broad smile and a silent shrug.

Ghote stood up and approached young Red.

'Can you take while he is sleeping?' he inquired in a whisper.

Red looked at the recumbent form deep inside the lower bunk.

'Not unless I use flash,' he whispered back. 'And that'd wake him.'

Ghote had half a mind to suggest that they should not be too tender, even despite the prospect of a whole day of multiple denunciation from an angry and awakened Mr Banerjee. But Mary Jane had other ideas.

'We can't wake him,' she hissed. 'Everyone has the right to sleep.'

Ghote privately considered the statement

rather sweeping. But he did not want to lose his new allies.

He set himself patiently to wait till the sleeping man should choose to wake, and resolved that if this did not happen till just before they got to Piparya he would not let the Bengali get even a foot beyond his grasp while the train was stationary or even going slowly enough to be jumped down from.

The early morning hours passed. Outside the sun climbed the sky and brought its unpitying dry scorchingness to everything. Inside the compartment the air-conditioning and the blued window glass preserved their isolation.

And then, at about half-past nine, Mr Banerjee did awake. He stirred, sat up a little in his bunk and consulted the watch on the inside of his wrist.

'Good gracious me,' he said. 'It seems that I have slept to an astonishingly late hour.'

He looked roguishly from the hippies to Ghote and back.

'And all the time you have been agog to see me photographed,' he said. 'Well, well, I must apologise. However, nothing has been lost by delay. I am still here. Your cameras, my dear young friend, are still here. Just as soon as I have completed my toilet the two can come face to face.'

He slid his long form from the bunk and made his way to the toilet compartment, swinging a gaily-checked sponge-bag that he had taken from his old leather case—those initials flashed derisively at Ghote for an instant—at the same time as he had put back into its fastness his scholarly-looking invariable reading-matter.

Well, Ghote thought, while he is in there he cannot get away.

He watched with interest while Red selected one of his two cameras and squinted at various corners of the compartment through his light-meter. So Mr Banerjee was going to allow himself to be photographed after all, and without the period of talk to allow Red to get to know him better that he had spoken of as so necessary the night before.

He did not know whether to be pleased or not.

And then Mr Banerjee, looking all the more bright-eyed for his fairly prolonged toilet, returned.

'Aha,' he said as he saw what Red was doing, 'I see you are eager for the confrontation, my dear chap.'

'If I'm going to do it I want to do it straightaway,' Red answered, without much graciousness.

'Excellent, excellent, my dear chap. The mark of the true artist, I am sure. To seize the inspiration and to be carried aloft on its wings. How fine. How fine. But—'

Mr Banerjee raised a long solemn finger.

'But,' he continued, 'awkward reality has, alas, intervened. I have seen, on examination in the mirror next door, the positively dreadful state of my face.'

They all looked at his face. It wore an expression of barely concealed glee.

'I don't see anything dreadful,' Mary Jane declared.

'Well, I must beg to point out that I am in an impossible state of unshavenness,' Mr Banerjee said.

'Hell, that's not going to matter,' Mary Jane bounced back. 'Red got some fantastic shots of an old boatman up in Kashmir one time. You could see every bristle in his beard. They sorta caught the light.'

'Yet do I want to find myself on a par with an aged Kashmiri boatman?' Mr Banerjee asked.

'If you look like a boatman,' Red said toughly, 'then you ought to be shown looking like him.'

'But,' asked Mr Banerjee with quick slyness, 'if I have been shaved will not the truth then be my clean-shaven self?'

'I suppose so,' Red acknowledged, though it was plain he felt that the unshaven truth must somehow be truer.

'Very well then,' Mr Banerjee said. 'When we halt at Piparya shortly I intend to get a shave from a station barber. Shaving oneself is an awkward business on a moving train.'

Ghote's suspicions awoke like the rising hair of a dog smelling a ghost.

'But, please,' he said, remembering the timetable he had studied with delight before setting out, 'we are not due to stop at Piparya long enough for anyone to be shaved.'

'Perfectly right, my dear fellow, perfectly right. However I have observed we seem to be running a little early and there ought to be, if not ample time, then time enough. Of course I shall have to watch my barber pretty carefully. They are often incorrigible rogues, you know. They will half-shave you very slowly and then when the train is about to depart demand an exorbitant dash for the swift completion of their task. But I think there should be no difficulty that cannot be overcome.'

So they had to concede him his right to the delay. And they had to listen during the ten minutes or less up to their arrival at Piparya to a short disquisition on the excellence of the barbers of Calcutta. But at length the train drew to a jerking halt and Mr Banerjee hurried off along the sealed air-conditioned coach to the exit door.

Ghote was on his heels every inch of the way.

Stepping down, inches behind him, on to the station platform he found himself assailed, in a way he had not altogether been ready for, by the sheer brutal reality of the heat of the day.

The stone of the platform was so hot it stung the soles of his feet even through shoe and sock. The noise too hit with all the more violence for his having come from the seclusion of the air-conditioned coach where the only sound had been the background thump and rattle of the train-wheels. But here in the harshly drying glare there was noise of all sorts. Away up at the head of the train their giant locomotive was hissing steam with a shrill squealing. And all round them on every side there were voices. Passengers were shouting to one another and to the red-headclothed porters. Porters and station staff were shouting back and shouting to each other. Tea vendors were making their way along the big train with large square wooden trays crowded with reddish earthenware cups. And, when passengers leaning from every window of the un-air-conditioned coaches were not shouting at them, the vendors were shouting for prospective customers. There were children too, by the hundred it seemed, some shouting, some yelling, some merely crying. And, from the sky above, came the incessant grating raw-voiced cawing of crows by dozens.

But Mr Banerjee had set off at a fast pace along the platform, and, ignoring the intense heat and the wild noise, Ghote set off at his heels. If that man was A. K. Bhattacharya and tried to make a bolt for it he would find himself lying flat on the ground in less than half a second with a pair of arms wrapped round his legs that he would not shake off whatever he did.

Dodging porters with items of luggage poised on their heads—tin boxes, wooden suitcases, leather suitcases, trunks, huge bulging bedrolls—he kept right behind his man. But Mr Banerjee did nothing other than make, as directly as the squatting families and indiscriminate piles of possessions all over the platform allowed, for the place where the station barbers sat beside their big bowls of lather.

And, while Ghote accompanied by the two leg-stretching hippies and even by the guru, stood and watched, Mr Banerjee rapidly agreed on the price of a shave. Then he seated himself on an old folding wooden chair with one strut missing, and was lathered up and had undergone the ministrations of a flashing-bladed razor well before a resplendently-uniformed station attendant had banged and banged on the hanging length of the departure-signal pipe to indicate that the Calcutta Mail was about to leave.

Still acutely suspicious however Ghote followed his man back closely as ever as they all went to their coach. Even when the train was in motion once more and the Bengali, looking very spruce and smelling of well-scented lather, was sitting in his seat, its bedclothes swept away in their absence, he still felt somehow cheated.

'Well now,' Mr Banerjee said, looking all round him, 'if the spirit still fires the photographer the victim is ready.'

'All right,' Red replied, and once more he took up his camera.

Mr Banerjee leant towards Ghote.

'We shall have to see that you too are submitted to the process, my dear Inspector,' he said. 'Though of course one knows that you are familiar with it all since your likeness only yesterday was staring at us out of the pages of *The Times of India.*'

Ghote ignored the gigantic impudence of that bland reference to the first trick the fellow had played on him.

'Most people have been photographed at some time in their lives, unless they are villagers only,' he replied prosaically.

He had wanted simply to puncture in advance any new flight of fancy on the part of Mr Banerjee—he was, surely, just Mr Banerjee now—but to his surprise he seemed to have actually disconcerted the Bengali, who broke at once into a flood of explanation about why he had not often been photographed and why he had generally objected to all photography. It was all so involved and confused that Ghote soon lost track of it.

Whether some coherent account would have emerged in the end he never knew because quite suddenly Red began clicking away with his camera.

At once Mr Banerjee fell tightly silent, watching the hippy ducking and weaving at him as if he were trying ineffectively to swat a dancing mosquito.

The darting, combined with the irregular, almost aimless clicking of the camera, soon began to irritate Ghote as much as it was affecting the Bengali. There was, he felt obscurely, something wrong about it all. It was out of proportion to the expected result.

Suddenly he remembered the first time he had actually been photographed himself. It had been on a family visit to Bombay, an event that occurred once a year at most. He must have been twelve or perhaps still eleven. They had been walking through the crowded city streets, then inexpressibly wonderful to him, now familiar as the marks and flecks on his own skin. Suddenly his mother had halted the family procession and had turned and pointed back at something they had passed half a minute before. At first he had not been clear what it was she was pointing out, then he had realized it was a photographer's stall. It must have been a pretty cheap affair, he knew now. And finally it had dawned on him that he himself was the reason for all the fuss his mother was making.

His father, a man who had never indulged in a flight of fancy in his life, had of course protested. But his mother, unable to read, leaving the immediate area of their home only rarely, knowing nothing beyond the traditional lore of the stove and the needle that she had learnt as a girl, his mother had a single-minded strength of will over such things as this which had not the least difficulty in overcoming all the sober reasons-against his book-reading upright father could put forward.

So they had all entered the stall, a tiny cramped area bounded by screens. He had been stood, to the awed envy of his brothers and sister, up against the back wall, where the strongly falling sunlight provided all the lighting the photographer could afford and on which long before had been painted, with more romantic ambition than skill, a grandiose scene of palace walls and high-towering minarets. There had been a plywood cut-out of a motor-cycle too and the photographer had been eager for it to be used. But his mother, with the brusque imperiousness of the grand shopper, had waved such gaudy reality away. And then the man had vanished under the enveloping black hood of the big camera on its tall tripod and, after due deliberation and a good deal of muttered counting, there had come one single resounding click.

And that had been his photograph. A stiff little figure in excursion-battered white shirt and shorts standing in front of those patently false palace walls had haunted him for years afterwards. It had seemed indeed to keep alive in its slowly fading browns and white the boy he had been then, all promise. And year by year it had rebuked him more pointedly.

But nevertheless it had been taken in the way a photograph ought to be taken.

However, that was evidently not the way a photographer of young Red's sort went to work, and the irritating, irregular clicking, light and insect-like, of his camera went on for a long time still, a gadfly counterpoint to the solid rumble of the train wheels beneath them.

But at last it was finished. Mr Banerjee, who had been encouraged by Mary Jane in her role as photographer's assistant to talk and 'just relax' while the process was going on, but who had remained almost as still as the little boy who had been Ghote, had dropped his pose and allowed his rapid Bengali gestures to resume their sway once more. Red, apparently exhausted from the effort of clicking away so much and darting and crouching for his differing angles, had flung himself down on his unpaid-for seat. And Mary Jane, still the dutiful helper, had taken the camera and was sitting, crouched over a little, preparatory to taking out the roll.

'We'll get it developed just as soon as we get into Calcutta,' she said cheerfully. 'You'll have prints that evening, Mr Banerjee, if we get in on time.'

'We arrive at eleven tomorrow morning, my dear young lady,' Mr Banerjee replied in high good humour.

To Ghote the words were the final verdict on his test of the Bengali. If in some absurd way he had been A. K. Bhattacharya, then he was bound to have avoided somehow being recorded on film. He had in the end agreed. He was only Mr Banerjee then, infuriating, dominating, imposing Mr Banerjee.

'Yeah, eleven should be fine, we could call in at the American Exp—'

Mary Jane stopped abruptly.

Something in the rigidity that had come over her whole sari-wrapped body drew the attention of every one of them, even the guru.

'What is it? What's up?' Red asked.

'Red, there's no film in it.'

Mr Banerjee spread his long-fingered hands in the air.

'And after all my efforts as a subject,' he said. 'Really, you are a culpably negligent pair, I fear.'

And you, thought Ghote, his mind racing and slipping like an out-of-gear engine, you are A. K. Bhattacharya.

But there was no time for hard thought about the implications of that. Mary Jane was going into battle, all guns firing.

'Negligent nothing,' she snapped at the Bengali. 'I put a film in that camera while we were waiting for the train to come in the retiring-room at Manmad Station. I know I did.'

'But, my dear young lady, you must have performed that service so often for your friend . . .'

'No,' said Mary Jane. 'I put that film in. Didn't I, Red?'

'Yes,' said Red thoughtfully, 'you did, Little Cloud. And I think you'd better take a look at the rest of our stock.'

And, while Mary Jane rummaged like a fury among their possessions, Red himself examined his other camera.

'No film in this either,' he said.

'And the box of films we had here,' Mary Jane added. 'Empty too.'

Red got up and marched across the gently swaying compartment till he faced the Bengali.

'Well,' he said, 'it doesn't surprise me there's no film anywhere. Does it surprise you, Mr Banerjee? Mr Banerjee, who has got some ridiculous objection to having his photograph taken.'

The Bengali looked back at him with immense and steady blandness.

'I noticed at Piparya,' he said, 'that the compartment door had been left open while we were all out on the platform. You know, my dear chap, however non-materialistic you are, you really ought to take some precautions against theft.'

Red's sullen face darkened with anger and his fists bunched.

Ghote decided he would wait and count five

slowly from the moment he saw a blow being offered. Then he would act. But after an instant Red swung round on his heel.

'I can't prove anything,' he said darkly, and stamped back to his seat.

The Bengali sat back and closed his eyes. Soon he seemed to have dropped off into a light sleep.

Ghote sat looking at him.

After all, he reasoned, he may not be A. K. Bhattacharya. Why would the man, if he was the man, choose to put himself where he was, of all places? And just because he had gone to such lengths to prevent himself being photographed did not necessarily mean that he was the arch-trickster who had never yet, to anyone's knowledge, been recorded on film. Perhaps those seemingly ridiculous reasons he had given for disliking the camera were real. It would certainly then be in keeping with the character that he himself was gradually coming to know to take such single-minded action to stop Red taking pictures.

Yes, when you thought about it, that was as cold-hearted and unpleasant a trick as could be played. Perhaps the two hippies were not as poor as the guru and his begging-bowl indicated. Mary Jane had said something about the American Express where traveller's cheques would be cashed. But on the other hand they were almost certainly not all that rich, and colour film cost a lot of money. To steal their whole supply and get rid of it like that just to avoid a business you happened to think unpleasant: that was spitefulness on a truly monumental scale.

But say the man was A. K. Bhattacharya? His mind began whirling again.

Firmly he anchored the clashing thoughts. Even if the fellow was the legendary confidence-trickster there was nothing that had to be done about it now. The train was passing at its best speed over a wide stretch of country. No one could get off it. There was no need to make any decision, either way.

All he had to do, in fact, was what he had wanted to do from the very start: to travel.

He turned to the window and plunged into quiet content.

Wheat-fields stretched for miles in every direction and the great train was moving through them as if it were on another planet, a steadily progressing little, long-shaped world cutting across the huge, slow and vast circular world of the peasants, their unvarying days, their little clustered unchanging village life, their slow rhythm of sowing, growing and harvest. The steadily thundering train passed them all by, sending up its huge but short-lived cloud of swirling yellowish dust, adding a few extra vibrations of heat to the pounding sun-heat that was there always and then vanishing away, a remote unconnected event.

For a quiet hour and more Ghote watched

the passing outer world and drew from the always changing, never different sights that intensely comforting feeling of journeying, of making progress without the nagging strain of minor decision-making that he had all along hoped for from his trip. He began bit by bit to feel secure. At the end of the journey a dose of bitterness awaited him with the miserable second-class criminal at Dum-Dum Gaol and the really miserable second-class journey back to Bombay. But now he could put all such thoughts out of his mind. There was absolutely nothing he could do at this moment to alter his situation.

Shortly before they reached the great steel bridge across the sprawling Narbada River not far from Jabalpur, their next halt, the Bengali woke up. Instantly Ghote raised up *The D.A. Breaks An Egg* which he had toyed with all morning whenever the hippies looked as if they might want to talk.

From behind the coarse yellowing pages of unseen print he surveyed his man with caution. But the Bengali seemed to realise that any attempt at conversation would still be adding insult to the hippies' injury, and he too resorted to literature. The large, smoothly white pages of his massive book soon screened him as much as Ghote himself was screened.

But his long forefinger stayed implacably over the title-lines at the head of the left-hand pages.

The long train rattled over the six-span bridge with its lattice-work of steel girders. Below, the Narbada River, reduced to wandering streamlets by the burning sun of the past weeks, glinted here and there in its dark bed like silver in a girl's dark hair.

Soon they would come to Jabalpur where the train was due to halt for twenty-five minutes. Would this be where the Bengali planned to leave? Ghote determined to watch him even more closely than he had done at Piparya, and for this reason he paid a precautionary visit to the toilet compartment.

It was an absence he was almost at once sharply to regret. When he left his seat he had left the Bengali isolated behind his massive book: when he returned the man was talking as volubly as ever he had done and the hippies, far from being antagonistic to the point of physical violence, were listening open-mouthed.

What had he done or said? As the great train shuddered to a halt at Jabalpur Station, Ghote asked himself the question. But the necessary strain of waiting for the fellow to make a move to break away was too much to permit him to give the problem any real thought. For the next twenty-five minutes, while the food they had been asked to order at Piparya was brought to them from the station refreshment-room and was eaten amid much coming and going of bearers and confusion over the telegraphed instructions for so many ready set-out trays of vegetarian or non-vegetarian luncheons with or without 'cold drinks', he watched the Bengali for the slightest sign that he was making ready to grab that old but good suitcase, with those incredible initials on it, and take a hurried departure.

But as time went by it became clearer and clearer that the Bengali had no intention of leaving. He was so evidently friendly with the hippies, referred so frequently to the rest of the journey with them—all question of their leaving the train had been forgotten now—that it could hardly be doubted he meant to go all the way to Calcutta.

Ghote did not relax his vigilance, however. The fellow was perfectly capable of bluff and double-bluff. But the rational section of his mind acknowledged that their journey together was to continue.

Who did this make the man, he asked himself. Was this evident intention of going the whole way to Calcutta the decision of an A. K. Bhattacharya? Or was it that of a more innocent, though still nastily malicious, Mr Banerjee?

Outside on the crowded and bustling platform ever faster charging and counter-charging teams of last-minute passengers, their porters and their relations indicated that departure-time was near and Ghote plumped almost certainly for Mr Banerjee. True, A. K. Bhattacharya might well want to go to Calcutta. From there he stood a much better chance of getting out of the country than he did from Bombay where he was much more likely to be recognised. But nevertheless to elect to travel with the very man sent to bring you back from Dum-Dum Gaol: that was an act of such ridiculousness that it was really impossible to believe anyone would undertake it.

No, despite all the coincidences and unexplained events, the man opposite him must really be one A. K. Banerjee.

The signs of imminent departure drew his attention to the still unclaimed reservation card for the seat at present shared by young Red and Mary Jane. Was the 'Passenger Jabalpur-Calcutta' not going to take his place after all?

He had hardly formed the thought when there was a tremendous flurry of activity just outside the blued window and it became clear that the passenger was at that moment entering the sealed fastness of the air-conditioned coach. And a moment later the door of the compartment was pulled back and the passenger himself came in.

At once Ghote began to assess him in the light of his possible reaction to the newly allied with Mr Banerjee hippies. If he were a tough customer who would angrily claim his rights, that might yet be the last they would see of the two youngsters and the guru. And though familiarity had, he found, altered considerably his first hostile feelings he would still on the whole be glad to part from such unpredictable people.

The newcomer did not look, at first glance, very hopeful as a potential expeller of brash young Westerners. He was short, an inch or two below Ghote's own modest height, and he was well advanced in years, a good fifty if not nearing sixty, and he wore spectacles. Then he was, too, if Ghote read the cocoa duskiness of his skin right, a Southerner, and though in his own steamily hot, distant parts he might be aggressive enough, up here in the north all but the most courageous were bound to feel a bit on the defensive and unwilling to court trouble.

Indeed, the newcomer was favouring them all now with a bobbing circular bow and a wide grinning smile from his large and elastic mouth.

'Excuse me please,' he said to the hippies. 'I e-see there is a reservation-card for me where you are e-seated.'

Yes, thought Ghote noticing the intrusive 'e' sound in front of words beginning with an 's', a Southerner.

He watched him as with placid persistence he waited for his place to be ceded up. It came to him that he looked like a frog.

'Is this seat reserved then?' Red asked a little sheepishly, contriving totally to ignore the card above his head.

'I believe e-so.'

Red heaved himself up, caught hold of one of his bundles of possessions from the rack above and dumped it down on the floor, almost, but not quite, over Ghote's feet. He slumped down on it heavily and gestured towards the vacated place.

'Help yourself,' he said to the Southerner. 'Mary Jane and I can sit anywhere.'

Especially, thought Ghote sharply, since you are not paying.

The Southerner gave Red another of his little bobs of bows and went and seated himself in his newly-won place. At once a red-headclothed porter came in with two small suitcases which he stowed with what looked like particular reverence on the rack where Red's bundle had been. When the man had been tipped and had gone and the great train had slowly begun to move off once more the Southerner looked all round at them.

'Most happy to make acquaintances,' he said. 'And if I may introduce myself, my name is Ramaswamy and I have the honour to come from the city of Madras.'

There were murmurs of acknowledgment, and Ghote saw, with mixed feelings, that Mr Banerjee was about to expound on the merits of the city of Calcutta. But Mr Ramaswamy contrived to forestall him.

'Now I wonder, gentlemen and madam,' he said, 'If any of you can guess what is my task in life.'

CHAPTER SIX

The Madrasi looked round at the assembled compartment, a smile of pure pleasure beaming out from his frog-like face at the simple suspense in which he was keeping them all. Even the guru, though it was hard to tell, seemed to be waiting to hear what the nature of the newcomer's life-work was. And certainly Red and Mary Jane, ever avid for new experiences from vast and mystical India, were almost goggling in their anxiety to hear. While even Mr Banerjee, balked of an opportunity to extol his native city and its wonderful sons by the Madrasi's riddle, was still unable to refrain from indicating in the tilt forward of his long body a certain eagerness to know, though Ghote suspected that it was more an eagerness to know what he had to cap than pure disinterested curiosity.

Mr Ramaswamy looked from one to another.

'I am in the service of Indian Railways, of course,' he said, 'but it is the precise nature of my work I am asking you to guess.'

Red and Mary Jane gave each other looks of some disappointment. A railways officer hardly sounded mystical. But when little Mr Ramaswamy, after one further look round in the hope of rousing an actual answer, came out with the exact nature of his duties their hopes really plunged.

'Very well then,' Mr Ramaswamy said, 'I will enlighten you: it will be my pleasure. My life is devoted, madam and gentlemen, to the duties of an Inspector of Forms and Stationery.'

'An inspector of forms?' Mr Banerjee pounced. 'My dear sir, you cannot seriously mean to tell us that your whole life is consecrated to the inspection of that most bureaucratic of objects, the form?'

Ghote thought he detected again in this a flick of that trait he had discovered in Mr Benerjee's character: the uncaring claw of cruelty. But the reply seemed only to please the frog-like Madrasi.

'Yes, indeed, sir,' he answered. 'That is precisely the nature of my occupation. I travel all round the area of the Central Railway and sometimes make forays into other areas, and, e-sir, I inspect the forms kept at any station I choose to descend upon. And, of course, the stationery. It is, you will agree, a curious form of existence.'

'It is laughable, my dear sir,' Mr Banerjee said, pushed into terseness for once by the other's continuing equanimity.

111

'Exactly, sir, laughable,' Mr Ramaswamy rejoined, apparently still pleased by the sharpness of the condemnation he was receiving. 'It is truly laughable, isn't it? Condemned to a life of form-examining. And I might have done other things. Yes, I might have done other things.'

'But you do not,' retorted Mr Banerjee. 'You continue to examine your forms. And your stationery. You—'

'E-sir,' said Mr Ramaswamy, raising a protesting hand at last.

'Yes, sir?' Mr Benerjee asked, a light shining in his tiger eyes.

'—Sir, not "your stationery". The stationery, and the forms are not mine, sir. They are the property of the Railways. Note, I do all that I do on behalf not of myself, but of the Railways. I am their jealous guardian.'

But this was all too much for your rebel Red.

'Let me get this straight,' he said. 'You spend all your time going from station to station counting up the forms?'

'Rather issuing permits for new stock,' said Mr Ramaswamy. 'Some of these station-master fellows are quite deplorable in their attempts to gain new stock, you know. Especially the ones with children.'

'With children, for heaven's sake?' Mary Jane asked now.

'Yes, yes, madam. Children have certain

112

requirements in the way of educational necessities, isn't it? And in many cases it so happens that railway property is quite suitable for this use. I tell you, I have to be devilishly sharp on occasion. Devilishly sharp.'

Mr Ramaswamy, wide-smiling frog-like looking beamingly bland, glanced from one to another of the compartment's occupants with pride.

'And so, my dear sir,' Mr Banerjee resumed his pointed interrogation, 'you take infinite pains to make sure these wretched fellows never have more forms and stationery than they are entitled to? You spend hour after hour, checking and counting, all to this end?'

'Not really counting, sir,' Mr Ramaswamy said blandly. 'Counting is considered to be beneath my status. My task is essentially one of comparison. I compare new requisitions with old. I draw my conclusions. And I cut down. E-savagely at times.'

Again he stared at them with innocent pride.

'And, my dear sir,' said Mr Banerjee, leaning forward persuasively, 'has it never occurred to you that you could make this tedious life of yours a great deal simpler?'

'E-simpler, sir? I should be most glad to hear of any suggestions you have to make. Though I must warn you, I think they are unlikely to be practical. A great deal of thought has gone, over the years, into the framing of the regulations which govern, as it were, my whole existence.'

'But I think my solution might have a certain overriding simplicity about it which would nevertheless, if you were to approve, relieve you of considerable burdens.'

'Very well then, sir,' said Mr Ramaswamy. 'What is your suggestion?'

Ghote, who had a very clear notion of the sort of suggestion Mr Banerjee would be likely to make, ran over in his mind with lightning quickness the central portion of the provisions of the Indian Penal Code on the subject of incitement of crime, and waited. If the man was not A. K. Bhattacharya, he was—or soon might become—another sort of criminal.

And then the fellow would come under the provisions of the law. At the very least he would deserve a sharp warning to take him down a peg or two. If nothing else, it would stop him scraping those claws he had proved to have on little Mr Ramaswamy.

'What is my suggestion, my dear sir? Falsify your returns. Yes, that is it. Falsify your returns. There you are working in a world of falsities: then work in it truly and submit returns that are purely and beautifully fictional. That is my advice to you, my dear sir.'

Mr Banerjee paused, with long finger raised up admonishingly. Ghote drew breath to leap.

'That is the advice I would give you, my

dear sir, if I were you. But of course I am not. I am not the voice of your conscience, and I cannot therefore give you advice. But listen to that conscience of yours, my dear sir, listen, I beg.'

No, Ghote thought, he has slipped off again. Damn it.

And then Mr Ramaswamy, in the politest possible way, explained how he could not possibly indulge in any falsehood. And Mr Banerjee, in the most theoretical terms, launched into a defence of falsehood in life. And Mary Jane dashed in with a passionate, youthful plea for truth and for the need to spread the truth, and Red sulkily held forth on the importance of just following the truth, and both were firmly put down by Mr Banerjee.

But neither of them seemed to resent it as much as Ghote, hidden again behind *The D.A. Breaks An Egg* but unable not to listen to every word, resented it on their behalf. They had not realised, he surmised, just what sort of a person was putting them so firmly in their place. They must think, as he himself had thought when the Calcutta Mail had started out on its journey, that this Mr Banerjee was simply a choice example of the wildly talking, lecturing, hectoring Bengali. But he now knew better. Indeed he had just had confirmation in the man's treatment of innocent Mr Ramaswamy: advocating falsifying those returns was nothing less than a casual attempt to wreck a chance acquaintance's whole life. If Mr Ramaswamy had actually been convinced, what would have happened? The whole framework of his existence would have rapidly crumbled away.

Yes, no doubt about it, Mr Banerjee was a dangerous man in his own right.

But none of the others in the compartment seemed to have an inkling of this as the Calcutta Mail swayed and rattled along over the miles and miles of dusty plain with the sun still high above it, though degree by degree plunging on its downward course, still leaving the dust-covered dead levels quivering endlessly from its accumulated heat. As the afternoon wore on, and the conversation in the air-conditioned coolness wound and twisted endlessly, the great train notched up little village after little village, flicking them off to either side, carelessly shedding the little black dots that were each a whole collection of mud-walled huts, with each hut in them a home, and over them a wisp or two of tall spindly palms and, scarcely rising above the level of the huts, a mud-walled temple, or, where the village was a Muslim one, no temple but a small collection of insignificant tombs.

At last dusk swooped down and the long train became a fiery comet dragging trailing lines of yellowy light through a night that was for mile upon mile almost unbroken darkness. Gradually the oven-hot earth lost its heat. But still the conversation piled idea on idea, and only Ghote and the guru took no part in it. The guru, it seemed, was to be privileged from Mr Banerjee's assaults, but Ghote knew that he himself was not and so had hardly dared even to look while it had still been daylight through the blued window glass at the endlessly passing monotonous countryside. In consequence he finished *The D.A. Breaks An Egg* though he got no joy, realising how few pages remained between him and the general conversation, in being completely fooled by the surprise dénouement.

And, as they neared their next stopping-place, Allahabad, he contrived, while Mr Banerjee was temporarily refreshing himself in the toilet compartment, to go back to near the beginning of the book and start to move through its swift pages once again.

But even these pages stood him in no stead when Mr Banerjee returned. Hardly had he been seated ten minutes when he leant forward and tapped Ghote sharply and implacably on the knee.

'You know what it is we are passing at this moment?'

Ghote looked up, trying to simulate the bewilderment of the disturbed faraway reader, and grossly over-acting.

'No, no,' he said. 'What was that? I am sorry.'

'I asked, my dear Inspector, whether you

realised what it is we are passing out there?'

Ghote dutifully peered at the now black window. In it he could see the glint of a slowly changing pattern of lights. The train, he realised, had slowed considerably.

'No,' he said. 'I do not at all know.'

'My dear sir, it is the notorious Naini Gaol.'

'Oh, indeed. Most interesting.'

Ghote made an attempt to get back to the D.A.

'Come, sir, leave that book, which in any case you are perusing for the second time, and listen to what I have to say.'

Ghote put down the book. Mr Banerjee rubbed the long fingers of his hands together. They sounded papery and dry.

'Have you, my dear sir,' he began, 'ever considered to what it is you are condemning the miserable wretches whom you sometimes capture? Have you any notion how appallingly unpleasant, for some of them, a gaol such as Naini there must be? Do you even know—'

'Stop,' Ghote barked.

He had spoken much louder than he meant. Mr Banerjee actually did stop and all the others turned and looked at him. Even the silent guru brought his unflecked gaze to bear upon him. He swallowed once and launched into what he felt he must say.

'Please, you must speak the truth. A police officer does not condemn any person to gaol. It is the magistrate or the judges who do that.

A police officer does no more than present a case.'

But Mr Banerjee was unconvinced.

'My dear sir, a fiddle for that. Oh, indeed, yes, I know that is the outward form of things. But let us look a little at what really happens. Take, for example, the case of that poor fellow A. K. Bhattacharya, whom you were on your way to drag from one gaol to another. Let us look at his particular circumstances.'

At once Ghote did indeed look at A. K. Bhattacharya and his particular circumstances. Why had this wretched Bengali dragged in that name again? Could it be because it was his own?

The very wildness of that idea for a moment appealed to him. But then common-sense in all its quiet legions of onward-plodding infantrymen tramped to the rescue. No, such an idea was in the realm of the purely fantastic. What was much more likely, and altogether more reasonable, was that Mr Banerjee, knowing as he did how the very name of A. K. Bhattacharya must gall him himself, had simply seized on this chance to thrust its thorny shape towards him.

'Come, my dear Inspector,' Mr Banerjee resumed, with a teeth-flashing smile, 'you will admit, will you not, that you and your colleagues have long ago made up your minds about the unfortunate Bhattacharya. You have condemned him. It is a matter of pride with

119

the whole police force of Bombay that a man they believe to have been operating the most daring scheme seen in all this century right under their very noses should not only be brought to trial but should be most humiliatingly punished. Now, my dear sir, it—'

'Objection,' Ghote snapped. 'You cannot in the same breath say that this A. K. Bhattacharya has been operating a daring fraud scheme and that the police have decided without evidence that he is a criminal.'

'A criminal, my dear Inspector? See what rigid thinking you are employing already. How can you say really that such a man as the great Bhattacharya is a criminal? What has he done when you look at it in a simple, common-sense, down-to-earth light? He has sold for valuable foreign currency a number of objects to people who were willing to pay for them. Is that criminal? Certainly not.'

Mr Banerjee leant forward even more persuasively.

'There have been some thoroughly wicked men, I grant you,' he went on, 'who have been stealing images from temples, as many as thirty have been taken recently in Nepal alone, I believe. There have even been thefts from museums, an utterly disgraceful business. But what the renowned Bhattacharya is doing is nothing of that sort at all. He, by his activities, is in effect preserving innumerable fine objects from the brutal depredations of foreign art-collectors. I have no hesitation in saying that his work is that of a supreme patriot. And yet you wish to condemn him to a stinking gaol like Naini back there.'

The great train began to rock and rattle over the long bridge that spans the Jumna at the approach to Allahabad. By the light streaming from the windows Ghote could see in the background the rising and falling pattern of rivet-studded girders as one by one the spans of the bridge passed by. He felt reassured by their solid presence, because all round him in the compartment he could sense hostility. The two hippies were clearly on Mr Banerjee's side—what could he have said to them just before they had got to Jabalpur?—and even mild Mr Ramaswamy seemed to be looking at him a little askance, while the guru was so neutral he might almost have been an insubstantial spirit floating there. And the hostility seemed so unfair.

'But please to listen,' he said. 'There are laws in this country. They are set out to protect us from the people who would harm us. We need them. We must have them. And it is one of these laws that A. K. Bhattacharya has broken.'

'Ah, you see,' cried Mr Banerjee, arms held high to either side, fingers eloquently spread in protest. 'Already he is declaring that the innocent, traduced Bhattacharya poor fellow, is a breaker of the law.'

'No, no,' Ghote protested, experiencing wave after wave of hostility battering against his frail defences. 'I am not saying. What I am saying is "if". If, only. If A. K. Bhattacharya is found guilty, then what he has done is to break the laws which are there to protect us all.'

Mr Banerjee fired off a white-flashing smile signalling supreme contempt.

'Now he is trying to go back,' he said, looking all round. 'Now he is admitting that after all A. K. Bhattacharya is absolutely innocent. And that was the man he was all ready to drag into gaol.'

'But, but—' Ghote protested.

But his desperate attempts to put things right were drowned by the loud squeal of the great Calcutta Mail once again coming to a halt as they entered Allahabad Station.

The train stopped here for three-quarters of an hour and there was time for a comparatively leisurely meal out in the station itself. Ghote simply followed Mr Banerjee when they all got out. For one thing he was determined not to let more poison against himself be spread in his absence. And for another, the fellow might, just might be— But, no, that was nonsense.

As they ate in the big, crowded vegetarian refreshment-room, to which Mr Banerjee had led them presumably in deference to the guru's religious susceptibilities, the aggressive Bengali continued to talk. But now his subject was Allahabad.

It seemed that this was another of the places he had had occasion to stay in for some time in the exercise of his still not yet completely accounted for business. But certainly he knew a lot about the city, about its incredibly distant past as a holy place (stirrings of excitement from Mary Jane and Red) and about its romantic Muslim period some four centuries ago when it had acquired its present name.

And before very long, interesting, even fascinating though what he had to say was, Ghote found that he could stand it no longer. All that knowledge, all that telling them what they ought to believe, all that superiority was intolerable.

'Excuse me, please,' he said, and rising abruptly to his feet he pushed his way out of the crowded, noisy room.

But promptly he felt obliged to come to a halt at a point on the platform outside where he could keep a watch on the refreshment-room door. He was not going to risk letting that man out of his sight, whoever he was.

The pushing, jabbering railway passengers all around him did nothing to quiet the fury he felt and, spotting a half-open doorway, he stepped back inside. He found himself in the station court-room.

At this mid-hour of the day it was deserted, except for a single almost naked sweeper who was standing shoving about on the wooden floor with one lackadaisical foot a big lump of almost completely blackened cleaning-cloth. But Ghote had no difficulty in imagining the procession of fare-dodgers who either must have appeared one by one in the railed dock, been brusquely questioned by the Magistrate from his high presiding bench and sentenced each in turn to a proper penalty under the Railway Regulations.

For a few moments he sought visibility to embody Mr Banerjee up in that same dock. And he himself would be opposite him in the unrailed witness-stand. And he would give evidence against him in a calm, rational and altogether inescapable manner. That the accused did yesterday with intent to cause fear and alarm to a section of the public induce, as heretofore stated, one so-and-so to commit an offence against the public tranquillity.

'You are wanting to inspect court, sahib?'

The sweeper had scented some easily earned baksheesh.

'No, no,' Ghote said hastily.

And, banishing these day-dreamings, he stepped back into the hurly-burly of the platform and a few minutes later saw Mr Banerjee come out of the refreshment-room. He joined the procession back to the train where he found that in their absence the four bunks in the compartment had once again been made up as beds.

But, once they were settled in their places,

the tall Bengali, not for the first time, did something that took him completely by surprise.

He turned suddenly to the guru.

'But what nonsense we have all been talking,' he said. 'All this chit-chat about art and antiquities is interesting enough in its way, but how it palls beside the subject of human beings. And, I may add speaking quite personally, how it palls beside the subject of A. K. Bhattacharya in particular. Since our conversation happened to touch on that man earlier I confess his presence has been in and out of my mind ever since. And it occurs to me now, Guruji, that you among us all as one who has devoted himself to truth are the one to pronounce on Bhattacharya's real worth.'

Ghote expected that the almost constantly silent guru would do no more than produce a sweet smile at this. But he had reckoned without Mr Banerjee's almost hypnotic power.

'I was hearing with great interest what you were saying about A. K. Bhattacharya,' the guru replied.

'You were? You were? Excellent, Guruji. Then we shall all be able to benefit from your opinions on the fellow.'

'But I have no opinion on him,' the guru said. 'What is it to me that a man should live his life all in one place like a prison, or in going about here and there and selling objects? He has only his life to lead whatever

125

he does.'

Mr Banerjee was not at all disconcerted at this.

'Most true, most true, Guruji,' he said. 'But let me nevertheless put before you a consideration which, naturally enough, may have escaped you. Tell me, essentially is not a man like A. K. Bhattacharya very much like yourself?'

'All men are men,' the guru replied tentatively.

But the comparison, if not striking him as anything out of the way, clearly presented itself to little Mr Ramaswamy as being something of an affront.

'Excuse me, e-sir,' he said, leaning forward and addressing Mr Banerjee, frog eyes shining through his round spectacles, 'I do not see how, employ what arguments you will, it is possible to equate our friend the guru here, a man dedicated to the holy life, with that extremely commercial fellow Bhattacharya.'

'Not at all, not at all,' Mr Banerjee replied at once and in high glee. 'Let me draw up for you, my dear sir, a brief table of comparison between the excellent A. K. Bhattacharya and Guruji here, who as a man beyond the vanities of the world will not mind hearing himself praised, I am sure.'

The excellent A. K. Bhattacharya. Ghote pondered the words. No, by themselves they probably would not really be said to constitute an offence under Section 505. But let the fellow watch out.

With a tremendous rustling of dry palm against dry palm Mr Banerjee began his catalogue.

'Now, first,' he said, 'both Guruji and A. K. Bhattacharya are men beyond the bounds of regular society. Does the guru stay at home with his family? No, he has reached the stage where such obligations are beyond him. Does A. K. Bhattacharya stay in some worthily respectable employment? No, he has reached a moral stage beyond that.'

Mr Banerjee regarded the guru with what Ghote thought was a touch of curiosity here, as if wondering whether he would actually get away with this curious concept of moral superiority. But the guru did no more than look back at him with good-natured interest. And equally Ghote decided that, so far, he too still had nothing against Mr Banerjee.

'Yes,' the Bengali resumed, with perhaps even greater confidence than before, 'now both you, Guruji and A. K. Bhattacharya are not only already out of society but both long to be even more out of this world. Is that not so in your case, Guru?'

'It is so,' the guru agreed peacefully.

'And A. K. Bhattacharya, I can assure you—I feel in some ways that I can see into that man's mind—A. K. Bhattacharya I assure you longs now for some place of distant happiness.

Say, Bali. You know the island of Bali?

No one admitted to much knowledge of Bali.

'Ah, it is a paradise, I promise you,' Mr Banerjee informed them. 'Think of that quite small island there in Indonesia, a distant stronghold of Hinduism, a rich and well-cultivated land and above all a haunt of beauty. If you have not seen the dances of Bali you have seen nothing.'

He looked ecstatically up at the curving roof of the carriage above him, once white, now somewhat brownish and stained with the bodies of dead insects.

'And there are there too,' he added, more prosaically, 'I am certain, hitherto untapped riches of sculpture and architecture.'

'Perhaps one day my travels will take me to such a place,' the guru observed.

'But, Guru, you said you would visit the States,' Mary Jane put in with some anxiety.

'He said no such thing,' Red broke in furiously. 'He's just going to go where it suits him, wandering in Holy India.'

And with these words he gave pretty, blue-eyed Mary Jane such a glare that Ghote wondered whether the pair of them would still be together even in the comparatively short time till midday tomorrow in Calcutta.

Mr Banerjee did not allow the interruption to influence him.

'Yes, Guruji,' he went on, 'you and I have

128

much in—'

He stopped abruptly for an instant, but resumed again almost without altering the flow of his discourse.

'You and I, Guruji, have something in common, I believe. But how much more have you in common with that elusive figure, A. K. Bhattacharya. I will tell you another—'

But to Ghote's astonishment, to everyone's evident astonishment, Mr Banerjee was here interrupted by the guru himself.

He held forward a long, bony, fleshless arm and waved it with an odd combination of imperiousness and vague directionlessness.

'I would like to say,' he began in a voice little more than a murmur, 'I would like to say that I have not got many things in common with you. In me you see a man who had cast off almost all except what belongs to every man. But you have been adding more.'

Mr Banerjee looked at him in utter surprise.

'Adding more?' he asked.

'Yes,' said the guru. 'There is your hair.'

And again Mr Banerjee was reduced to two words of query, while Ghote with sudden running joy knew quite well what it was the guru had meant.

'My hair?' asked Mr Banerjee.

'To that you have added colour, black colour,' the guru stated placidly.

'No. Nonsense. Utter—It is a—'

Mr Banerjee stopped himself talking and

forced a waxen smile on to his fleshy Bengali face. His white teeth looked like over-long fangs stuck on to a carnival mask.

'Well, my dear sir, my dear Guruji,' he said after a pause long enough for the never-ceasing rhythm of the train beating over the rails to come into the foreground of their minds. 'My dear Guruji, I confess to it. Yes, I plead guilty. Guilty to vanity. It is a hard thing to have to avow, and in public, and before such young people too.'

Mr Banerjee leered awkwardly at Mary Jane.

'Yes, I admit it,' he said, 'I have on occasion had recourse to the dye bottle. I wish to be other than I am. But it is a harmless wish surely?'

It was a question to which embarrassingly he plainly wanted an answer. No one spoke.

'Well, perhaps back in the friendly warmth of my native city I shall have the courage to throw off this—Yes, this disguise. Why not call it that? After all, this is what it is. A disguise. I have disguised my true self, I admit it.'

He looked round at them all now with his confidence entirely restored. The smiling grin no longer looked like stuck-on carnival teeth.

'But we were talking of A. K. Bhattacharya,' he said briskly. 'Not of myself. By no means of myself. No, Bhattacharya and our friend Guruji here. Both you and he, I venture to claim, above all, teach your fellow-citizens the valuelessness of mere property. You, my dear Guru, by your evident example. A. K. Bhattacharya, as forcefully, by showing the world that a forged work of art can be more costly indeed than what might be called the real thing.'

Incitement? Not quite, Ghote regretfully decided.

'And finally,' Mr Banerjee said, bringing his oration to a conclusion of sweeping majesty. 'Finally, both you, Guruji, and A. K. B., if I may call him such, possess that most wonderful of gifts, a belief in the intangible. You with your life devoted to the spiritual. He with his life devoted to the arts.'

And again this was too much for the diligent Inspector of Forms and Stationery.

'But, e-sir, no, no, no, no,' he burst out. 'I really cannot accept that. How can a man who, isn't it, has perpetrated really disgraceful forgeries, how can such a person claim to be a lover of the arts? Sir, the suggestion is perfectly e-scandalous.'

He sat bolt upright to the last inch of his five feet of height and regarded Mr Banerjee with all the shocked disapproval of the little succulent frog for the rearing, fangwide snake.

And Mr Banerjee did seem somewhat put out, to Ghote's pleasure. He looked from side to side in silence, and then with something of a shrug he turned to take from his fine but battered leather suitcase a fat volume that had, occasionally, beguiled the journey for him.

And as he did so once more the light fell squarely on top of the case, and once more, plain to see, were those old stamped initials A. K. B. Ghote regarded them with that curious uneasiness that he had felt every time he had seen them or even thought of their existence.

But their effect on little Mr Ramaswamy, who it seemed had not yet chanced to catch sight of them, was far more dramatic.

He looked. He goggled. His whole right arm raised itself as if attached to some system of visible pulleys and chains. The finger at its end pointed.

'A. K. B.,' he said in a voice of strangled intensity. 'A. K. B., the very initials.'

He swung round rigidly in his seat till he was facing not the old but fine suitcase but Mr Banerjee himself.

'E-sir,' he said, 'an astonishing idea has presented itself to me. E-sir, I believe that you are none other than A. K. Bhattacharya himself.'

CHAPTER SEVEN

Ghote felt, as little Mr Ramaswamy uttered his impossible challenge to Mr Banerjee (if that was his name), that some immensely distant

132

beneficent being had done for him something he could not even have dared to ask for. The really impossible had been uttered as words. What would A. K. Bhattacharya's reaction be to this piece of unimaginable daring? But no, Mr Banerjee was not A. K. Bhattacharya. He could not be. For all Mr Ramaswamy's denunciation it was simply too much of a coincidence that the man he had been going to fetch from Calcutta should have landed up in the very same compartment as himself. It was flying in the face of fact to believe it. And this he would not do.

Ghote forced himself not to lean forward, forced himself to look as if he was regarding Mr Ramaswamy with mild surprise. But his gaze was dragged round as by a magnet to the fleshy-faced Bengali. Who was . . .

The eyebrows that for the first part of their journey had been so tantalisingly hidden behind the rims of Polaroid sun-glasses rose in astonishment. But were they rising too slowly? Was this a desperate effort not to acknowledge the shaft, not to leap up and get away somehow down the length of the great train now moving steadily past the outskirts of the great old holy city of Benares?

Ghote tensed himself to spring up and pinion the fugitive.

Yet Mr Ramaswamy seemed to believe that the astonishment being elaborately registered on the Bengali's face was just what it appeared to be, shocked dismay. He began at once to babble out a series of excuses for his outrageous remark.

'My good sir, you will forgive. But nevertheless perhaps you will equally acknowledge that I have a case, isn't it? Oh, gracious me, yes, such facts that kept presenting themselves to my mind.'

He gave a quick, patently nervous smile.

'To begin with,' he said, 'only this moment, just before observing the dreadful coincidence of initials, I had the fact drawn to my attention that you are, in some way, wearing a disguise. One knows of course that a great many people do employ a hair dye, but nevertheless it is a disguise, and A. K. Bhattacharya at this moment no doubt is in disguise somewhere.'

'No doubt he is,' Mr Banerjee assented, with a smile of such tigerish whiteness that Ghote, at whom for once it was not directed, still quailed.

'And then, e-sir,' Mr Ramaswamy ploughed nobly on, 'you had shown earlier such an acquaintance with antiquities, and surely that fearful fellow Bhattacharya must have a like knowledge.'

But evidently Mary Jane had too in some part shared Mr Ramaswamy's horrible suspicions, because she now joined in his public act of penance.

'I guess you acted pretty suspicious when Red wanted to photograph you too,' she said to the tall Bengali. 'Why, at one time we thought you had taken those films from Red's cameras, till you told us—'

She came to an abrupt, filly-in-a-field halt and looked at Ghote as if she wished he was just simply not there.

And at once Ghote realised what it must have been that Mr Banerjee had said to the hippies when he had them on their own just before they had arrived at Jabalpur. He must have told them that he himself had taken the films. No wonder he had been regarded so blackly.

He longed to be able to stop and think about this. He knew, after all, that he had not taken the films. And surely it had been Mr Banerjee who had done so, almost to the point of being proven. But then if he had, surely this meant that after all he was A. K.—

No. He forced himself to stop. That was a perilous path indeed.

'And then I feel bound to add also,' Mr Ramaswamy went bitterly and bravely on to the end of his confession. 'Also that you did, my dear good sir, advocate that I should falsify my returns. E-sir, that was ultimately what put the thought in my mind. Only a man as terrible as A. K. Bhattacharya himself, I said, could think of a thing like that.'

Mr Banerjee smiled again, more blandly and hurtfully even than before.

'But, of course, my dear sir,' he said, 'I did not for one moment advocate any such terrible thing, as, if you recall, I am sure you will be the first to acknowledge. I asked only that you should look into your own conscience and see if such a course lay within your powers.'

'E-sir, I acknowledge it,' said Mr Ramaswamy. And he got up from his seat, delivered a last bow of humiliation to Mr Banerjee and sought the refuge of the toilet compartment, clutching the smaller of his two suitcases.

* * *

Ghote decided that if Mr Ramaswamy emerged from the toilet compartment in night attire he too would risk the complications of Mary Jane's stare and change for this night out of his day clothes. But when, after a considerable interval, Mr Ramaswamy rejoined them, wearing a pair of orange-spotted pyjamas in unexpected contrast to his notably sober suit, claim to the toilet compartment was instantly exercised by Mr Banerjee.

Plainly nobody felt that they could stand in the way of a person who had had to endure the terrible affront that had been offered him. Nor did anybody feel able to console Mr Ramaswamy for his gaffe. So the poor frog-like Madrasi crept into his berth and hid his head.

Mr Banerjee exercised his rights to the toilet compartment even more lengthily than Mr Ramaswamy had done. But Ghote was in there like lightning after him, concerned above all not to be within range of the Bengali after such an incident.

He got himself ready for bed in less than four minutes and when he came back into the main compartment dived into the security of his sheets with all the speed of a mongoose burrowing into an inviting under-rock crevice. It took him, face peering up into the milky white of the cotton counterpane drawn up over his head as high as he could, a considerable time to get off to sleep nevertheless. He felt, in fact, as if he had not succeeded in getting his eyes really closed by the time the train halted at Gaya Junction for ten minutes or so shortly after 3a.m. But he was certainly obviously asleep shortly after they had set off again.

When he was woken finally, outside the blued glass of the windows the white light of dawn was beginning to show up the shape of the country. To the north now were mountains, a low range, dark against the paling sky.

It was Mr Banerjee who had woken him. The tall Bengali was already dressed for the day in his fine kurta and many-folded dhoti and he was looking desperately fresh and ready for battle.

Ghote at once became acutely conscious of his own dark jowl, no doubt all the worse for the fiasco over shaving the day before. Would things be any better this morning? He saw no reason why they should be.

And in less than seven hours he would be in Calcutta too, meeting his opposite numbers in the Calcutta force, giving them an appalling impression of Bombay smartness and turn-out, and having humbly to take delivery of that second-rate crook, A. K. Biswas, card-sharper, in place of the renowned A. K. Bhattacharya.

He would be looked down on as well, he knew, for his force having allowed Bhattacharya to give them the slip. And all the more so because in some measure that man had got away owing to the Calcutta force arresting the wrong fellow.

'Good morning, good morning, my dear Inspector,' Mr Banerjee said. 'I thought I would take the liberty of waking you because I very much want you to share something with me.'

I do not want it, Ghote thought.

'Yes?' he said.

'I want you, my dear chap, to share with me every moment of our coming into Bengal today. I have told you about the virtues of my native place, and you have been so good as to take them on trust.'

Ghote was aware of two eyes looking at his sharply.

'Yes, yes,' he said. 'I have taken what you have told me with complete trust.'

'But now, my dear Inspector, my dear

professional distruster, you shall see that every word I have said to you has been nothing less than the purest truth.'

'Yes,' said Ghote.

'But, my dear fellow, if I may make a suggestion?'

'Yes?' Ghote said.

'Let me speak quite personally, my dear sir. As man to man, as friend to friend, may I say? My dear chap, you are looking most abominably unshaven. I suspect that something went very wrong when you attempted to shave yesterday morning. Not everyone can do it in a rocking and swaying train, my dear chap.'

Mr Banerjee stroked his own, long fleshy jaw. His barber-shave of the day before had lasted extraordinarily well.

'Now, my dear fellow,' he said, 'take the advice of an old-hand, a seasoned traveller, a man whose hard lot it has been to go travelling all over this country of ours looking at—Well, looking at this and that in the course of my business. Take a tip from me, old boy, and get yourself properly shaved by a barber when we stop at Hazaribagh Road in a few minutes.'

'But the train is scheduled to stop there for four minutes only,' Ghote said, remembering the timetable.

'Perfectly right, Inspector. As always. Yet I think you will find that we are some six minutes ahead of schedule and that we will thus stay at Hazaribagh Road a good ten minutes. More than time for a shave, my dear sir, as you saw yesterday. And at Hazaribagh Road the barbers are devilish quick fellows. I know them well. I am on first-name terms with the rogues.'

Ghote did not much like the sound of falling into the hands of Mr Banerjee's rogues.

'I think nevertheless I will try to shave myself,' he said.

'And look a mess when you greet your colleagues, my dear, Inspector? When already you have to collect from them, not the renowned A. K. Bhattacharya, but the petty card-sharper, A. K. Biswas?'

'Perhaps you are right,' Ghote said, thinking of the missing tube of Lakmé for Men. 'Yet the train may not be early at Hazaribagh Road after all.'

But, of course, the Calcutta Mail did roll into Hazaribagh Road Station just precisely six minutes early. And almost before the long line of dust-thick carriages had ground to a halt Mr Banerjee, long thin fingers clasped hard on Ghote's elbow, had the inspector out on to the broad cement platform and was marching him briskly over its phlegm and betel-spit spattered surface. Spurning the clamorous attentions of the squatting shoe-shine boys who to Ghote's mind rose up at their approach like so many squawking gulls beating up from Bombay Harbour at the slight hope of a prize of food,

Mr Banerjee called aloud to a group of razor-wielding barbers established with a number of masseurs on their own section of the platform. And he called in Bengali.

Ghote's spirits simmered even lower. Bengali, the fellow's own much vaunted language. It was beginning to be spoken now and soon it would be so everywhere till that miserable second-class carriage in the train home had rolled a good way on its journey back.

He understood a word or two of the language, but he found now he was missing most of what Mr Banerjee, talking it seemed faster and more vigorously than ever, was saying as he approached the squatting group.

And, to Ghote's continued annoyance, Mr Banerjee proceeded to arrange the whole matter of the shave. He selected which barber Ghote would use, a man with—surely this was not a good idea—only one eye; he instructed him at considerable length and still in very rapid Bengali.

'Stop,' Ghote said once. 'Please, I do not follow Bengali well. What are you telling?'

Mr Banerjee switched momentarily into English for an explanation.

'My dear fellow, I am making sure you get the treatment you deserve. A distinguished visiting police officer. Yes, indeed.'

And then back to that quick, flicking, mysterious Bengali.

Furiously Ghote sought to pick out the meaning of the darting stream of words. What was the man arranging for him, for heaven's sake? Surely just to say to the barber—and why had he picked on the one-eyed one?—just to say to him, if he really did have to be addressed only in Bengali. 'Here is a friend of mine who wants to be shaved before the train goes', surely that would be enough? But, no, Mr Banerjee was going on and on.

But mounting fury blocked his ears, and even his scanty Bengali vocabulary deserted him. And, to double his rage, the two hippies, out on the platform stretching their legs in the early morning air, also now appeared to be joining in the conversation and to be doing so in Bengali that was at least fair. Ghote could not properly make out what they were saying either, though the belicose Red seemed to be enjoying some joke or other and was holding up one of his useless, filmless cameras by its neck-strap, perhaps explaining he was unable to photograph any of the barbers or the bare-chested masseurs at work.

Ghote wished he would go away. And besides the minutes of their stay at Hazaribagh Road were ticking past.

But a moment later he found himself taken by the barber of Mr Banerjee's choice, his one eye darting hither and thither at tremendous speed, and being sat down on a low, wide canework stool some distance away from the spot where Mr Banerjee himself was already under the razor.

He attempted to adjust his position on the stool, less because he was uncomfortable than in order to assert a little bit of independence. But the one-eyed barber simply put a hand on the top of his head—his fingers were appallingly bony and quite as long as those of Mr Banerjee himself—and held him firmly in exactly the position he wished. And an instant later the other hand had come up from the cement floor of the platform where there was a large enamel basin full of grey and sticky lather with a short, stubby brush that plainly prickled had covered his face from deep down on his neck to within centimetres of his eyes with stiff bubbles.

They were cold too, cold and clammy.

Ghote nerved up his forces for one good twist of his head that would get him out of the fellow's grip. All right, he would consent to be shaved by him—there was very little time after all—but first he would choose at what angle he was going to hold his own head.

The one-eyed barber's open razor appeared in his free hand as if by magic and sizzled towards Ghote's stretched neck. Ghote held himself desperately rigid.

The razor swept into the glutinous and clammy foam. It seemed to be much less sharp than it had looked. It could be felt scraping along the skin like a hot thin jagged wire.

And at some moment too the one-eyed fellow—could he really see what he was doing?—had dexterously transferred his grip with his holding hand. No longer were those digging, wooden-peg fingers on top of his skull: they were now holding his nose.

But at least, he said to himself as that agonising blade worked jerkily up first his left cheek and then his right, at least the fellow is being quick about it. Unless the train left early, and surely—surely—it would not do that, then he ought to be through this terrible process in decent time to get on board again.

And then quite suddenly the rapid razor-strokes ceased. For a moment Ghote wondered whether the shave was over, though he could not recollect any attention having been paid to his upper lip and that was an area—he had once ventured on a small moustache—that had always been particularly sensitive.

But, no, the barber was still holding his nose clamped tight as in an iron vice between his long fingers and he was making small tentative, though still good and painful, jabs at an area round his right ear, a part that already, unless his sense of touch had completely deserted him, had been swept clear of lather.

What on earth was the fellow doing?

Squinting ferociously he was able to see Mr Banerjee, presumably shaved already, walking back towards their coach. But the finicky, painful work under his right ear was still going on. It was not as if there were usually a stiff patch of bristle there. What was happening? If the fellow carried on at this slow pace he would have hardly finished before the train was due to leave. It would be a question of running along the platform back to his boarding door, with lather perhaps still lying in stiff white lines on his jaw, after hastily dipping out too much money to the one-eyed devil and then scampering aboard the train at the very last moment.

Too much money. That was probably the whole idea.

Ghote boiled.

Could he get a hand into his pocket and pull out a decent sum, correct, generous even, but not ridiculous? When the fellow saw that he was found out would he stop this absurd game?

But held by the nose like this it was difficult to move even an inch. At this rate he would miss the train altogether.

Miss the train.

A sweat broke out beneath the half-scraped layer of cold, gluey lather on his face. He might miss the train. That would mean he would arrive in Calcutta heaven knows when. There would quite likely be someone from the Calcutta CID waiting to meet him. They knew of course when he was due to arrive. And if he was not there they might do anything. They

145

might telegraph to Bombay. To D.S.P. Samant. And that would crown it all. Not only not to be collecting A. K. Bhattacharya but instead some two-anna card-sharper, but not even to be there to collect him.

He wriggled hard from side to side.

The grip on his nose increased in intensity till that organ actually throbbed with pain and the tears pricked at his eyeballs.

What the hell was the man doing?

'Let me up,' he shouted in English.

The eye did not even blink.

What the devil was the Bengali doing?

Ah, yes. Something like this.

He tried it.

The bloody impertinent fellow actually grinned at him and twisted his nose. Yes, he had done it on purpose. Twisted—

Oooooh.

And then, penetrating with difficulty the bell of pain that hung over his whole face there came a sound.

A terrible sound. A sound not to be allowed.

It was the shrill pipe of a guard's whistle. The Calcutta Mail was departing. It could be nothing else.

Ghote put his hands to the edges of the canework seat and pushed upwards. The barber leant right up over him and with the hand still gripping and gripping his nose pushed downwards. Ghote swayed quickly to

146

the left. He felt himself at last beginning to get from under the madman's hold.

The jagged edge of the too-little-sharpened razor presented itself half an inch away from his left eyeball.

He froze into stillness.

In the quiet that followed he could distinctly hear every sound that came from the huge train at the edge of the platform, the heaving gasping of the great steam locomotive as puff by puff it gathered energy to drag the immense weight behind it, the sharp release of agonised pain from the iron wheels of the serried carriages as they were at last jerked out of their station stillness, the deep clanging mutter chasing back and forwards as the carriages in turn began to receive motion.

The train was off. The train was off.

The one-eyed barber's razor remained deadly still within its half-inch of Ghote's left eye.

The squealing of train wheels ceased as they got fully into motion. The back and forth bumping of the carriages became a more regular rhythm. The panting of the huge locomotive grew less massively laboured as the long train began to gather some momentum, and this last sound now too could be distinctly made out as going away from him.

The Calcutta Mail was leaving, and leaving him stuck here.

CHAPTER EIGHT

Ghote made up his mind he would not endure it. And almost at the instant the resolution came into his head he acted. The jaggedy razor was still hovering steadily just half an inch away from his left eye. He flung himself in one sharp, firm movement hard to the right, away from the direction in which the great Calcutta Mail was leaving the platform, wrenching his hard-held nose clear of the one-eyed barber's pinching grip. Above him the barber lurched forward on to his hands and knees with an equal suddenness to that with which his victim had disappeared from under him. His razor flashed uselessly in the air.

Ghote leapt up, swung round, jumped over a masseur's muscle-working back as he slap-slapped at the legs of an elderly gentleman in a white atchkan and Congress cap, and ran.

The train was not so far away after all. It never left any station at much above a walking-pace and it was often a mile or more before it had gathered any considerable speed.

How else could the dozens of ticketless passengers get aboard?

So, although some time had now elapsed since it had begun to pull out, its guard's van was still well in sight. Ghote set out after it at a steady run.

What spurred him on even more than the notion of an impatient colleague of the Calcutta CID failing to find him at Howrah Station and urgently telegraphing Bombay was the thought that the train pulling away contained the person of Mr Banerjee. Because from the moment of his escape it had been quite clear to him that the one-eyed barber had been holding him there of set purpose and that here was the object of that inexplicably long talk in fast Bengali that Mr Banerjee had had with the man.

He weaved and ducked round the people gathered on the long cement platform even at that early hour—passengers for local trains clutching anxiously old bulging suitcases and bundles of cherished possessions, porters swaggering about in the aftermath of the departure of the great Calcutta Mail, beggars beginning the new day by attempting to secure themselves an early supply of food.

But at last the end of the platform was reached and Ghote adjusted his pace as his feet struck the packed stones of the permanent way. But he had, in spite of all the dodging and pushing, already decreased considerably the distance between himself and the Calcutta Mail's steady red rear-light. He quickened his stride.

'Stop. Stop. Stop thief.'

The voice behind him, frantic and

screeching, was loud in the morning air. Darting past a trotting man in a flapping and faded blue-check shirt who was cradling in his arms all his worldly goods collected in a gunny sack, Ghote ventured to turn his head and look backwards.

As he feared it was the one-eyed barber.

And not him only. He was accompanied by a ragged pack of his fellow-tradesmen, most of them waving open razors which glinted like a miniature forest of spears in the morning sun.

Ghote turned back and increased his pace yet again. But he had not gone more than thirty yards or so when it seemed to him as if the shouting of the barber and his friends had grown louder. He glanced backwards once more. Yes, the man might have only one eye but he had two very long legs and he had definitely reduced the gap between them.

Still running hard, Ghote plunged his hand into his trousers pocket and milled his fingers round amongst the notes and coins he found there. At last he secured a note that he felt was a fair sum for a shave plus a generous tip, little though the fellow deserved that. He pulled the note out and glanced down at it.

Damn, it was the two-rupee not the one-rupee. Still, to get rid of that pack of screeching barbers would be worth nearly that much.

He held the note well out in his left hand, feeling it flipping in the wind caused by his running. He hoped the barber could see it and would realise his customer had not been attempting to avoid payment. Certainly the yelling and shouting seemed to have stopped.

Ghote fixed his eyes on the rear of the Calcutta Mail, now only some fifteen or twenty yards away, and concentrated on closing the gap. In a little he became aware of a harsh, grunting panting just behind him. He flicked a look back. The one-eyed barber. He agitated the note in his left hand even harder, hoping to feel it tugged away by eager fingers.

'Not enough,' said a voice from behind.

It did not altogether surprise Ghote to find that the man spoke good Hindi. But it enraged him.

He quickened his pace. The end of the train was at his right shoulder now.

But glinting over his left shoulder was that jaggedy razor.

He dipped his hand into his pocket and produced the one-rupee note as well.

'More.'

Damn and blast the fellow.

He put his hand into his pocket again, gripped the bottom of the lining and jerked it up. He felt a shower of coins shoot past his hand and at the same moment he released the two notes. Then he made a furious spurt and jumped for the running-board of the train.

Looking back from his high perch, he saw, to his considerable relief, that the barber was industriously picking up the money from the permanent way, assisted or hindered by the man with the gunny sack of possessions who apparently preferred a little tangible wealth now to whatever prospects his journey might have had for him.

Secure at last, with his feet well braced on the footboard of the great train and a barred window of the guard's van providing him with an easy handhold, Ghote clung where he was for a while and let the one-eyed barber and his razor-wielding fellow tradesmen slide out of his mind. Now he had foiled the attempt to make him miss the train he could turn to look ahead.

He speculated on what the appalling Mr Banerjee would be doing at this moment. Would he be telling the others in their compartment about the success of his malicious trick? If he was not doing so already, he would soon enough. A talker like that would not be able to hug such a delightful secret for long. Well, he would learn pretty quickly that he had not been so clever after all.

The train was now going at a fair speed, but Ghote set off with bouncy determination to swing his way along its length till he could find somewhere to get inside. He would just like to see Mr Banerjee's face when he pulled back the door of the compartment and stepped in.

It was not altogether easy to make his way along the train side. The carriages had begun to sway and rock with the increasing speed and it was necessary to make sure of a firm hold at all times. But he heaved his way forward with all the confidence of one buoyed up by a prospect of dramatically and satisfyingly turning the tables on an enemy.

At last he spotted a window a little way ahead that was open an inch or two at the top. He swung and scraped towards it.

In the compartment there were half a dozen women, mostly middle-aged matrons, comfortably fat and gossiping hard. He bunched his knuckles and rapped sharply on the dust-thick pane in front of him. No one seemed to hear. He turned his fist sideways and thumped time and again on the heavy glass. And at last one of the gossipers, a woman in a pale pink georgette sari, not ideal for the wear-and-tear of travel, swung round. She wore gold-framed spectacles.

It took her a long time to realise what it was she was looking at. When at length she had done so she gave him a brisk, jerkily dismissive wave of the hand and turned away at once.

Fizzing with impatience to begin his tables-turned scene, Ghote swung out from the train side as far as he dared and looked along to see if there were another open window not too far away. There was nothing. He hammered at the window in front of him again. For a considerable period all the hard-talking matrons inside contrived to ignore him, though he could see from the increased intensity of their conversation that the noise of his thumping could be heard clearly enough above the drumming of the train-wheels. He hammered all the harder.

And then quite suddenly, as if a secret signal had been made, all the women rose up together and advanced on the window. The one in the pink sari, evidently from the extra expense of her clothes the elected leader, spoke in the direction of the narrow gap at the top of the window.

The noise of the train was too great for him to be able to catch a single word. He mimed as well as he could without taking a hand from the window-top and cocking it to his ear that she would have to speak louder. He saw her draw in a deep breath and stretch up on tiptoe. And this time with her face right up between his two clutching hands what she was saying did penetrate his thrummed-at ears.

'This is "Ladies Only" compartment. Go away.'

Gritting his dust-rimmed teeth, he went.

He had noticed earlier far along the train where the third-class carriages were that there had been a scattering of fellow clingers-on. Now, he saw, they had all succeeded in scrambling aboard. He set off, still determined though weary, to work his way right up to the place where they had disappeared.

He put behind him coach after coach and

gained a substantial layer of caked dust all down his left side, the one that faced the wind caused by the train's clipping speed. But still there was no other open window. He resigned himself to perhaps an hour's toil in all before reaching the traditionally hospitable third-class, a part of the train which experienced ticketless jumpers-on waited for in advance.

But then suddenly there did come another window that was open a crack at the top. Hooking his fingers on to this comfortable and easy hold, he looked in, ready for another compartment full of 'Ladies Only' ladies. Instead he found musicians.

The compartment, a second-class one, seemed to have been taken over entirely by the group and they were busy holding a rehearsal sitting on the floor in a circle. The plaintive sound of a morning raga came tinnily to his ears through the thunder of the train. He tapped hard at the window in front of his face. As he had expected, no one paid the least attention.

He decided that there was a tribute he owed to art, and heaved himself onwards again.

His gesture towards the higher flights of the human imagination was quickly rewarded. The first window but one of the next coach was also open a crack, but at his touch it slid down to a point where he could just squeeze himself in. And, with not so much as a good precautionary look at the passengers inside, this he did. He was not going to be balked of his prey in the air-conditioned coach by any more considerations of politeness.

He landed head and arms foremost on the floor of the compartment and shakily picked himself up. Between him and the far corridor door four people were sitting, three men and a smartly-dressed woman. They were playing canasta, with the cards spread in front of them on an up-ended suitcase.

'Excuse, please,' he said.

None of the players took any notice. From the hypnotized way their eyes were fixed on the cards it was evident they had been at play all night. No doubt someone would have to break up the game when they got in at Calcutta.

'Excuse me, if you please,' he said in a louder voice.

Still no one paid him any attention.

He sized up which side of the suitcase looked easier to pass and, turning sideways, he blundered through. The woman player looked up at him briefly through dark glasses.

'Who was that?' he heard her say as he broke out into the corridor.

But the malicious Mr Banerjee was almost under his grasp now. He set off, stiff-limbed, at a fast walk, bumping and banging the walls to either side as the great train swayed.

And then, at last, he reached the air-conditioned coach. His feelings of imminent triumph were such now that he could barely suppress them. Almost at a run he went along glancing in at each compartment to spot the familiar forms of the tall Bengali, the two Indianised hippies, the ever-contemplative guru and little, frog-like Mr Ramaswamy. And then he was there. In one heavy jerk he lugged back the door and spoke.

'Hello, Mr Banerjee.'

The Bengali, sitting right leg carelessly crossed over left knee, glanced up, and, to Ghote's delight, just for one instant he looked totally put out. This admission of guilt, however momentary, confirmed all his feelings that he was indeed to deal out justice to a malefactor.

'You did not expect to see me again, I think,' he said.

He ought perhaps to have left it there. But there was more he wanted to make clear.

'You considered you had left me behind in the care of your one-eyed barber friend,' he went on. 'You did not worry yourself one jot that if I failed to arrive in Calcutta as instructed that would be a black mark against me of very bad effect to my whole career. You did that for the sake of a joke only, but well knowing how much real harm it would bring.'

Mr Banerjee was still regarding him with defeated blankness. He should, he knew, stop his indictment here. Perhaps already he had gone a little beyond the sober truth. But a sudden self-induced vision of long years of failing to rise in the service because on his record there stood an indelible note made him abruptly set sail on a sea of self-pity.

He tumbled into a new denunciation of the fraud that had been committed on him. He added nothing new to what he had already said, but the words poured out. And even as they did he was able, with another part of his being, to observe Mr Banerjee recovering from his shock. Signs of dismay, of fear even, that had been there to see were one by one eliminated to be replaced soon enough by a smile, a smile that lurked on the well-formed lips waiting to flash.

'My dear Inspector,' he said when Ghote at last sputtered to a halt. 'It is good to see you. We were all of us considerably concerned. It was, if you will forgive me, a little foolish of you to indulge in such a very long shave.'

Wildly Ghote struck back with whatever weapon lay to hand.

'Please do not be thinking you can get away with a practice of that sort,' he stormed. 'I require to know your address in Calcutta. Once there I shall institute the strictest inquiries by telegraph to the Railway Police at Hazaribagh Road. If I get confirmation that I was indeed victim of an illegal act you can be sure you will hear further in the matter.'

This random blow seemed to be effective. Mr Banerjee ceased to smile.

Ghote made up his mind that he would indeed tell his Calcutta colleagues about Mr Banerjee, even if it meant making himself a nuisance with awkward inquiries from an unregarded and lowly Bombayite. He would give someone in Calcutta a full description of Mr Banerjee and insist that inquiries about him were made. And if there was anything known to his discredit, then he would see that the fellow learnt that he could not play his tricks on anybody he pleased and get away with it.

And when the Bengali replied it was in a noticeably conciliatory way.

'My dear Inspector, I quite see why you are disturbed. But let me assure you, you are under a complete misapprehension. Of that I am certain.'

And abruptly he switched from his elaborate and beautifully pronounced English into staccato, t-spitting Marathi.

'My friend, I suspect the two foreigners. They are afraid you will denounce them for not having visas.'

And back to English.

'I am sure there has simply been some dreadful mistake. Let me beg you to say no more about it.'

His hand stretched out, almost tentatively, to where beside him there lay his impressive reading matter and he plucked it up, just before Ghote had a chance to see the front cover. In a moment the pages were open and the reader absorbed.

Ghote went across and took his seat, which had been left symbolically unclaimed. He wanted to think, to sort himself out. He felt he had somehow been cheated of his due, although he could not see what it was that had happened—except that he had just once let himself foolishly get carried away.

And yet, after all, he reasoned, Mr Banerjee might be perfectly correct in his swiftly-conveyed Marathi hint about what had happened at Hazaribagh Road. It was true that young Red had also spoken to the barbers. And Red and the girl would perhaps have been happier if there was no policeman on the train when they arrived at Calcutta.

But all the same Mr Banerjee could not be wholly a white figure. What a pity there had been no catching him out on Section 505 before this. And time was slipping away. It was already nearly half past six and at 11.50 hours precisely the train was due to come to a halt at last at Howrah Station in Calcutta.

In his head there danced the words that ought to have already tripped his man. 'Whoever makes publishes or circulates . . .' and 'alarm to the public or any section of the public . . .' and 'an offence against public tranquillity.'

The train thumped steadily over the interminable steel ribbons of the rails, running almost south-east now, coming down from the hills of Bihar into the river tangle of the many-mouthed Ganges in Bengal. The sun climbed steadily in front, soon beating down in desiccating heat on everything that lay under it. The hours ticked by. The distance between them and the terminus of their journey where each would depart on their different ways, probably never to see each other again, mile by mile diminished.

CHAPTER NINE

At last they came to the final stages of their long journey. The view from the windows ceased to be of fields and villages and instead there reigned a grimmer industrial landscape, grey acres of hovels interspersed with the dark bulk of factories, their heavy chimneys pointing implacably sky-wards. From time to time now it was just possible about half a mile away on their left to get glimpses of the Hooghly River which runs through Calcutta itself, glints of sunstruck water with the tall black bulks of mills strung along it.

Suddenly Mr Banerjee closed his book with a joyful snap, and buried the volume instantly—now I shall never know, Ghote thought—in his old, fine leather suitcase with those disturbing initials just visible on it.

'My friends,' the Bengali said, 'allow a seasoned traveller to remind you that before arriving in Calcutta one has to adjust one's watch. Calcutta Time is twenty-four minutes ahead of Railway Time.'

Ghote fumed. The remark could have been directed only at him. Mr Ramaswamy was as 'seasoned' a railway traveller as could be and neither of the two hippies, much less the guru, bothered with anything as everyday and necessary as a watch, although Mary Jane at this hint did begin to collect up their possessions—the useless cameras, the Kleenex box—preparatory to packing them.

But nevertheless in Calcutta, Ghote realised, he would need to know the correct time. Dutifully he pulled the winding-knob of his watch and twirled it round till the minute-hand had advanced by exactly twenty-four minutes.

He was suddenly smitten with sadness at the thought that it was Railway Time he was parting with. Railway Time: it was as if it was something set apart. And now he was going to have to emerge from its cocoon and face, unprotected, the pricks and batterings that a not particularly high-ranking policeman might expect in carrying out a minor task in someone else's territory.

If only he had still been fetching A. K. Bhattacharya. If only looming, brass-faced Mr Banerjee had turned out to be A. K. Bhattacharya, arrestable A. K. Bhattacharya, after all.

But Mr Banerjee, who had got to his feet to make the solemn adjustment of his own watch, worn so smartly on the inside of his wrist, was now favouring them all with another white-teethed smile.

'Madam and gentlemen,' he said, 'we are within a short time of the end of our period of companionship, so let me tell you all, with complete sincerity, that I think I have never enjoyed a journey more.'

His glance travelled over his odd assortment of companions with a smile of proprietorial joy. It passed over the simple and almost always silent guru, who yet had furnished him with some extraordinary comparisons for his hero figure, A. K. Bhattacharya. His eyes halted too for a few seconds on Mr Ramaswamy, perhaps remembering that moment, which surely the frog-like Madrasi hoped no one would ever again recall, when all the decencies had been flouted and a perfectly innocent traveller had been accused of being in disguise the most notorious confidence-trickster of the age. Then the eyes lingered briefly on the sullen face of young Red and dipped to the two useless cameras dangling in front of him. They lingered longer over the unexpungeably pretty Mary Jane, a flower of youth despite the sari wrapped in such a business-like way round her, patently a believer in good things despite the moment when it had seemed that she too had shared something of Mr Ramaswamy's terrible aberration. And finally that gaze came to rest on Inspector Ghote, the one of them all who had shared the journey right from the moment two and a half days before when the huge Calcutta Mail had set out from V. T. Station, Bombay.

Sitting with the now useless copy of *The D.A. Breaks An Egg* dropped in his lap, enduring that gaze, Ghote tried vainly to analyse its meaning. One thing was clear: it was nothing like the expression that had regarded him at the start of the journey when the tall Bengali had leant forward and said 'So we are to be travelling companions, my dear sir.' That look—Ghote found he remembered it with extraordinary clearness—had been one of outwardly polite greeting masking an imp of simple mischievousness. The gaze now still masked, under an outward appearance of politeness, something. But that something was quite plainly real malice.

If that had been all there was to it, Ghote might not have been perturbed. So his 'travelling companion' had proved to be less of a pleasant fellow than he had seemed. But besides the hardly hidden malice there was something else, and this was harder to pin down.

The nearest Ghote thought he could get to it was to describe it as a feeling of just successfully repressed triumph. And why should Mr Banerjee be triumphing? All he had done was to make a long, but really very ordinary, rail journey from Bombay to Calcutta.

'My dear Inspector,' Mr Banerjee said at last, 'what words shall I leave with you, the one amongst us who so nearly did not arrive, and one who has yet to experience all the delights of this vast, infinitely varied, deeply mysterious city of palaces and contrasts where, too slowly for me, we are at last about to come to rest?'

He looked down at Ghote still. Ghote thought that Section 505 would never now come into play, so little time remained.

'I think,' Mr Banerjee said slowly, 'that I will leave you, cunning fisher of slippery fish, just one recommendation. During the short time that you are in my city, before you depart, alas by second-class with that second-class criminal A. K. Biswas, before you go: eat, fisherman, the most delectable of dishes that the city provides, eat in any of the little restaurants that run back from the Chowringhee hilsa fish curried in mustard. Eat that and know bliss.'

He looked out of the window.

The converging tracks of all the lines that end in the huge Howrah Station were all around them now, a criss-crossing pattern of interlaced steel. A crowded suburban train, passengers crammed inside and hanging clutching outside, overtook them in a last spurt to its destination.

Mr Banerjee looked back into the compartment.

'Do you know, my friends,' he said, 'I feel that there is one other person who has been with us on this journey that I must take leave of.'

He looked round at them. The air of mystification he had hoped to create had taken swift hold. Young Red, frowning like the very criss-crossing rail lines outside, looked up at him.

'Was there someone who left before we got in at Manmad?' he asked.

Mr Banerjee favoured him with his flashing smile.

'I am afraid, my dear hippy friend, that you do not take me mystically enough. It was not a solid, flesh-and-blood person to whom I was referring. Rather it was a presence that I feel has been with us all along.'

Ghote knew who it was going to be. So, he thought, judging from that shame-faced expression, does Mr Ramaswamy.

Mr Banerjee smiled at them.

'My friends,' he said, 'let us take a last farewell of A. K. Bhattacharya. After all, did not his daring exploits provide us with many and many an hour of pleasant dispute? Has not that master criminal truly been with us in this very compartment?'

Will he even now make a mistake, Ghote

asked himself, even though, surely, that is the famous Howrah Bridge glimpsed there. Will he even now incite the silent guru here to such fear or alarm that might make him commit an offence? Too late to think of a magistrate, perhaps, but the criminal could still be trounced, trounced to the last shred of flesh on his Bengali back.

'Yes,' said Mr Banerjee, swaying to the short, interrupted rhythms of the train as it began to enter the vast extent of Howrah Station, 'let us at the last hymn that poor misunderstood fellow Bhattacharya. Do you realise that with the profession he had chosen for himself he had to have a knowledge of the arts of India that it would be hard to rival in any university in the land? He had to have a real love of beauty, that man. And to be prepared to trade objects of beauty in the manner he did, I suggest to you, gentlemen and madam, he had to be above the sordid cares of this world, a real mystic.'

The guru shifted sharply in his invariable cross-legged pose at this, and Mr Banerjee went on with some haste.

'But consider this too. Not only was the man above the sordidness of commerce, but at the same time he was responsible, entirely on his own, for a most thriving export business for India. My friends, that is something very near genius.'

And is it something very near an incitement

167

to commit a felony, Ghote asked with anxious inward insistence? Not quite, he decided. Not quite.

'But, my friends,' Mr Banerjee flowed majestically on, 'But A. K. Bhattacharya is yet more than this. He is a very important force in the social structure of our country.'

He turned and regarded Red and Mary Jane from an Olympian height.

'You two young people,' he said, 'you pride yourselves on what you do to upset the over-rigid order of things. You think that you are doing the world a service in breaking up too fixed patterns of society. Well, I for one do not dispute that claim. You are doing excellent work, I say. Keep it up. Keep it up. But the work that you are doing in that direction is nothing to the work that A. K. Bhattacharya did. Just think how much more disruption of the social order that great reformer achieved, and sink to your knees before him. To your knees.'

Is this it? Ghote asked. Well, no hippy had been successfully brought before a magistrate on a disruption charge. So presumably holding up A. K. Bhattacharya as a master-hippy was not a crime. Still, the fellow did not look as if he had finished yet although the train was only just moving now.

'Yes,' said Mr Banerjee, 'a magnificent upsetter of the over-rigidities of our society. But more than this even. I give you A. K.

Bhattacharya as the prime persuader of his day, the most eloquent man in the whole of India, and I am not sure that I should not extend that to the uttermost shores of the world. My friends, this is the age of persuasion, and A. K. Bhattacharya is the prince of persuaders.'

In a minute, in a second.

'Oh, my friends, yes. When I think of the brilliance of that individual I gasp. I positively gasp. And when I think of how that unexampled brilliance fell to pieces just because of one stupid American and his cigarlighter, I weep. Gentlemen, madam, if only there was someone to take up that fallen banner. That man was an example to all of us. Oh, my friends if only any one of you were good enough to follow him. Do it, I beg, tread in his steps if you can. Try, try each one of you to be a smaller A. K. Bhattacharya.'

Now.

The blood raced in Ghote's head.

Now the words had been said.

The Calcutta Mail even at that moment jerked once as it began to slide to a final halt at its appointed platform. The time was 11.49 hours. Ghote swayed sharply forward but kept his balance.

'Sir,' he said, 'I am a police officer and I have to tell you that you have committed an offence. A grave offence. I am considering bringing a charge under Section 505 of the

Indian Penal Code.'

Mr Banerjee, who had been standing magnificently for his final flourish, sat down with abruptness.

'Yes,' Ghote said, 'by your words just now you have committed the serious offence of inciting others to break the law. It is as bad, in every way, as breaking the laws set over us yourself. Words only you have used, but they have been wicked words.'

Mr Banerjee looked hastily to the others in the compartment. But the two young hippies had turned and were busy stuffing their goods into their bundles of possessions. Mr Ramaswamy was suddenly deeply concerned with a small notebook he had taken from his pocket. The guru, still cross-legged, was staring into his distant inwardness.

Mr Banerjee licked his well-formed lips.

'Inspector,' he said, 'forgive me.'

The Calcutta Mail ceased to have any motion. It was 11.50 hours precisely. The thousandfold shrill hubbub of huge Howrah Station replaced in their ears the steady rhythmical thundering that had accompanied them all the way from Bombay.

'Inspector,' said Mr Banerjee, 'I acknowledge that I was wrong. I have been carried away. My feet left the ground. I was wrong.'

Silent and implacable, Ghote let him talk on. He watched while, still apologising, the tall

Bengali saw to it that his luggage was all fastened up. He watched without a word while his man secured a porter—he had no difficulty in doing that—and he climbed down from the train in his wake, as he still threw apologies over his shoulder.

Brushing aside the attempts of more porters to relieve him of his own small case, Ghote walked closely behind the tall Bengali all the way down the long platform towards the ticket barrier. And still Mr Banerjee apologised, although it was plain now that he was not actually to be arrested.

At the barrier they were halted for a few instants while passengers ahead of them filed one by one through the narrow gap in the iron railings where a proudly cap-badged ticket-collector presided. Mr Banerjee was silent now, busy taking his ticket out and preparing to present it at the gate before going on out into the vast wilderness of his native city.

He turned, on the point of surrendering the ticket, and gave Ghote one last, lingering, just sickly smile.

'My dear Inspector, again forgive me. And now, my dear sir, goodbye.'

'No,' said Ghote.

'But, surely—'

'No,' Ghote said. 'A. K. Bhattacharya I take you into custody as an escaped prisoner.'

A. K. Bhattacharya attempted with one wild lunge to get past the iron barrier to freedom.

171

But Ghote had chosen his moment well. The bars ahead prevented the master confidence-trickster from running forward, and he himself securely blocked the way back. Anywhere else his man might have made a successful bolt for it. Here he was penned as neatly and securely as a tiger in a trap.

A. K. Bhattacharya's shoulders slumped suddenly in admitted defeat.

'So you knew,' he said.

'Yes,' said Ghote, still grim-faced. 'From the moment you were talking so much in praise of air travel and yet were seated in a train I felt there was something wrong. But, even when I knew A. K. Bhattacharya was not in Dum-Dum Gaol, I could not believe it was possible he was there in front of me. It was against sense.'

'Yes,' said A. K. Bhattacharya with noticeable plaintiveness, 'that is what I had calculated on when I decided to find you at V.T. Station and place myself just opposite to you in the train if I could. It was a conception of magnificent daring. Where was it that I went wrong?'

'The stupid American with his cigar-lighter,' Ghote quoted. 'Only the police and the man whose schemes collapsed when that cigar-lighter was lit knew about that. The moment you had uttered those words I was waiting the time to make arrest.'

Behind them at the barrier Mr Ramaswamy,

172

the two hippies and the guru stood looking on. Ghote noticed, with sharp amusement, that Mary Jane had her purse out to pay.

He spotted a man on the far side of the barrier who looked like the Calcutta colleague come to meet him and prepared to take A. K. Bhattacharya off with him to somewhere where he could be kept in safety till their journey back to Bombay that evening.

A. K. Bhattacharya resignedly watched the CID man approach. Just before he arrived he turned to Ghote again.

'Well, Inspector,' he said, with something of his lost confidence back again, 'it looks as though, after all, you will be travelling in high style back to Bombay, and that I shall be with you.'

And then the white teeth flashed their old smile.

'I shall start with you at least,' A. K. Bhattacharya said. 'But will you be able to keep me?'

CHAPTER ONE

BACK

Inspector Ghote's departure from Calcutta at the start of his return train journey was a very different affair from his quiet leave-taking at V.T. Station, Bombay, almost exactly forty-eight hours earlier.

This time he was to travel by another Calcutta Mail, one taking a different, more southerly, slightly shorter route to Bombay. It left Howrah Station at 19.50 hours and, as his previous train had done, it departed on time.

But there the similarities ended. To begin with Ghote was to travel on this occasion in even more luxury than by air-conditioned class. This time he had hired, on instructions, a self-contained bogie car, one of the wonders of Indian Railways.

So he had found himself entering not a conventional compartment with seats that could be used as bunks but nothing less than a drawing-room on wheels. Its walls were panelled in polished woods. Long curtains in a flowered print hung to be drawn over the windows. There was a well-sprung sofa covered in the same domestically pretty material and softened by large cushions. There were two matching arm-chairs. A low

174

coffee-table with curved legs stood beside the sofa, another beside one of the chairs. On one of the gleaming walls hung a picture of a starkly isolated and romantic-looking hill-fort perched on a tumbling bluff.

But the luxury in which he was to travel did not end there. The bogie incorporated, he knew, a four-bed sleeping compartment, two small bathrooms and a kitchen complete with a cook, who was now standing awaiting inspection, a man whose whole existence was to be devoted to ministering to his own creature comforts.

It was an arrangement fit for millionaries and maharajahs. But Ghote knew it had been given to him not as a reward for capturing that criminal of criminals, A. K. Bhattacharya: it had been given him so that he would have the best possible conditions for obtaining from that same A. K. Bhattacharya, before their arrival in Bombay in something less than forty hours' time, a full and complete confession.

The fact of the matter was, Deputy Superintendent Samant had made clear during a long, long telephone call, that the State of Maharashtra which would have to bear the costs of prosecuting A. K. Bhattacharya in Bombay was extremely disinclined to face the enormous expenditure of a very lengthy series of court appearances. A plea of guilty, on the other hand, would reduce expense to a manageable sum, for which perhaps the

175

Bengali might get in return a decently lenient sentence so far as the prosecution's representations could ensure it.

So, Ghote had found, instead of his feat having done him the immense good he had allowed himself to hope it would, it had simply presented him with a yet more formidable task. And a task in which failure would bring its usual and inevitable drop-down in the estimation of those who had control of his eventual promotion prospects.

The thought had of course ruined his day in Calcutta.

Before putting through his call to Bombay, in a spirit of bubbling triumph he had seen himself being shown around Police Headquarters by respectful and admiring Calcutta colleagues. He had pictured a stroll along the crowded and exotic Chowringhee, secretly hoping that it would not seem more modern and sophisticated than Dadabhai Naoroji Road in Bombay. He had hoped to get as far as the Botanical Gardens where he could satisfy a quiet hankering to see the Giant Banyan, two hundred years old and a whole grove in itself, an item that had featured in a geography primer in his schooldays, and that he had never afterwards quite forgotten.

But that long-distance conversation with the D.S.P. Samant in Bombay had taken the joy out of everything. The D.S.P. had congratulated him on his capture naturally, and the words had been sweet. But hardly had they been said when they were followed by the practical details of bringing the captured man back to Bombay and that sudden and totally unexpected thorn of an order to obtain a full confession.

So when later he did make his tour of inspection of the Calcutta CID headquarters he had hardly been able to take in what his Bengali colleagues were telling him about their latest technological advances in the fight against crime, and he was afraid later that the champion Bombay thief-taker must have appeared a very dull fellow in their eyes. But blotting out in his head all their excited talk about possible computerisation, and X-ray diffraction units, and improved spectographs was the thought that before long he would have to engage the man he had known as Mr Banerjee in perhaps a forty-hour conversation during the course of which he must master that formidable talker and bend him to his will.

He had indeed taken his stroll along Chowringhee, with the roadway tar yielding under his shoes from the heat of the day. But he had not felt able to make any comparisons at all with the sights and shops of Bombay. What did such trivialities matter?

Yet he had felt almost impelled at about two o'clock to eat the very meal that Mr Banerjee had recommended, at one of the restaurants running back from Chowringhee. He had tried the dish which that intolerably confident figure had told him he ought to eat, hilsa fish in a mustard curry. It had seemed like dry rice in his mouth.

He had not succeeded in seeing the Great Banyan in the Botanic Gardens at all.

Instead he had had to take the five-mile trip out to Dum-Dum Gaol there to collect (D.S.P. Samant had forgotten nothing in the course of the telephone call) the prisoner, A. K. Biswas, card-sharper, once mistaken by over-zealous Calcutta detectives for the legendary A. K. Bhattacharya himself. He had to be brought back to Bombay for trial as well: Ghote was coming: he could bring him.

And when he had signed, time and again, for the body of this prisoner and had eventually been put in charge of the man himself, Ghote took an instant and strong dislike to him. He was a grossly cheerful person. Certainly he was somewhat similar in outward appearance to the man he had known as Mr Banerjee, being much the same height and having too a fleshiness about him as well as a prominent nose and long fanning grey hair. Of course, Ghote had thought, A. K. Bhattacharya's hair was almost white, not the dyed black that had once drawn his attention to Mr Banerjee. But in essence A. K. Biswas was not at all like A. K. Bhattacharya.

Where the confidence-trickster had been polished and formidable, the card-sharper was awkward and sloppily friendly. He smiled more than the false Mr Banerjee had done but his smile was not at all tigerish. It simply revealed a set of broken-stumped teeth and loosed on the world every time it broke a sharp waft of bad breath.

And the worst thing of all about the fellow was that he was delighted that he had been mistaken, if only for a few hours, for the great A. K. Bhattacharya.

'You taking me back to Bombay, bhai?' he had said at once to Ghote. 'Going with A. K. Bhattacharya, isn't it? That what they told. So I get to see that man. That is a man for you, bhai. A real genius crook.'

Ghote had made no reply.

But at Howrah Station that evening the moment had come when the admiring petty criminal had met the great example-setter to his whole profession. Ghote had come with A. K. Biswas alone, linked to the fellow with handcuffs and thus catching at frequent intervals further shocks of foul breath. A. K. Bhattacharya had been brought from the Calcutta CID headquarters by a whole squad of important-acting detectives, puffing out their chests and hoping that the Press and the cameramen would be there.

The actual encounter had taken place on the platform alongside the new giant Calcutta Mail waiting to begin its long journey. And at the moment the Calcutta squad had come up, tightly surrounding A. K. Bhattacharya, the man standing beside Ghote had plunged forward till the handcuffs joining them dragged.

'Pleased to meet, Mr A. K. Bhattacharya,' he had shouted. 'You done a good job, bhai. Damn' pity they ever caught.'

A. K. Bhattacharya—still to Ghote retaining the last vestiges of Mr Banerjee, businessman—actually smiled at the card-sharper.

'You are the Press?' he asked.

'The Press?'

A. K. Biswas grinned appallingly and jerked high the arm linked to Ghote's by the handcuffs.

'Ah,' said A. K. Bhattacharya quickly, 'no, I see you are not a reporter. You must be a detective then.'

He peered towards Ghote and the card-sharper through the ring of plain-clothesmen surrounding him, pretending to have difficulty in seeing in the hazy lights of the dark station.

'And who is that you have with you, my good fellow?' he asked. 'Some miscreant or other?'

Angrily Ghote jerked his chained arm down.

'Oh, no,' said A. K. Bhattacharya. 'I see now it is my old friend, Inspector Ghote.'

He turned to the ring of detectives round him.

'You have met Inspector Ghote of Bombay?' he asked loudly. 'He nearly got left behind at Hazaribagh Road on the way here, poor fellow. He got set upon by a little, one-eyed barber, you know.'

'Get him in,' Ghote said, taut-faced, jerking his head towards the open door of the waiting bogie.

And so first A. K. Bhattacharya and then A. K. Biswas, linked still to Ghote, had been pushed into the bogie and there they had stood while the cook had presented himself as if those the bogie had been ordered for were top-class American tourists or maharajahs themselves.

The cook, an almost spherical little fellow, looking as if he himself consumed everything he prepared, and with relish, had attempted at first to present himself to A. K. Bhattacharya, veering towards that stately presence like a magnetic globule trickling inevitably towards a lodestone.

But Ghote was not going to stand for that.

'Very well, very well, I will attend to you later,' he said sharply. 'My name is Ghote, Inspector Ghote, Bombay CID. This bogie is booked in my name, and you will take orders from me only.'

The little round-shaped cook bobbed a salaam at him with joined fat little hands.

'Whatever the sahib wishes for dinner, he shall have it,' he said. 'There is prawn curry.'

But he did leave the bogie drawing-room clear and Ghote was able to release A. K.

Biswas from the handcuffs and take a ceremonial farewell of his Calcutta colleagues.

These latter, he could not help registering, did at last pay him something of the attention the man who had captured A. K. Bhattacharya ought to have been given. There were discreet murmurs of congratulation, not without covert looks at the tall elegant Bengali who had seated himself in the flower-print covered armchair farthest from the door and was ostentatiously taking no part in the proceedings.

And then the last one of the Calcutta detectives had worked his way to the door and was about to go.

'Well,' he said to Ghote, 'the best of luck to you, and I must say you Bombay fellows are smarter than I thought.'

He took a final glance at A. K. Bhattacharya over Ghote's shoulder.

'And yet I would keep my eyes pretty damn' well bloody skinned if I were you,' he added.

'Goodbye,' Ghote said.

With some pleasure he began swinging the door of the bogie closed, already feeling in his pocket for the sturdy key that would keep it, he hoped, locked right until they had reached Bombay. It nestled next to a police-whistle he had secured as a means of calling help should he need it. The two small clinking metal objects gave him a comforting sense of security.

And then, pushing past the knot of detectives on the platform, came two figures he had never expected to see again, the young hippies, Red and Mary Jane. And they came shouting.

'Inspector, Inspector.'

'Mr Ghote, Mr Ghote, we demand to see you.'

Ghote saw his departing Calcutta colleague take an appraising look at the hippies, Red with his bare chest, dangling beads and dangling cameras, Mary Jane, startlingly pretty and American-looking with that same sari wrapped round her with brisk efficiency. He stepped aside to allow these highly unconventional figures to get to the man who had taken A. K. Bhattacharya. There was an open expression of sharp curiosity on his face.

'Mr Ghote,' Mary Jane said, looking at him with blue-eyed intensity, 'Mr Ghote, we're here to help Mr Banerjee.'

'And we mean help,' the burly, sulky-looking Red added with terseness.

'He is not Mr Banerjee,' Ghote said stiffly. 'He is the man he himself spent so much time praising on our journey here, the notorious A. K. Bhattacharya.'

'Sure, we know, we know,' Mary Jane burst in. 'We listened to all that when you arrested him. But that's not the point. We think the guy needs moral support.'

Ghote looked at her, trying to conceal his

183

feeling of sheer astonishment.

'A. K. Bhattacharya needs no support of any kind,' he said.

'Not if he's been falsely arrested?' Red snapped in.

'Falsely arrested? Are you telling he is not A. K. Bhattacharya?'

The idea was ludicrous. Yet it presented a moment of wild hope, the possibility of not having to engage after all in a combat of wills with the Bengali still lounging at ease on the flowered arm-chair behind him.

'Sure he's who he says he is,' Mary Jane declared with all her Montana forthrightness. 'But he still needs help. Hell, that man is just one sensitive human being. And you're dragging him back to Bombay in chains. The least you can do is let us talk to him.'

'No,' said Ghote.

'I think you had better, you know.'

It was that smooth, detestable voice, and it came from close behind his shoulder.

Ghote squared his back to the half-open door and braced his whole body against it. He looked over towards the Calcutta men. Were they near enough to be certain of stopping a last-second breakaway attempt? There were too many other people nearby on the platform now for his liking. Passengers were trotting along to take their places in the train before it left. Porters were hurrying by shouting loudly. Food vendors were rushing to and fro with their high-piled barrows and wide trays making last-minute sales.

Yes, it was possible the Bengali might make a successful break for it.

Ghote swung round and bawled a brutal order into the long-nosed, fleshy face not far behind him.

'Get back to that seat. Back at once, and do not move. Get back or I put the handcuffs on you.'

A. K. Bhattacharya retreated, step by step. He sank down on to the sofa, still looking at Ghote. Ghote advanced on him.

Behind him he was aware that the hippies were getting into the bogie.

Well, they could be put out at the first stop if there was not time to get rid of them before the train left.

And at once the long piercing shriek of the departure whistle sounded in his ears, followed by a volley of banging sounds as the last doors were slammed. Someone even had banged closed their own. There was a single heavy jerk shuddering through the floor under his feet. The Calcutta Mail had begun its journey to Bombay.

Ghote turned away from A. K. Bhattacharya, went over to the closed door of the bogie, took the key from his pocket, locked the door firmly and returned the key securely to its resting-place.

Then he turned round and looked at the

185

gleaming travelling drawing-room to which he was condemned for the next forty hours. Red had already taken over one of the arm-chairs and Mary Jane was lugging over their dust-smeared bundles of personal possessions. Through the narrow door leading out to the tiny kitchen compartment could be heard a vigorous clashing of pans as the tubby little cook prepared to serve his prawn curry. A. K. Biswas had taken himself off to the far corner where he was cheerfully sitting cross-legged on the luxurious carpeting and was engrossed in picking his nose. And, seated comfortably now, at the far end of the flowered sofa there was A. K. Bhattacharya.

How to begin trying to persuade him to his confession, Ghote wondered with level grey pessimism. Could these two hippies, with their support for him, somehow be used to achieve this end? What even should be the first words he himself spoke?

'My dear Inspector, this is not going to be pleasant for you.'

So the first words, the opening shot, had fallen to his opponent.

'Not pleasant?' Ghote demanded sharply. 'Why not?'

'The responsibility, my dear Inspector. After all, I have no intention of arriving at Bombay to go through that ridiculous process of a trial. So it must be a considerable worry to you. I am, you know, a formidable man.'

'You are a prisoner under escort,' Ghote said. 'There is no reason why you should not arrive at your destination.'

'No reason? My dear fellow, perhaps you consider that you are a match for me. Well, perhaps even you are. You showed, I must say, an unexpected resourcefulness on our way here.'

Then the Mr Banerjee of old, then A. K. Bhattacharya, flashed out again his white tiger smile.

'But has it not occurred to you, Inspector,' he said, 'that I am a man of considerable wealth? And that wealth buys help when it is needed? Inspector, a match for me on my own you might just possibly be. But where are my accomplices?'

And, so saying, A. K. Bhattacharya dipped a hand down into his open suitcase beside him and produced a familiar, heavy, thick-paged book. Keeping his long fingers insolently over the top-of-the-page titles he began calmly to read.

CHAPTER TWO

Inspector Ghote strode across the carpeted drawing-room of the self-contained bogie as the Bombay-bound Calcutta Mail swayed and rumbled over the many points of the crisscross of lines leaving Howrah Station. He went up to the sofa where A. K. Bhattacharya was sitting with offensive calmness reading his massive book. He leant down and, using only the minimum force, he plucked the heavy volume out of the Bengali's long-fingered hands, flipped it closed, turned it over and read at last the bold print of its title.

It was *Art Treasures of Bali.*

Ghote tossed the volume down on to the other end of the sofa.

'I do not think you will ever be considering what profit you can make out of the treasures of Bali,' he said.

He watched out of the corner of his eye A. K. Bhattacharya's hands clench at the soft edge of the flowered sofa.

By managing during that long journey from Bombay to hold on to the plain truth of things, Ghote thought to himself, he had succeeded in beating this man once. So he would show him again just what the real situation was, and then perhaps he would beat him a second time. But it would not be easy, and it would not be quick. There was no point, for instance, in just asking for a full confession now. It would be a matter of waiting till the fellow realized just what his position was, and then suggesting to him where his interests lay.

In the meanwhile he turned to the two hippies.

Red, seated comfortably in the arm-chair,

was divesting himself of his two cameras. By the care he showed for them, Ghote realised, they must have been re-loaded with freshly-bought film in Calcutta. Mary Jane was busy, for the second time in Ghote's short acquaintance with her, in unpacking a selection of possessions and disposing them here and there in a railway compartment in which she had no actual right to be.

Yet, somehow the domesticated way in which she carried out her task robbed it of the offence it ought to have had. Ghote found himself positively leaning forward to peer into the half-opened bundle when the familiar box of Kleenex failed to appear as quickly as he had expected.

He spotted it safely, and a moment later Mary Jane took it out and put it neatly half out of sight under Red's arm-chair. But almost at once something else Ghote glimpsed in the open bundle sent spurting up in him his former sense of fruitless anger with the hippies which Mary Jane's unconscious housewifeliness had countered.

He was not certain, but he thought he had spotted deep in the bundle a very characteristic object, a thin, two-foot length of hollow bamboo tipped with white mouthpieces, the customary device used by smokers of chandu. It pained him immensely to think of Mary Jane, and even of Red, as having anything to do with that fantasy-

189

enthralling, and illegal, habit of opium-smoking.

He looked at them both.

'And the guru?' he asked. 'I did not see at Howrah.'

'No,' said Mary Jane. 'I guess it turned out we were going around with him and not him with us after all.'

Red glanced up at her meaningfully.

'If you hadn't gone on about wanting to parade him through the States, he'd have been with us yet,' he stated.

'Not so—' Mary Jane began.

But evidently she thought better of resuming an old quarrel and with a shrug went back to her bundle and began tying it closed.

'Anyhow,' said Red, 'we've got something more urgent to do now than be chelas to a guru.'

He looked across at A. K. Bhattacharya, sitting book-less on the edge of the sofa and looking, for the moment, unprotected as a shell-less crab.

'You are meaning this idea of helping my prisoner,' Ghote said, taking the bull by the horns. 'Well, let me tell that I will not tolerate any interference whatsoever. He is under my custody and I am taking him directly to Bombay where he will stand trial as charged.'

No harm, he thought, in underlining for A. K. Bhattacharya the end that awaited him.

'He isn't guilty of anything,' Red declared.

'You can't take him to gaol.'

'I am not saying he is guilty,' Ghote answered sharply. 'And I am taking him to gaol only until he appears before a magistrate.'

'Legal quibbling,' Red announced. 'My God, there's nothing makes me so angry as petty legal quibbling.'

He sat up straighter in his appropriated arm-chair.

'Let me tell you one thing,' he went on. 'I'm going to do my best to see Mr Banerjee here goes free as he ought to be.'

'He is not Mr Banerjee,' Ghote banged back. 'He is A. K. Bhattacharya, a man who has cheated to the sum of 72.85 lakhs.'

Now it was Mary Jane's turn to leap to the defence.

'There you are,' she said, whipping up from her bundle like a spring-stick. 'You're convicting the guy before he's even been brought to trial. The pigs are the same all over the world.'

'Very well,' Ghote said, 'if you are insisting, let us put it that he is accused of fraud to the value of Rupees 72.85 lakhs. And if he is accused he must stand trial.'

He glared furiously at the girl.

'I never said he shouldn't stand trial,' she retorted. 'That's just like the cops again, always twisting every damn' word you say.'

'But you did say you were going to attempt to see the prisoner went free,' Ghote came back at her, all the more angry for having got involved in any dispute at all.

'She didn't say that,' Red shouted now. 'She's got some crazy idea of just sticking round and seeing the fellow gets legal aid and home comforts. I'm the one who says he doesn't need legal aid. What he needs is getting out of your hands.'

'And I say you're wrong,' Mary Jane flung back at him.

Ghote, restraining himself with his last dregs of commonsense, stepped back and left them to it.

Their quarrel raged for all the time it took for the train to work its way out of the intermeshing of converging lines that left Howrah Station and to progress at increasing speed past the outskirts of sprawling, turbulent Calcutta. No one had drawn the flowery curtains over the windows. And while the row between the hippies went on, with A. K. Biswas grinning and grinning at it all, outside Ghote half-consciously took in the varying patterns of light as they passed some huge patch of hovel-like dwellings where mostly the glow of cooking fires was the only thing to be seen, or where they went by some huge dark mass of a factory eerily illuminated by the never-extinguished bright glare of a furnace.

And even when the tubby cook brought in the prawn curry, which ingeniously he had stretched to provide enough for them all, the two hippies contrived to snarl and snap at each other between gobbled mouthfuls. Ghote and his charges ate in silence.

It was an excellent curry.

Long after the meal was over Ghote, becoming thoroughly irritated by the loud voices twanging merciless English at each other, looked at his watch. It would be two hours or more before the train made its first official halt at Tatanagar about midnight and he could expel the two contestants.

Would they go on slanging at each other in this way for the whole period? And how could he start working on A. K. Bhattacharya when all this was going on?

Then another thought occurred to him. What if all this loud talk about trying to free or not trying to free A. K. Bhattacharya was simply bluff? What if the two of them were not such convinced, unpractical hippies as they made out? What if they were in fact working together as the very accomplices A. K. Bhattacharya had spoken about?

That sort of bluff would be just what would delight the man who had deliberately sought out a place in the train to Calcutta opposite the person who was meant to be escorting him back to Bombay. And were those fellows in the Calcutta force truly reliable? It was possible, just possible, that A. K. Bhattacharya could have got a message to these two young Westerners while he had been in detention.

All this noise and disturbance, in that case, would be planned with one end: to make him want to put the pair of them off the train and in doing so unlock the bogie door. He had wondered about getting rid of them when they stopped to change from the electric locomotive that had pulled them out of Calcutta to the steam engine that was to take them over the major part of their 2,000-kilometre journey to Igatpuri and the diesel to Bombay. He saw now that to unlock the door of the bogie while the train was standing still at the remote engine-changing station at a late hour of the night would be asking for trouble.

No, he would not fall for that one. The hippies could stay where they were right to Bombay and the bogie key would not leave his pocket at any stop anywhere.

He had only to keep his head. While the train was moving they were all of them prisoners: when the train was stationary he was the one with the key to the door and he had his whistle to summon help if any one of them threatened to attack him. It was as simple as that.

He picked up the discarded copy of *The Art Treasures of Bali* and settled down to immerse himself in its pages. A. K. Biswas, he noted, was attempting to approach his great exemplar in the art of criminality to strike up a conversation. But A. K. Bhattacharya, no longer using the petty crook to score cheap points as he had done at Howrah Station, made it perfectly clear that he was not interested. And that meant that for once he too was silent.

And soon, Ghote noticed, since *The Art Treasures of Bali* floated so far from his usual world that he could summon up little interest in it, the lids had drooped over those eyes that had sparkled at him so brilliantly on the way from Bombay. The wide mouth that had flashed out those devastating smiles had sagged open in mere sleep. A. K. Biswas, too, not much put out by his rejection, had curled himself up comfortably on the floor in a corner and had fallen asleep. He soon began snoring disgustingly.

Gradually Ghote too felt himself becoming more and more inclined to nod off despite the intermittent jangles of sound from the quarrelling hippies.

And soon he was aware of *The Art Treasures of Bali*, glossy and heavy, slipping from his grasp. For a few seconds his mind fought with the problem of how really necessary it was for him not to sleep, and then it decided that no one was going to get that key deep buried in his pocket without bringing him to full life at once. And he was terribly tired: it had been a long, long day since Hazaribagh Road. He allowed a light doze to blot out all his problems.

The Calcutta Mail rocked and swayed at its

full speed through the blue, star-illuminated night eating away at its forty-hour journey time.

*   *   *

It was probably the glare from the copper works at Galudih that woke Ghote. Certainly he came to with a start and found the bogie drawing-room momentarily filled with curious bright greenish light.

He jumped up and peered out. In a short while he realised that the square, looming shapes he saw in the greenishly-lit dark were the works, of which he had heard talk somewhere. Reassured, he turned back from the window and glanced at his watch. It was just after 11.15 p.m. In about half an hour they were due to halt for ten minutes at Tatanagar.

The two hippies, he saw, had at last ended their quarrel. Mary Jane was asleep in Red's arms on the chair they had commandeered. Ghote envisaged a sudden reconciliation, an embrace and puppy-like instant sleep, the sleep of the innocent. Both his charges were also still asleep. A. K. Bhattacharya was lying almost full-length on the sofa now, looking as he had looked when Ghote had watched him sleeping off the effects of his vigil when he had stolen Red's films, as if even in sleep he was striving for higher things. A. K. Biswas, on the other hand, was as gross asleep as he had been awake. The green light flashing in on them must have disturbed him a little because he shifted his position on the floor and loudly broke wind.

But in a moment he was soundly snoring again. And now Ghote realised that the time had come to tackle the confidence-trick giant.

Going closer, he was able to see right into the sleeping tiger's mouth. The flashing white teeth, he observed, were tartar-covered on their backs.

He put out a hand and tapped briskly. But the eyes in the fleshy face were alert as soon as they were open.

'Sit up, sit up,' Ghote said. 'There is much to talk.'

A. K. Bhattacharya heaved himself upright, shook himself a little and smiled.

'My dear fellow, about whatever you wish. I am all attention.'

'It is about your course of action when we have reached Bombay,' Ghote said.

The tall Bengali, now comfortably leaning back on the flower-print sofa, looked at him calmly.

'As to that, Inspector,' he said, 'I do not anticipate that it will be of great concern to you. Indeed, I do not anticipate actually getting even as far as Bombay before I take my liberty once more.'

'That is nonsense only,' Ghote said. 'You cannot escape from a locked bogie on a moving train. Nor even from one that is resting at a station. So you ought to bring your mind to it: you will appear before long in court in Bombay.'

'Well, my dear fellow, I am naturally not going to enter into a detailed discussion with you. But let me assure you that there are many, many ways in which I can terminate this pleasant, but not altogether satisfactory, return journey.'

'You have already been charged in Calcutta,' Ghote said. 'Probably the very afternoon of our arrival at V.T. Station, at 11.30 a.m. on the day after tomorrow, you will appear in court. I strongly advise you then to intimate that you will plead guilty.'

'Not a very spirited course of action, my dear chap. Even assuming I am ever in a position of having to consider it.'

'But please to listen,' Ghote answered, moment by moment feeling the utter blankness of the wall he had been ordered to get over. 'On our journey to Calcutta you as good as admitted the various offences with which you have been charged. Speaking with another voice, you boasted of them even. Very well, since you agree that you have committed these crimes, admit to them in court.'

'You really seem, Inspector, to have decided I am a very craven fellow.'

'No,' said Ghote loudly. 'That is not being craven. That is admitting the truth of what is.

It is being sensible.'

'Yeah, I guess he's right.'

It was a slightly unexpected voice from behind him. Ghote turned to see Mary Jane sitting upright on Red's knees, her eyes bright, her sleep-bemused but still simply pretty face rapidly bringing things into focus.

She leant forward now and earnestly addressed A. K. Bhattacharya.

'Listen, you don't have anything to be ashamed of. You certainly convinced me of that on the way here. You're nothing short of a force for good in society. You know it. Well, what you've got to do is let the world hear it. You should take pride in what you did. All right, so society says it's a crime. Well, admit you committed their crime. And I'll make sure you get the very best advocacy to see you get as short a sentence as can be.'

A. K. Bhattacharya looked at her with clear coldness.

'Let me assure you,' he said, 'that if by any extreme chance I was to come to court I am quite able to secure lawyers to see that any charges the police are foolish enough to bring are made to look thoroughly ridiculous.'

Visions of character attacks on prosecution witnesses, of interminable side-issues raised at interminable length, of willing defence witnesses leaping up to say that even the nub of the prosecution case, Professor Frankenheimer and his cigar-lighter, must be a fiction since they could happily swear the professor never smoked. All this and more Ghote saw, and his determination somehow to make sure it did not happen gritted itself stubbornly down.

And, it seemed, visions of a hero failing to live up to his own high ideals must have entered Mary Jane's head.

'No,' she cried loudly, 'I won't let you do that. If I have to argue with you every mile of the way back to Bombay I won't let you let yourself down that way.'

Her shrill exhortation, of course, woke Red. And Red, of course, produced his own very different opinions of what should happen to A. K. Bhattacharya. In seconds the pair of them were at it again like a couple of screaming hard-beaked parrots disputing a morsel of fruit.

Before long Ghote caught himself exchanging a look of baffled complicity with A. K. Bhattacharya himself.

Hastily he checked it. He must keep a grip on the real situation. The Bengali had openly boasted that he might have confederates. The hippies' quarrel could well be a disguise for their real intentions. A. K. Bhattacharya was perfectly capable of trying to charm him into forgetting all this.

He set his face into a stony mask. And it was still held like that when with the hippies' battle yet raging they pulled into Tatanagar Station.

There Ghote merely sat looking out of the window at the lighted platform as people rushed up and down endeavouring to board the giant, waiting, puffing train.

But the thought was strongly present in his mind that among the crowds there might be a band of goondas hired by some unknown helper of A. K. Bhattacharya's. It did not have to be the two hippies who were his accomplices. He could have bribed somebody in Calcutta to get in contact with a friend at any halting-place on the journey. The paying of a band of toughs to attempt a rescue would be nothing to him. If any one thing was sure about him, it was that he had acquired a total of Rupees 72.85 lakhs. With that enormous sum at his disposal he could easily hire ten or twenty goondas wherever it was easiest for him to arrange an attack.

Yet there was always the whistle. He would not go down without a fight. If there was the slightest sign that anyone was about to tamper with the bogie door or try to smash in the thick double-glass windows, then he would blow, blow, blow till every policeman and railway official there was came to his aid.

Keenly he scrutinized the hurrying passengers. But not one of them seemed to show the least interest in the bogie. It was, he found, even a little disappointing when he had nerved himself up for a fight to the last.

He had just acknowledged the feeling to

himself when he saw among the people he was watching an unexpected and familiar face.

Ushered along by a bobbingly deferential station official, Mr Ramaswamy was coming down the length of the platform with the evident intention of boarding the train somewhere further along.

Without even having to think Ghote rapped hard on the window in front of him. The sharp sound attracted the attention of the official, who looked round in fury at such a manifestation in the chaotic calm of his station. But, seeing that it came from as distinguished a part of the train as a bogie car, he hastily assumed an expression of the utmost deference.

Ghote took a quick look at A. K. Bhattacharya to make sure he was planning nothing, scrabbled the key out of his pocket and rapidly opened the bogie door to a small extent.

'Mr Ramaswamy, Mr Ramaswamy,' he called out. 'Would you do me the honour of joining me in this bogie?'

He felt no doubt that the little Madrasi, who had been so shocked at the proposal the so-called Mr Banerjee had put to him that he should falsify his returns as Inspector of Forms and Stationery, would be firmly on his side while he put pressure on the confidence-trickster.

Mr Ramaswamy had turned at the sound of his name. Now he came up and greeted Ghote with evident pleasure.

'My dear sir,' he said, 'to resume my acquaintanceship with, may I say, a colleague and one whose enforcement activities have an actual grasp on reality, it would be a pleasure indeed.'

'I must tell you of one difficulty,' Ghote said, wishing he could be other than honest. 'I am travelling to escort the man A. K. Bhattacharya to Bombay. He is in the drawing-room of the bogie now, together with also the young foreigners who travelled with us.'

For a quarter of an instant little Mr Ramaswamy hesitated. Then he drew himself up to his full five feet of height.

'I shall take pleasure in resuming my acquaintance with you under whatever circumstances, Inspector,' he said.

Turning cautiously to make sure his prisoner was still well on the far side of the bogie, Ghote stepped down on to the platform and held the door open for Mr Ramaswamy, the station official and the two porters who were carrying Mr Ramaswamy's modest luggage. And all the while that the entourage was still aboard the bogie he stood beside the door ready to slam it with all his force at the least sign of movement from A. K. Bhattacharya.

But there were no difficulties. A. K. Bhattacharya did indeed rise to his feet, but he rose slowly and it was only to make a formal greeting to Mr Ramaswamy. The frog-like Madrasi returned his bow with a stiffish little nod and remained admirably silent. The hippies, beyond a brief 'Hi', did nothing, and A. K. Biswas on the floor continued happily to snore.

Soon enough, and not without Ghote experiencing a good deal of relief, the Calcutta Mail drew out of Tatanagar Station. With the bogie door securely locked once again and its key deep in his pocket, he felt able to give Mr Ramaswamy his full attention.

'My dear sir,' he said to him, 'I would be delighted to pass the hours in conversation with you. But doubtless you have had already a hard-working day. Would you prefer to take one of the bunks in the sleeping compartment?'

'Not at all, my dear Inspector, not at all,' Mr Ramaswamy replied. 'I would be deceiving myself and you also if I were to pretend that my duties at Tatanagar and at the other stations I attended this afternoon were such that they involved any real degree of fatigue. I would very much like to talk.'

'I am glad of that,' A. K. Bhattacharya said abruptly from the sofa where he had resumed his seat.

Ghote's heart sank.

'Yes,' said A. K. Bhattacharya, flashing at both of them his old, white-teethed tiger grin, 'I felt that on our journey to Calcutta there were many things I would have liked to have said to this distinguished railways officer that I failed to find time to express.'

He paused for a tiny space, long enough for them both to wonder what it was that he had wanted to speak about, not long enough for either of them to get in a word.

'Yes,' he resumed, 'there was, for instance, the question of the astonishing difference that I suspect lies between the Jabalpur he had just been visiting when we first met and the Jabalpur that I happen to know.'

How was it, thought Ghote, that the fellow held one's attention in that way? Why did he now find himself wanting so much to know why A. K. Bhattacharya's Jabalpur was different?

The confidence-trickster looked from one to the other of them, a smile coming and going on his well-formed lips.

'Did you know, I wonder,' he said at last, 'that Jabalpur, once famed for the number of members of the cult of Thuggee confined there, still harbours devotees of that curious, and quite deplorable, sect? I doubt whether you did. Yet they are there. And their life is whole worlds away from the forms and stationery that brought our friend here to their city.'

He blazed at them both now his tiger smile.

'You ask how I know?' he said. 'I reply: many of the thugs are my personal friends.'

CHAPTER THREE

In the cocoon of the drawing-room of the Calcutta Mail bogie little Mr Ramaswamy, Inspector of Forms and Stationery, looked at once extremely modest and somewhat apprehensive. The whole notion of Thugs and Thuggism, that extraordinary cult of wayside murder as a religious activity which once flowered for years completely unsuspected in British India until it was discovered and suppressed in the latter part of the nineteenth century, hung like a band of vultures in the air.

'Yes,' A. K. Bhattacharya went on happily, 'there is a lot that goes on in this great and multifarious country of ours that does not appear in the compilations of statistics, or even in the newspapers. The worship of Kali in the form of the strangulation of various innocent people, notably travellers, is a practice that is perhaps not as dead and buried these hundred years past as most people believe.'

He looked down at his hands, long-fingered and quietly reposing on his lap.

'My dear e-sir,' said Mr Ramaswamy, 'I must declare that I am convinced that you are joking, isn't it?'

A. K. Bhattacharya looked at him straight in the face and smiled. Mr Ramaswamy's Adam's apple rose and fell once as he swallowed hard.

'It is impossible that murders should take place on religious grounds in this day and age, and especially of travellers,' he declared with stoutness.

Ghote was certain that A. K. Bhattacharya was inventing everything he was telling them. He also saw that he was doing so with the aim of frightening Mr Ramaswamy into neutrality in the struggle between the two of them. He decided he must do something to restore the balance.

'Let me state,' he interrupted, 'that I do not believe that Thuggism exists at all today. Certainly it does not come to the knowledge of the police. And I can assure you that very little that happens escapes us.'

'Though the rate of successfully solved murder cases is deplorably low,' A. K. Bhattacharya said, looking down at his hands again.

'That is as may be,' Ghote snapped. 'But I promise that not many murders are committed without the police being aware. And I add also that I believe any experienced police officer has a much greater knowledge of such people as murderers than you yourself.'

He glared at A. K. Bhattacharya and was unable to resist trying one more blow.

'However,' he added, 'your acquaintance with murderers is going to become considerably more extensive during the course of, let us say, thirty years in prison.'

'Thirty years!'

But it was not A. K. Bhattacharya who exclaimed in horror: it was Mr Ramaswamy.

Ghote looked at him in some surprise. Yet it was plain that the thought of a cultivated man like A. K. Bhattacharya spending thirty years in the company of gaol-birds had considerably upset the little Madrasi.

And of course his horror, which Ghote had not at all counted on, was swiftly reinforced by the two young hippies, who had been struck into doubtful silence by the mention of Thuggee and who now, because of that doubt, were all the more vocal.

Mary Jane took it out directly on Ghote.

'Thirty years?' she said. 'Is that what he'll get? A guy like that? You're nothing short of a monster.'

'It is not for me to say what sentence a court will impose,' Ghote answered, conscious he must be sounding prim but unable to speak otherwise.

'But you did say it,' Red exploded now. 'You're the one who wants him in prison for thirty years.'

He got to his feet and hung menacingly over Ghote.

'And I'm the one who's going to see you don't get him there,' he added.

This, however, started off once more the dispute in the hippy camp. Mary Jane was quick to point out that it would be better to let A. K. Bhattacharya come up for trial and ensure—she was vague about how it would be done—that he got a purely nominal sentence. And this made Red all the more determined to free his man, though he seemed to have no immediate idea of setting about it.

Through all this renewed row Mr Ramaswamy was silent, and plainly deeply thoughtful. But as soon as there was a momentary halt for breath he spoke.

'Excuse me,' he said, 'but I find after all that I am not so inclined for conversation as I had thought. I think I will retire to bed.'

And he went, carefully bidding them all good night. The two hippies were already too busy with their renewed quarrel to hear him. A. K. Biswas was still gruntingly asleep. Ghote, seeing his brand-new, almost heaven-sent ally withdrawing into neutrality, if not worse, simply lacked the impetus to reply.

It was left to A. K. Bhattacharya to speak for them all.

'Good night, my dear sir,' he said. 'Or, if by chance I am no longer on the train when you awake, goodbye.'

*   *   *

For some time Ghote sat listening to the hippies fighting—their recriminations wandered further and further from the subject of what ought to be done about A. K. Bhattacharya—and wondering whether he would get another opportunity of attempting to persuade the confidence-trickster to confess. But the hippies showed no sign of needing sleep and he himself felt so tired, as well as being discouraged by Mr Ramaswamy's defection, that he came to the conclusion that he might as well follow the Madrasi's example and get some rest.

So with an abruptness that secretly pleased him he simply ordered the Bengali into the sleeping compartment and followed him there himself. And the night passed, to his mild astonishment, very well. He did not sleep with perfect soundness, but he was content to wake from time to time, push himself up on one elbow and, peering through the dim light, observe A. K. Bhattacharya safely asleep in the bottom bunk opposite with Mr Ramaswamy, equally sleeping, above him.

At some stage the two hippies, seemingly reconciled again, came and took the vacant fourth bunk. And after the small disturbance of their arrival he lay on his back for a while, feeling underneath him the slow swaying and steady jogging of the great train eating up the miles to Bombay.

He even felt happy then. He had decided not to do anything about A. K. Bhattacharya till the morning and so the old precious sense of being removed from his responsibilities, which he had hoped to savour to the full on both parts of the journey, came back to him for a little. Soon he fell asleep again.

At just after three o'clock he woke for a slightly longer period when the train came to a halt for ten minutes at Rourkela. But all seemed to be quiet outside. Once more he looked down at the Bengali confidence-trickster. Again he was just able to make out his sleeping face in the gloom, its long white teeth inert. All the others slept too, and again he felt he could relax.

It was while he was doing so, and on the very verge of sleep, that his plan exploded softly and fully-formed in his head just as the great train jerked into movement again.

He would do it by sympathy.

That was all there was to it, but he felt at that mid-hour of the night totally confident. In the morning he would approach A. K. Bhattacharya in a completely new spirit. He would offer him all his sympathy, he would win him over, and then he would just show him that a full confession was the best course.

He had, at that hour, no doubts of his ability to carry out his task, and when he slept once more there was a smile on his face.

*   *   *

With the new day he hardly felt as cheerful. But as their tubby cook served himself, A. K. Bhattacharya and A. K. Biswas with an excellent, and extraordinarily plentiful

211

breakfast while the others still slept, he dutifully opened his campaign.

'How pleasant it is,' he observed to A. K. Bhattacharya, busy wiping his lips after doing voracious and happy justice to the cook's efforts, 'how pleasant to be sitting here in comfort, with good food inside one and all the while to be making progress.'

He looked out past the Bengali's fanning hair, now just perceptibly grey at the roots, to the large window of the bogie drawing-room and the wide stretches of the plain beyond, its level flatness broken here by frequent villages.

'Yes, making progress,' A. K. Bhattacharya replied, with distinct sourness. 'Making progress towards Bombay and the prison you hope to see me in for thirty years.'

A. K. Biswas, sitting on the floor in the far corner, and still eating, belched loudly.

'Prison for me too, bhai,' he said. 'But air-condition rail travel on the way. Is very good.'

Ghote looked over towards him.

'Get out,' he said. 'Go and see the cook, go anywhere. But get out.'

The card-sharper pushed himself to his feet, still noisily chewing.

'You want to be getting round Bhattacharya sahib,' he said to Ghote. 'Okay, I go. But you won't ever get round that man, not you. No, sir.'

'Get out,' Ghote shouted.

With a belly-rumble so loud that it was

easily heard over the steady thud-thudding of the train wheels A. K. Biswas took himself off.

Ghote resumed his softening up.

'Please,' he said, 'I am a police officer and I have been given the duty, certainly, of escorting you to Bombay. But please do not be thinking of me as desiring to see you in prison for thirty years. That is not my pigeon at all.'

A. K. Bhattacharya cocked a quick eyebrow at him.

'Then you will hand me the key that you take so much trouble to hide in your pocket?' he asked.

'You know I cannot do that,' Ghote said. 'But that does not mean there is nothing I can do for you.'

'You could unlock the door without giving me the key.'

'No, no, no, no. Nothing of that sort. I have my duty. But I am also a police officer, and I have a certain experience of the courts and judges and the sentences they are inclined to pass for various forms of illegal activity. I could give you good advice, if you would let me.'

'And I could give you good advice, my friend,' A. K. Bhattacharya said with the sharpness still present in his voice. 'Give me that key. You will not suffer by it, I promise. But keep the key and you may well have to be hurt.'

'Please, let us not be talking in such a

manner. I cannot do anything for you now. But in Bombay, then there is much I could do.'

A. K. Bhattacharya was silent for several minutes. Ghote watched the countryside go by. They crossed the nearly dried-up bed of a wide river. The hard shadow of the lattice-work bridge could be seen far below on the zig-zag cracked mudbanks. A small station on the river bank, sleepy and sun-blasted, was left behind.

Then the Bengali opposite him spoke, now in a quiet and speculative way.

'Just supposing that I do consent to make the rest of this not too pleasant trip with you, my friend?'

'Then, by way of thanking you for making my life easy . . .'

'You could . . . ?'

'There are people I could speak to,' Ghote said. 'I am, as you above all must realise, in most excellent standing with my superiors just at this time. If I put a word in their ear about your conduct I have no doubt whatsoever that they would pay the most strict attention.'

He listened to the sound of his words. There was a logic about them. They fell into a fine pattern.

He suppressed a suspicion that somehow D.S.P. Samant would pay him no more attention than before on his return to Bombay, even though he was dragging the great A. K. Bhattacharya with him.

'Yes?' the Bengali said, now in a distinctly thoughtful manner.

Ghote could not but go on.

'It is all a matter of police discretion,' he said. 'It is often a matter left to our discretion which charges are made when an illegality has occurred. And, as you know, each offence carries a different sentence in the Indian Penal Code. A different maximum.'

'So?' A. K. Bhattacharya said, his eyes beginning to shine.

'So,' Ghote went on, feeling the stirrings of a similar excitement, 'if we were to investigate very carefully exactly what charges might be made on the evidence we have, then by selecting such a charge or charges as carried the smallest maximum sentences we could effect a considerable reduction in the term you might have to serve.'

'Yes,' A. K. Bhattacharya said thoughtfully. 'But nevertheless I fear these maxima you speak of might add up in the end to a total that I could not altogether appreciate.'

He looked at Ghote, his fleshy face keen and sharp.

'But if . . .' he suggested.

Ghote thought hard. Things were beginning to run his way now. It would be a pity—it would be absurd—to let this favourable current slacken.

'If,' he said, as thoughtfully as A. K. Bhattacharya himself, 'well, if, for instance—

and it is an instance only I am giving—if the police were carefully to examine the evidence they had, they might come to consider that some of it was not strong enough to justify presenting in court, and in consequence . . .'

'In consequence,' A. K. Bhattacharya picked him up, 'in consequence the number of charges on which a judge would have the duty of passing sentence might be greatly reduced?'

He sounded suddenly so starrily hopeful that Ghote found only one reply to make.

'They might be very considerably reduced,' he said.

'To a mere handful?'

'Even, I suppose, to a mere handful.'

'These minor charges that you are proposing to make,' A. K. Bhattacharya said after a short pause for reflection, 'what sort of sentence do you envisage might be imposed on anyone found guilty of them?'

'I am certain that for minor charges it could be as little as one year only,' Ghote said with a heartiness designed to cover his actual uncertainty.

'One year,' A. K. Bhattacharya replied, with a sad movement of his prow-nosed head. 'You know, that would hardly do for a man in my position.'

He looked very depressed. Ghote thought hard. But with the best will in the world he could not see how he could progress any further.

'Now, look at it this way,' A. K. Bhattacharya said, with a smooth inclination of his long body forwards that Ghote found irresistibly confiding. 'Consider the matter in this light. We have reduced the number of charges, certainly. And we have dropped those that carry the heavier penalties. But supposing we were to do the two things simultaneously: one, to find a charge which carried only the very lightest of sentences, and, two, to put forward only that one count.'

Ghote shook his head sadly.

'I do not see how that could be done,' he said.

A. K. Bhattacharya's long-fingered hands flew up into a fan of disclaimer.

'My friend, I am not asking you to make any sort of promise,' he said. 'All that I am doing is putting forward a purely hypothetical situation.'

Ghote brightened.

'In that case,' he said, 'I would have no hesitation in answering. With just one charge, and that carrying the lightest penalty, it is not at all impossible that you would receive a purely nominal sentence, one corresponding only to the length of time you had been in custody awaiting trial.'

To his relief A. K. Bhattacharya made no attempt to convert his pure hypothesis into any sort of concrete reality. Instead he broached another subject.

'Ah, yes,' he said, 'this matter of being in custody awaiting trial. That is something that has always interested me as a subject. Tell me, what sort of conditions obtain for gentlemen in this situation. I mean, they are after all most probably completely innocent of the charges made against them, you know.'

'Ah,' said Ghote sharply, 'that is not so. In the great majority of cases brought by the police a conviction is obtained.'

With a bland wave of his hand A. K. Bhattacharya conceded the point.

'Let it be, let it be. But tell me something about the conditions of such custody. They are comfortable, yes?'

'Oh, yes, yes indeed. They are as comfortable as the circumstances will permit. Such prisoners may send out for the food of their choice. They may obtain newspapers. There are all sorts of privileges.'

'So a period in prison on those terms would not be an unduly harsh experience?'

'Not at all, not at all,' Ghote assured A. K. Bhattacharya with the utmost conviction.

'Then,' said the tall Bengali, 'I feel that you and I can truly co-operate, my friend.'

And Ghote experienced such an all-spreading glow of confidence and trust that it seemed to him at that instant as if there could not possibly be any obstacles in the path of a successful co-operation between himself and the smiling and pleasant Bengali. In the heat of his desire to help he found himself taking on a role in the case that he knew really was hardly likely to be his.

'The very moment we get to Bombay,' he cried, 'we will straightaway examine the charges that could be made against you. We will reduce them to the very minimum.'

'We will reduce them to one, you and I,' A. K. Bhattacharya exclaimed in unison with Ghote's mood.

Ghote could not introduce a black slur now on the radiant path opening out before them.

'Together we will reduce them to a single one,' he agreed. 'And on that one we will present only such evidence as we cannot in conscience omit.'

'The merest trifle,' said A. K. Bhattacharya.

'The merest trifle.'

'And as soon as the trial is over I will go free,' A. K. Bhattacharya chanted.

A fraction of doubt sent a tiny frown on to Ghote's face.

'But, of course, I shall have served a term while awaiting trial,' A. K. Bhattacharya hastily put in. 'I shall not get away with this scot-free. Ah, dear me, no, my good Inspector. But, having served my term, and having served it with a good grace, I shall be free.'

He leaned forward suddenly and gave Ghote a smile so warm that it would have melted the very snow on the highest Himalayas.

219

'And, my friend, when I am free again,' he said, 'I am going to take you into partnership. Yes, I insist. I insist.'

With sweeping gestures of his well-fleshed right hand he waved down the protests he obviously saw Ghote as making.

'Yes, into partnership,' he declaimed. 'And, my friend, we will go to America. I have plans for America. And you can be of immense assistance to me there. Immense assistance. Immense. We will fly there side by side on the very day that I am released.'

CHAPTER FOUR

Inspector Ghote listened to A. K. Bhattacharya's words, which seemed to echo and rebound in the empty chamber of his head, as hard to catch and hold down as a demented bat in some tree-ringed temple ruin.

We will fly there. Side by side. To America.

What was this the man was saying? What was this that A. K. Bhattacharya, the notorious confidence-trickster, was saying to him, Ganesh Ghote, Inspector of Police, Detection of Crime Branch, Bombay CID?

We will fly—

Suddenly these words at least he caught and held.

'No,' he said.

He shouted it loudly.

Mr Ramaswamy, coming into the bogie drawing-room, newly shaved and preceding the fat little cook carrying his breakfast, savoury and fresh, stopped abruptly.

'No,' Ghote said, looking fixedly at A. K. Bhattacharya. 'I am not going to fly. Flying is wrong.'

A. K. Bhattacharya smiled with a great flash of white teeth.

'My dear fellow, forgive me. I had forgotten, momentarily forgotten, your objections, which I confess I never altogether followed, to that mode of transport. But do not be concerned. You can travel in whatever way pleases you. The main thing is we shall be set up in partnership together.'

'No,' Ghote explained, more calmly now. 'You do not understand. Flying is wrong for me, because it is part of the world you are offering me. I do not belong to the flying-here-and-there world, and I do not think I ever will. I do not belong to your world, and I am certain I never should.'

'My dear chap, I am not sure that I understand you.'

Mr Ramaswamy coughed tactfully behind them.

'I have not heard exactly what this proposal was,' he said, 'but let me tell you that I certainly am able to understand the objections of my good friend, Inspector Ghote, to this planned air-flight, wherever it is to. I have spent my life travelling all over the systems of Indian Railways, and I quite understand anybody saying that air travel is another world. And one to which not all of us feel suited.'

The support gave Ghote time to make the last stages of his descent from the high and rarefied plateau on to which with A. K. Bhattacharya's enthusiastic co-operation he had strayed.

'Let me make myself clear,' he said to the Bengali. 'I decline to become your partner in any enterprise. I decline to fly anywhere at your behest. I am not in truth in a position to ensure that you do not go to prison. But what I can do is promise you that, if you are willing to plead guilty, police will not press more charges than necessary.'

A. K. Bhattacharya's eyes glinted hard.

'What sort of a fool do you take me for, Inspector?' he said.

*   *   *

This was a day of uninterrupted progress for the train. Not until they were to come to Nagpur, in the very centre of India, at the end of the afternoon, were they to have a single scheduled stop. A distance of some five hundred miles was to be traversed, starting across a treeless extent of plains with peasants coaxing crops from the embanked rice-fields, each separated from the next by a sandy red ridge, over the wide beds of rivers dried into sometimes half-mile wide stretches of caked and baked reddish-brown mud under the incessant sun, and moving on up into hills where the jungle grew ever thicker. The sun, now rapidly climbing into the still blue sky, would have to reach its full height, whitening the whole heavens with its glare, and to sink almost to the horizon again before they came to a full stop.

The prospect somewhat pleased Ghote. In the locked bogie, proceeding at a fair speed, the situation could not take on any new and disturbing factor. A. K. Bhattacharya, he felt reasonably confident, was at least safe. But there remained the problem of manoeuvring him round to the point where he would agree to plead guilty at the trial. And that, with the disastrous check of their shared excitement falling like a spent Diwali rocket into the sea, was certainly an enormous difficulty to surmount.

Yet there was the whole long day ahead, and the night after that, and even then almost all of a morning still to come. There was hope.

He decided to leave matters to simmer.

They simmered, as it turned out, all that morning, despite some attempts that he made to explore new ways of bringing the subject of the trial into the conversation. About half an hour after the collapse of the joint flight into impossibility, and just when the two hippies had at last appeared, sleepy and once more bickering, A. K. Bhattacharya had stiffly requested to have *Art Treasures of Bali* back. Ghote had let him have it, and thereafter he had remained immersed in its pages.

It was, however, Ghote's turn to notice that not much actual reading was being done. But he decided there was nothing to be gained by pointing this out.

The sun reached its mid-point. Outside, Ghote watched from time to time the tiny motions of distant cultivators, like miniature black cut-outs. Or, bringing himself back to the small world inside which they were locked, he chatted in a desultory fashion with Mr Ramaswamy who, to his considerable pleasure, now patently abetted him whenever he tried to bring the talk round to a point where it would catch the attention of the loftily distant A. K. Bhattacharya.

Yet it was in the middle of the long, immune period that the Bengali went far to take the game completely into his own hands.

The first signs of it occurred when the little balloon-shaped cook entered the drawing-room, offered a profound salaam and asked what he should serve for lunch. He extended a choice of either chicken curry or mutton vindaloo, and Ghote, who supposed that for dinner that evening they would get whichever he now rejected, simply asked for the chicken

224

that the cook had mentioned first. But abruptly A. K. Bhattacharya looked up from his book and spoke.

'Might we have the vindaloo?' he said, and turning to the cook he added: 'Your breakfast was so delicious I can hardly wait to sample your skill on what is a favourite dish of mine.'

The little tub of a man appeared highly pleased, as well he might, and Ghote simply agreed to have the mutton. He thought no more about the exchange, especially as A. K. Bhattacharya did nothing to follow up the small moral advantage he might have gained in insisting on the substitution.

It was only when the cook came back into the drawing-room with his basket of cutlery that Ghote realised what A. K. Bhattacharya's apparently insignificant remark had been aimed at.

Because the Bengali at once resumed his flattery of the globular cook, making a great play of sniffing at the aroma that had drifted into the drawing-room.

'Ah,' he had said, 'I believe I am about to be proved correct. To judge by the extremely delicate smell of those spices we are in for a treat indeed.'

The cook's moon-round face broke into a beaming grin, and he waddled across to where A. K. Bhattacharya was sitting and with immense care drew up the low table beside him and laid cutlery out on it, puffing and panting and pausing over each item to make sure it was the best in his basket.

But by then Ghote had seen what the whole business was about: A. K. Bhattacharya was acquiring an ally.

And when the cook slammed down some cutlery beside where he himself sat, leaving it all crooked, he began to see that he would have to act fast if he was to counter the Bengali's move. And the cook, he realised now, would be a useful ally indeed for a would-be escaper. There was no door leading from his little crammed kitchen to the exterior world, but Ghote thought he remembered from seeing the outside of the bogie that its air-conditioning did not extend to that little area and so it had a small window that could perhaps be opened.

'Luncheon coming soon,' the cook said, directing his whole attention to A. K. Bhattacharya. 'Very important to eat quickly. Long tunnel when we get to the top of the hills here. Not good to eat in dark, but not worth getting lights to work.'

'My dear friend,' A. K. Bhattacharya said, 'the flavours you are about to provide us with one could no doubt eat with pleasure wearing a blindfold. And yet, you are right too. I would not willingly miss the sight of what I am eating when it is prepared with skill.'

The cook made A. K. Bhattacharya another salaam, deep as his spherical shape allowed, and trotted back into his kitchen. Ghote got up quickly and quietly followed him out.

What he saw in the narrow, steam-filled little kitchen-compartment confirmed his worst fears. There was a window and it could be opened. It was very small, but with perhaps a little assistance a man could probably scramble out of it.

The cook turned, his neck-embedded face no longer looking so sunny.

'What is it you are wanting?' he said.

Ghote smiled.

'After I am hearing so much about how good this meal is to be I have come to see the cooking,' he replied.

The cook looked at him suspiciously.

'It is coming,' he said. 'It is coming. And if it is all to be eaten before we get to Darekasa tunnel it must come soon.'

He swung himself ponderously round to his stove. But Ghote thought that all the same he did not look too displeased.

He went back to the drawing-room and sat expectantly beside his laid place. A. K. Bhattacharya looked at him sharply, and when a minute or two later the cook waddled in holding in his two short arms a large steaming dish of mutton vindaloo the tall Bengali at once gave the man a broad smile.

'Here, here,' he said with great gusto. 'I beg to be served first. Really, I so much want to taste this delectable dish that I think I am entitled to a certain priority. And, besides that, I claim to have had a greater experience in sampling the culinary arts of the various parts of India than anyone else present.'

And he gave Ghote, as a hopelessly limited provincial, a look of plain disdain.

'Here,' Ghote said to the cook, 'serve me first, if you please. I have been in the kitchen and seen the dish in its last stages of preparation.'

To his pleasure, he saw that this gross and illogical piece of flattery seemed to have touched the ball-shaped cook. The serving dish was brought across to him and a substantial portion spooned on to his plate. A. K. Bhattacharya looked furious.

'Serve my guests next also,' Ghote said. 'I cannot wait for them to taste.'

So the cook, smiling now like a fat tickled baby, hurried round to serve first Mr Ramaswamy and then Red and Mary Jane.

But with the two latter Ghote's system of blatant flattery came sharply unstuck. All the while that he had been busy counteracting A. K. Bhattacharya's move the two hippies had been quarrelling, though for once in hissing whispers. But he had been too occupied to take any notice of them. Now however their quarrel seemed to have come to a head, and it proved to be the oddest yet of their disputes.

No sooner had the puffing, puffed-up cook ladled out a mound of steaming vindaloo on to

Red's plate than he simply pushed it aside.

'Damn it, no,' he said. 'I am going to do it.'

'Red, no, no,' Mary Jane exclaimed.

'I say "Yes",' Red declared.

And he rose to his feet and started to sweep the strap of one of his cameras over his head.

Ghote looked at him in puzzlement. Was the fellow going to start taking pictures now, when they were just about to eat? And what on earth was it he wanted to photograph?

The latter question was answered immediately. Red advanced on Ghote himself.

'Just act naturally,' he said. 'Just act naturally.'

Ghote would have liked to have asked why a photography session had to take place at just this moment. He would have liked to have known what it was about him that Red wished to capture on film. But he yielded to the mystique of art. If he must at all costs act naturally, to ask questions about what was happening was obviously quite wrong.

Stiffly he picked up a fork and plunged it into the savoury mound on his plate. Or would Red expect him to eat with his fingers, he wondered bemusedly.

'No,' said Red with impatience, 'put that stuff away. I don't want a picture of a railway traveller eating in the height of comfort.'

But he did not say what he did want a picture of. He only approached Ghote, peered at him hard, danced away back across the drawing-room and shook his head morosely.

Ghote felt sharply that he had failed a test.

But he could not for the life of him think what it was that he ought to be doing, how he ought to be looking so as to please. He leant back in his armchair and tried hard to take on the appearance of a traveller simply travelling. But what does such a person do? Again imagination failed him.

Red advanced once more with the camera, and Ghote thought that this time his finger really was about to click down. He tried to intensify the expression he thought he had been holding at that instant. In the background he was dimly aware of the globular cook making a sort of wailing sound.

'But you must begin to eat. You must begin. When we come to Darekasa tunnel it would be too difficult.'

He ignored such earthly considerations. But he could not help noticing that his stomach was beginning to feel extremely hollow as the spicy odours from his nearby plate of vindaloo reached his nostrils. He began furiously salivating.

Somewhere beyond Red's heavily dancing figure he heard too the voice of A. K. Bhattacharya, though he did not dare turn his head as to be able to see him.

'Cook, you can at least serve me. I shall eat your food.'

He saw that he must stop the whole process

of photograph-taking at once if he wanted to keep the cook's favour. He began to move.

'No, no,' Red said fiercely. 'Stay there, stay there. I've got to do this while the mood's right. This may not happen again the whole journey.'

Hastily Ghote resumed his pose, glaring even more fixedly than before approximately in the direction of the far window, beyond which he was aware vaguely that they were climbing steeply and that dense bamboo jungle was waving in stiff fronds right up close to the track. Even as he looked, or half-looked since the angle at which he felt bound to hold his head prevented him from really seeing, the train began to enter a cutting which moment by moment got deeper and deeper.

The Darekasa tunnel will be here soon, he thought, and then we shall not be able to see to eat.

Hurriedly he tried to put that idea out of his head and to replace it with thoughts fit for a traveller, doubtless to express themselves in countless subtle ways on his features ready to be captured for all time on Red's film.

Only why was he suddenly so worth photographing just now?

At last Red began actually to click away with his camera, uttering short grunting sounds which Ghote despite intense effort was unable to allocate either to appreciation or to disgust.

He sat submissively, stiffly holding his

expression. Once more he recalled his first experience of the camera as a boy visiting Bombay. A lot had happened since then, but the two experiences seemed equally demanding.

And all the while loud noises of appreciation for the fat cook's achievement were coming from A. K. Bhattacharya. The odours from his own plate were also still making their insistent claims on his gastric juices.

He wriggled.

'Keep still, keep still,' Red snarled.

He froze again.

Dimly he was aware too that the light in the compartment was altering. It was getting greener and greener, darker and darker, as they advanced into the long deep cutting. Would this spoil everything for Red? Ought he to have got into this expression—only what expression was it?—earlier?

And then with startling abruptness, despite it so long having been heralded, the tunnel came. The whole drawing-room was instantly converted into the thickest blackness.

'The tunnel, the tunnel, and you have not begun to eat,' he heard the cook moan.

There was a lot of scuffling going on too that he could not account for, unless it was Red making his way back to his seat in disgust, the grand opportunity lost.

If it was he, he was making a very bad job of

it. The plate beside him clinked sharply as, no doubt, the bullock-like hippy bumped into the table.

The darkness was still impenetrable. He sat in it, waiting. The odour of spices still impinged on every square centimetre of his nostrils. Could he reach out and get hold of his plate? How long was this tunnel?

Cautiously he extended a hand. It encountered a body. A moment later he registered that the body was covered in smooth cotton. It must be the sari that Mary Jane wore. Hastily he withdrew his hand and placed it primly on his lap. There must be no misunderstandings when he was engaged on such an important task as escorting A. K. Bhattacharya. And the Bengali was just the person to try and take advantage of an accident like that.

But what was the girl doing so near his chair? Perhaps trying to guide Red back to his place? She seemed devoted enough to him really, despite their frequent quarrels.

And then the daylight returned. Blindingly and suddenly.

But Ghote could think of only one thing. He seized his plate and began shovelling the vindaloo into his mouth. His hunger had been appalling.

So it was not for some time that he realised that the food he was putting away so quickly actually tasted extremely unpleasant.

He checked himself abruptly with a perilous forkful on the way to his mouth. Cautiously he brought it nearer his nose and sniffed. It was impossible to distinguish any particular unpalatable odour among the thickly rich smells of mingling spices. He put the mouthful in.

But there could be no doubt about it: it tasted repulsively bitter.

And then he realised the full extent of his problem. It was not that while still screamingly hungry he would have to stop eating. It was that he had to go on eating. He had to please the fat cook and the cook was still there, watching over him.

He glanced swiftly at A. K. Bhattacharya's plate. Empty. And clean almost to the last smear. Slowly he began eating again. If A. K. Bhattacharya thought the vindaloo was that good, it could not be so bad.

All the same it tasted horrible.

'Cook, Cook,' A. K. Bhattacharya said. 'Can it be that all is eaten? Are there no second helpings?'

The cook beamed. He beamed like the sun and went waddling off to his kitchen to reappear moments later bearing a second dish of vindaloo, as big as the first, all steaming and odorous. He helped A. K. Bhattacharya liberally, to almost inarticulate words of encouragement. Each of the others, even down to A. K. Biswas who had eaten so noisily it was like hearing a drain gurgle, declined a further helping. The cook turned to Ghote.

Closing his mind to everything, Ghote resolutely tackled the remains on his plate, eating as quickly as he could, determined to get the stuff down somehow.

At last he had succeeded.

'Now the Inspector sahib will take more?' the cook asked.

Ghote looked at him. The fellow was smiling ingratiatingly, but not without a look of power. Ghote hated him.

'It was excellent,' he began doubtfully.

The cook rocked forward.

'And certainly I will have more,' Ghote added, noticing at that moment that A. K. Bhattacharya had actually left some small remains of his second helping.

How he was going to get down the large mound the cook spooned on to his plate he could not think. But he was not going to let A. K. Bhattacharya win an ally in the narrow confines of the bogie if it was at all possible to avoid it. Especially not an ally who was in effect guardian of the only way of getting out of the train bar the key safely hidden in the depths of his own pocket.

But when, with sick reluctance, he eventually forced himself to take a first mouthful of his new helping of vindaloo he found that it seemed much less unpleasant. Hastily he ate some more while he was still able to tolerate the taste. And soon, to his considerable relief, he had finished the whole helping at the cost of nothing worse than feeling extremely full, and, he had to confess, not a little sleepy.

'It was excellent, excellent,' he said to the cook.

And, glancing over to A. K. Bhattacharya's still not perfectly cleaned plate, he laid a detaining hand on the man's arm as he stooped gruntingly to clear his place.

'No, wait,' he said. 'There are some small remains still.'

And he polished them off to the last smear. 'There.'

The look of devoted respect he got from the rotund cook was reward enough, and the casualness with which the man removed A. K. Bhattacharya's smeary plate was pure bonus.

Ghote leant back contentedly.

The great train was slipping downhill now, emerging from the far side of the cutting leading away from the long tunnel. Still there was dense bamboo jungle on either side of the unnatural straight path formed by the double set of wide-spaced rails and their artificially flat and even-textured bed of permanent way. The beat of the wheels beneath them made a wonderfully soothing clack-clack, regular and steady.

Ghote stretched and yawned.

And he had beaten A. K. Bhattacharya, he thought with sleepy contentment. He had, at a bit of a cost—really he had eaten much too much—foiled the fellow's plan to recruit the fat cook. Marvellous. He could relax now.

His eyelids drooped.

For a few seconds he dozed, dreaming briefly that it was very important for him to get into some particular position to be photographed, and being obscurely puzzled at the thought that this was somehow to be standing on his head.

The puzzlement brought him to life again, and he sat up and shook himself.

It was vital he should not go to sleep.

Then he asked himself why. Why on earth should he not doze off after an enormous meal like that? It was natural. And there was no reason not to give way to that natural impulse. Certainly he felt very much as if he wanted to. He did not know when he had felt so purely sleepy.

So why not sleep?

Once more he dozed. And this time he dreamt that A. K. Bhattacharya was being photographed. By the cook. And it was important, vital, that he should be photographed just as he fished the bogie key out of his own pocket.

Ghote jerked so far forward in waking himself up that he nearly fell off his chair. He looked round blearily. He could hardly make out the others in the drawing-room his eyes were so heavy, but he thought that for some reason Red was observing him with great intentness.

Did he want to photograph him again? Had he been anxious to get a shot of a traveller about to nod off? That would be a great success, to catch a traveller just—

His mind was beginning to wander again. And it must not. He knew this, though he could not at the moment quite think why.

He had to make an effort. A great effort, cost what it might.

Slowly he forced his mind back to clarity, as if he was manoeuvring into position some heavy wooden object, a temple juggernaut on clumsy wooden wheels. And then he had it.

It was important not to go to sleep because if he shut his eyes now it would be into a darkness so thick that he would not know what was going on around him. Because in that thickness A. K. Bhattacharya could come across and take the bogie key from his pocket with no trouble at all. Because he himself had been doped so that the key might be taken.

For a moment this lucid clarity hovered over him like a cloud of light. And then it dispersed into vanishing droplets and his head lolled forward.

CHAPTER FIVE

From down among the black banks of stifling, fantasticated somnolence into which he had fallen, Inspector Ghote, finding some tiny spark of basic self-preservation, slowly forced his way to the surface, head down and obstinately forward-pointing.

He made his eyes open.

He knew now why he was feeling so sleepy and sick as well. He had been drugged. He even knew when and how he had been drugged. Young Red had done it, with the help of a slightly reluctant Mary Jane. That was what the whole absurd, sudden photography business had been about. It had been a hasty dodge on Red's part to delay him eating until the train had plunged into the thick darkness of Darekasa tunnel. And under cover of that darkness Mary Jane had helped him put some of the opium they carried into his food. It was almost certainly crude Indian opium they had used, to judge by the strong feeling of sickness he was experiencing. And he had gobbled up that whole first large helping. No wonder he felt so dragged down by sleep.

But he knew too what he must do now: he must get rid of the stuff before it could do any more harm.

He made himself sit swayingly upright while

he forced the sleep-choked channels of his mind to consider step by step just what it was that he had to get done. First, he must get to his feet. Second, he must swing round till he was facing the door leading to the two bathrooms of the bogie. Third, he must set off in that direction. Fourth, he must get the door open without leaning on it because if he did that he would inevitably slump into sleep. Fifth, he must get into the first bathroom. Sixth, he must make himself immediately vomit.

Holding this list firmly in a mind on which pillows of sleep were bulging in from either side, he set it into effect.

One. Get his hands on to the arms of the chair. Each hand was like manoeuvring the iron claw of an excavating grab on the end of a long, double-hinged girder bar. He could see the hand moving unendurably slowly towards its destination. It hovered uncertainly. And then it was there. Now he must use it as a lever.

Two. After a long, long time he was up now, on his feet. He had to swing round and find . . . Find something. What was it? Desperately he sought for some tiny patch of hard, grating facts in the billows of dream that softly flumped together in his head. Wait. Door. Yes, he was to turn to the door to the bathrooms. Which way? Think. Yes, to the right.

He had to peer hard to see the narrow,

240

gleamingly polished wooden door though it was only some six or seven feet away. But at last it came into blurred focus.

Three. Set off. What was that? Again his mind floundered, hopelessly seeking some tiny foothold. And again his will forced it to succeed in the search. To set off: it meant to walk. Walk.

He found the narrow dark oblong which he had his eyes fixed on was getting mysteriously nearer and getting clearer too. It was a door. The door to the bathrooms. He must be walking towards it. And then he must vomit. Cling to that. He had to vomit.

Now, four. Do not lean on this door. He ached for the comfort of it. To lean there and to slip away from the niggling grit that lodged like a minuscule-hard irritation in his mind and to sleep. He leant backwards a little, slowly pushed forward his hand, tapped like a blind man two or three times at the squat, many-sided doorknob, remembered that what he had to do was to turn it, wondered for a while how that was done, then somehow conducted the operation and was saved from having to think what the next stage was by a happy lurch of the great train that sent the opened door swinging forwards and dragged him into the little lobby beyond.

What now? Now it was five? What was five? He had to vomit. Why? Do not know. How to do it? A blankness faced him. For a long time he stood there in the lobby swaying to the motion of the train, the blankness seemingly permanent in his mind. But still there was something needling the will forward. A something that eventually produced the stubbed thought 'Bathroom' and urged him blunderingly into the nearer small compartment.

Next? Six. Six was to vomit. He leant forward over the stainless-steel toilet pan and, since this part of his plan must have been in his mind as the longed-for final stage from the very beginning, without at all knowing what he was doing he got his hand up to his mouth with the idea of putting his fingers down his throat.

But then the occasionally lurching train that had helped him once went against him. There came the one heavier sway among the others, and it toppled him over.

He lay crumpled on the floor of the bathroom and at last let the sleep that he had fought against and wanted to welcome take over completely.

What woke him—and some deep internal clock let him know for certain that it was only a minute or two later—was the feel of a pair of strong hands tugging at the waistband of his trousers in an effort to turn him over. The jerking and poking brought his mind to the surface, but only just. He was able to take in what was happening to him, but only enough of his brain to observe this was above the thick black surface of sleep. To act against the prying hands was totally beyond his capacities. All he could do was experience. He could feel. He could hear. He could see in front of his immovable head a small triangular section of the bathroom floor, grey with whitish splodges and a rime of dirt caught where the wall rose up eight inches from his nose.

He could hear.

'Stop. You want to leave him alone. You shouldn't have done that to him, neither you nor Red.'

It was the girl, Mary Jane.

'My dear young lady, please restrain yourself. I cannot complete this journey like a dog tied with a rope. This is necessary.'

A. K. Bhattacharya's cold voice. And A. K. Bhattacharya's strong-fingered hands were working now at his trouser top. He felt himself rolling over, like a sack.

He must get back. That was what he had to do. A small voice, still alive inside him, put first things first.

He fought.

He was hardly conscious of what it was he had to fight, or how it was that he could fight it. But he fought. And, after what seemed as long a tunnel of time as he could imagine, he emerged. The possibility of movement was restored to him.

He heaved himself upwards on one straightening arm. Above him he was

243

conscious that someone had moved. Moved away. It was A. K. Bhattacharya.

He shook his head, hoping to clear it. He was going to have to stop that man stealing the key. Because once he had that, the moment the train slowed down at all, as on some sharper-than-ideal bend it was bound to do sooner or later, then the fellow would be out on the running board and dropping down into the jungle on either side of the track. To be lost. Utterly. Within minutes.

He swung himself round, managed to balance for a second or so on his stretched arm and lunged out with the other.

'It hasn't worked.'

That was Mary Jane's voice again. And she sounded triumphant, triumphant on his behalf. A new surge of strength came back to him. He heaved again with his spirit at his reluctant body and succeeded in turning himself right round before he slumped backwards into a seated position on the bathroom floor. But now he could see the open door. He could see Mary Jane standing there and he could see A. K. Bhattacharya, tall and white, there now. And in a moment retreating, baffled.

Then it was Mary Jane who was helping him to his feet.

'Sick,' he managed to blurt out. 'Must be sick.'

She guided him with tough, confident young arms towards the toilet pan. And there was no

244

need now even to get his fingers into his throat. The nauseating crude opium did the job for him.

'Can I help some way?' Mary Jane asked when it appeared to be finished.

'Yes,' Ghote said. 'Please. I need tea now. Can you get the cook to make a great quantity of tea?'

Weak from his vomiting and still under the heavy menace of sleep from the drug that had got into his bloodstream he made his way lurchingly back into the drawing-room and fell into his chair. But he knew he could relax a little. He had an ally. Mary Jane would see that the cook made tea, would see that he drank it. He would before long be in full control again. He had won.

*   *   *

Ghote took his time about drinking the tea. Slowly he consumed cup after cup and quite soon he began to feel the beneficial effects of the hot and strong liquid. His mind cleared. But he did his best to maintain the doped look he must have had on his return to the drawing-room. He wanted to think, and he wanted to think without being disturbed.

A. K. Bhattacharya, he had seen shortly after Mary Jane had put the first hot, refreshingly steamy cup into his still dopy hands, was sitting at the far end of the

245

flowered sofa pretending to be immersed in *The Art Treasures of Bali* but sitting with such a deep scowl on his long face that it was plain, even through the haze in his own mind, that the Bengali was hardly benefiting from the beauty of the illustrations and descriptions in his heavy volume.

So much for him. He had been beaten off. And, though no doubt since he had shown so much active and ruthless determination to escape he could not be counted on for long to remain quiet, he was at present held in check.

But there was Red also to be considered. If A. K. Bhattacharya had failed to secure the cook as an ally he had at least shown that he had a strong supporter, and one prepared to act, in the sullen-looking British hippy. In some three hours the train would stop at Nagpur for a halt of twenty-five minutes or so. Should he then expel the hippies, since it was now plain they were not A. K. Bhattacharya's hired accomplices, calling on the railway police to help him if necessary? On the one side there was the enmity of Red, though that might well be exhausted with this one effort to achieve his idealistic end. And on the other hand there was his own, new-found ally, Mary Jane. And it certainly did not look as if her sympathy was used up.

He looked into her fresh picture-pretty face as she handed him another strong brown cup of tea and was rewarded by a broad smile and a wink.

It was the wink that decided him. It spoke of an uncomplicated friendliness, and that at this moment seemed so precious that he made up his mind there and then to take no action against Red.

By the time they reached Nagpur Ghote was fully recovered and was able to keep a particularly acute watch for the whole twenty-five minutes the train was stationary for any signs of a possible attack by goondas hired by his prisoner. But no one seemed at all interested in the bogie, and before long he came to the conclusion that, if A. K. Bhattacharya had succeeded in getting a message through to some paid confederate, then it was not at Nagpur that the attempt was to come.

His feeling was confirmed by the action of A. K. Bhattacharya himself, who, with the sharp bulk of the fort-crowned Sitabaldi Hill slipping past on their right as they pulled slowly out of Nagpur Station, stood up and moved along the length of the drawing-room sofa until he was near enough to where he himself sat to be able to hold a confidential conversation.

As the romantically grim fort disappeared from view to be replaced by glimpses of the foliage-shaded city, A. K. Bhattacharya pushed himself to the very edge of the sofa and leant forwards.

'Inspector,' he said, 'I think the time has

247

come for you and me to have a quiet chat—about certain matters.'

His fleshy face looked so untypically quiet that Ghote was in a flash convinced that all the seeds he had been sowing were about to come to light in the long-awaited confession. The thought spread rosily in his mind. A full confession. What a magnificent thing that would be to bring back to Bombay. To arrive there with the notorious A. K. Bhattacharya, not only safely held, but tamed.

The prow-nosed face inched one tiny bit nearer.

'Inspector,' said A. K. Bhattacharya. 'I am a man of very considerable wealth. If you wish, I will admit that that wealth was not come by in a fashion which society considers proper.'

This was hardly the tone of a suppliant, Ghote noted. But on the other hand his man was making an admission he had hitherto avoided. The diminishing rosiness in his head took on once more a finely pink hue.

'Yes, yes,' he said. 'Go on, go on.'

A. K. Bhattacharya's eyes lightened.

'Good, good, my dear Inspector. I see you are not as unsympathetic as I feared you might be. Now as I was saying, I have, by means which I know you have not approved, acquired a really very considerable fortune. And, with my excellent contacts with foreigners of many kinds, I have taken the precaution of putting a large part of that wealth far beyond the reach

248

of the authorities in our native land, authorities who, I am bound to say, take an extremely petty view of my activities.'

Ghote felt that he ought to object to this. But if it was A. K. Bhattacharya's way of getting round to making that full confession then he was not going to quibble.

'Yes,' the Bengali went on in low tones that Ghote had constant difficulty in catching above the heavy continuous rumble of the train. 'Yes, I have acquired all this money by means which hitherto you have not approved. But I begin to suspect that perhaps you are coming to see that it is not necessary to hold the same strict views all your life. You are—'

'Not necessary?' Ghote interrupted sharply. 'I am afraid I do not understand.'

A. K. Bhattacharya smiled.

'How shall I put it then?' he asked. 'Let us say that with the passing of years a man takes a different view of life.'

'But, no, I do not,' Ghote said. 'There are some things which you ought to hold on to. Always.'

'Yes, yes, no doubt. But there are things too which change. When a man is young he believes he can happily conduct his life with very little money. He is tough: he is prepared to endure hardships then. A small house. Poor schooling for his children. Only an occasional coarse cotton sari for his wife. All this seems nothing to a man who is young.'

The Bengali looked at Ghote assessingly. And Ghote, in himself, had to admit that for whatever reasons he was doing so the fellow was painting an accurate enough portrait of his young self.

'All the same,' he said doubtfully, 'I am not sure . . .'

'Of course not, my dear Inspector. No one makes a radical change in their life without having doubts. But let me continue. We have on the one hand the man who is young, who has hope still. He does not care that he is poor, that his wife and children suffer.'

'Excuse, please,' Ghote interrupted. 'I have one child only.'

'Ah, one child. One child only. The apple of his father's eye. But he is now—How old is the boy? It is a boy?'

'Ved is nine.'

'Good, good. And let me ask. Is Ved at nine still the whole bundle of high aspirations that he was in your eyes at the age of two? I venture to reply on your behalf. He is not. There are things, you have to admit, fond father that you are, that the boy is incapable of, things that he will never achieve.'

Ghote, in all simple reality, had to admit to himself that this was so. Ved was not good at arithmetic. It was something all his teachers agreed on. And he did not even shine exceptionally brilliantly at anything else.

His face showed the acknowledgment.

'So,' said A. K. Bhattacharya, 'you see now that your earliest, wildest hopes are false. The boy will not become such a man as never to need any protection, he will not become such a youth that nothing can cause him to fall. He will need all the protection you can give him. He is only human. He will need protection, and therefore you need money.'

It was a thought Ghote had often had, and one which believing with everything that was in him that what cannot be cured must be endured he had always thrust utterly away. All this too showed in his eyes as he leant forward to catch the almost whispered words of the Bengali above the heavy rattle and throb of the Calcutta Mail as it began to bite into the last half of its journey to Bombay.

'Yes,' A. K. Bhattacharya said, 'as an inspector of police you will never have all the money you will need. But, by what must be something of a miracle for you, here am I sitting in the same bogie drawing-room as you and possessed of really very considerable wealth. Inspector, it is simple: name your price.'

Despite the obvious drift of the confidence-trickster's conversation, Ghote had not for a moment expected to hear these last words. Although he well knew that sometimes police officials had accepted bribes in the past and that therefore it was not really out of the ordinary that he should be offered one, and one calculated with extreme skill to appeal to his deepest instincts, still the brutal request bemused him.

So for measurable seconds he sat there with his mouth actually a little open like an idiot's.

'Come,' A. K. Bhattacharya said sharply. 'I ask you to mention a price. Do not be afraid to pitch it too steeply. If I do not think your game worth the candle, do not be worried: I shall tell you so pretty quickly.'

And then the flame-orange rage shot up in Ghote's mind.

'You are attempting to corrupt an officer of the law,' he barked. 'There will be charges made. You have spoken before witnesses. You will serve a term for this. This will finish you, I promise.'

'Keep your voice down, you fool,' hissed A. K. Bhattacharya. 'The others will guess what we are discussing. Listen, you and your precious family could live a life of ease with me in Bali, if you will only hear reason. All of you, all the rest of your life, free from worry. Do you know what Bali is like? Do you? It's a paradise, I tell you, a paradise. The climate is magnificent. The people are friendly, and astonishingly beautiful. Everything there is generous. There is art, beauty, everything you could wish. And it could be yours, yours easily, if you will only pay some attention.'

Inspector Ghote rose to his feet. He swung round on his heels and went across to the door to the bathrooms. He went through, entered the cubicle where he had mercifully been so sick, and very thoroughly washed his face and his hands and swilled out his mouth.

*   *   *

When Ghote returned to the drawing-room they journeyed on, all of them, in a constrained silence. No doubt his short outburst after he had, in his entrenched innocence, realised that A. K. Bhattacharya was attempting to offer him an enormous bribe had eventually made the others fully aware of what was happening. In any case Mr Ramaswamy seemed to feel the atmosphere very keenly, and sat there with some enormously complicated returns spread out on his lap but not looking at them at all. The two hippies, who in any case were still smouldering from their quarrel, equally sat in silence. And even A. K. Biswas, cheerful and crude, seemed chastened and sat without a word industriously picking his nose. Darkness fell and quite shortly afterwards the train came to a halt again at the important junction of Wardha.

When it did so none of them moved from their frozen positions, and so it came as a shock, which made little Mr Ramaswamy actually utter a short sound somewhere between a gasp and a scream, when on the window on the platform side there sounded abruptly a staccato tattoo of knocks.

Ghote leapt up and hurried to the window, rapidly working out that its double glass was so tough that to break it would need something a good deal heavier than the stick it sounded as if it was being hit with.

All the same, was this the start of an attempt to free A. K. Bhattacharya?

He glanced swiftly back and felt for his whistle. No, surely the Bengali looked genuinely surprised.

He peered through the blued glass of the window out into the dark station. Close to, it was immediately obvious what the cause of the tattoo on the glass was: the pane was being sharply rapped by an elderly but vigorous-looking woman with the butt end of her umbrella.

The moment she saw Ghote she began to shout.

Her words, thanks to the thickness of the double panes, were quite inaudible and Ghote turned away. No doubt, for all the respectability of the woman's neat white sari and bespectacled face, it was some poor mad creature.

The knocking on the glass was resumed more imperiously than before.

'Kindly take no notice,' Ghote said to the others.

They obeyed in so far as they did not move

from their chairs. But not to take any notice of the noise of the peremptory and continued rapping would have required the powers of a yogi in the Himalayas.

Eventually Ghote decided that he would have to do something. Taking a cautious look at A. K. Bhattacharya, he went to the bogie door, slipped the precious key from his pocket and cautiously turned it in the lock.

Immediately he opened the door a crack he was confronted by the lady with the umbrella, who he now saw was even more respectable than he had realised. She clutched in her other hand from the umbrella a battered but efficient-looking briefcase.

'Young man,' she said in the voice of someone used to having people do what she told them to. 'Young man, I have been tapping on your window for a full five minutes and no one has answered.'

'The bogie is reserved,' Ghote replied, stiffly.

'I am well aware of that. A bogie is not put on a train to take ordinary passengers.'

'Why are you knocking then?' Ghote replied, beginning to feel distinctly resentful of the calmly authoritative tone.

'Because I want to come in, of course.'

'I have already said: this bogie is reserved. It is reserved for police purposes.'

'Ah, good. I was afraid it was some maharajah or other who would object to me sharing with him.'

And up she marched as if to brush Ghote aside like a badly-dressed clerk.

He stayed put.

Certainly this imperious lady was not his idea of an accomplice for A. K. Bhattacharya. But you could never tell. And in any case he did not wish to complicate the situation inside the bogie one bit further. There was only the night ahead, and what there was of the next morning, in which to get the confession.

'Young man, stand out of the way.'

'I regret, madam, I cannot give permission for any member of the public to enter the bogie.'

'I am not a member of the public. I am Mrs Sulbha Chiplunkar.'

Ghote had heard of her. He knew from the newspapers, in which her name often appeared in the duller and more formal items, that she was a person of consequence. Just why she was so he could not exactly recall. But she had strong connections with the old India of the freedom-struggle days. And, the thought struck him, Wardha was of course the station for Gandhi's former ashram at Sevagram. She must be coming from there.

He could of course still stand by his rights and refuse to let her in. But he had his respect for the cloud of glory that hung round this battle-axe frame, steel spectacles, knobbed umbrella and all.

'Mrs Chiplunkar, madam,' he said, 'please to enter.'

Mrs Chiplunkar entered. Ghote, commonsensically locking the door behind her, issued an explanation.

'It is Mrs Sulbha Chiplunkar.'

A. K. Bhattacharya leapt to his feet and joined his hands in a profound namaskar.

'Madam,' he said, 'I will not burden you with my name, but allow me to say I have long nourished the most deep respect not only for you yourself but for all that you stand for and have stood for over the long years.'

And the floweriness of the speech sent a niggle of suspicion through Ghote. Was it not surely too readily produced? Did this mean that the long-threatened accomplice had succeeded in getting into the bogie after all?

It was just at this instant that, thanks to the chance of his angle of vision, from where he stood just behind the new arrival's shoulder, he was able to see that the steel-rimmed spectacles clamped so firmly across her nose had lenses of plain glass.

The words of Dr Hans Gross came back to his mind and sonorously rolled there: 'Everything which appears unnatural should be considered as suspicious and unauthentic.' Behind him he heard the shrill scream of the guard's whistle. The Calcutta Mail lurched into movement again.

CHAPTER SIX

For an instant Ghote contemplated swinging round, unlocking the bogie door, seizing the stringy-looking figure standing just in front of him by her waist and hurling her off the train, umbrella, briefcase and all, while it was still moving at a speed which would do her little harm.

But, despite the tell-tale spectacles, the woman grasping the battered briefcase looked so like the person Mrs Sulbha Chiplunkar ought to be that he could not but hesitate. Were he to arrive at Bombay with two dozen A. K. Bhattacharyas, each one ready to plead guilty to any number of frauds, and if there was awaiting him a telegraphed complaint from the real Mrs Chiplunkar, respected and influential voice from a distant and glamour-rich past, stating that he had flung her bodily out of a moving train, he would be dismissed from the force in no time at all.

So he did nothing.

He was able to reflect, however, that he did have one advantage: neither the false Mrs Chiplunkar (if she was false) nor A. K. Bhattacharya knew that he had penetrated the secret of the plain-lensed spectacles. So, provided he kept an unremitting watch, he should yet be able to put a stop to any plan they might have.

If only, he thought with grey irritation, he did not already feel tired. To keep as unremitting a watch as he ought seemed like a burden even now too heavy to lift. No doubt the effects of the opium were still lingering in his system, and in any case he had had nothing but bad nights since he had left Bombay. That very first evening A. K. Bhattacharya in the guise of Mr Banerjee had kept him up talking till well into the small hours and then there had been that awful awakening at about three in the morning with the news that the man in Dum-Dun Gaol was not the Bengali confidence-trickster. The second night had hardly been better, with its 5a.m. stop at Hazaribagh Road. And last night, though it had been an improvement on the other two, had not been by any means one of unbroken sleep, and he had been up early too to have that dreadful, fly-away talk when his man had proposed they should enter into unholy partnership together.

Inwardly he shuddered at the remembrance.

And now he had the prospect of keeping doubly alert because of the intrusion of this person pretending to be Mrs Chiplunkar. What was she aiming to do?

It was certain that she was a woman, and not a very strong or young one. So a direct attack with that knobby umbrella was not to be expected. But what had she got in her so

259

respectable and work-worn briefcase? A gun?

He took a quick step forward.

'Madam,' he said, 'allow me to put your briefcase and umbrella in a safe place.'

And he swept both out of her hands and carried them over to a far corner of the drawing-room. Standing for a moment with his back to them all, he flipped open the briefcase's old brass lock and took a rapid look inside.

There were papers in one compartment, voluminous and dog-eared with frequent perusal. Just exactly what Mrs Chiplunkar ought to be carrying. And in the other compartment were a few toilet articles and an efficiently wrapped-together white night sari. He squeezed this quickly between his fingers.

No gun hidden in the folds. Not a file. Not even a key to fit the bogie door.

The false Mrs Chiplunkar seemed a very unprepared accomplice.

'What is it that you are doing with my briefcase?'

Her voice, sharp and authoritative, hit him in the back of the neck like a slap.

He turned.

'The lock appeared to have sprung open,' he said. 'I will make quite certain it is properly fastened and then I will put the case in the corner here.'

'Good, good.'

Mrs Chiplunkar dismissed the matter from

her mind.

But A. K. Bhattacharya, who had taken a sudden interest in Ghote's activities again, was far from ready to let the subject drop.

'Yes, yes,' he said. 'Your case will be entirely safe in that corner, Mrs Chiplunkar. You can be sure of that. Although, if I may make so bold as to guess, I would hazard that it contains nothing that a thief would want. Some papers only, and a few necessaries, yes? Of inestimable value to you, no doubt, madam. But not to a thief. A thief would want something like valuables. Or a gun even.'

He flashed on Ghote his old Mr Banerjee, white-teethed smile at its most tigerish.

'Is that not so, Inspector?' he said. 'Would not a thief hope to find a gun in that briefcase?'

Do what he might, the smile and the suggestion could not but put back into Ghote's mind all his suspicions of the new arrival that his inspection of the admirable and innocent briefcase had begun to dispel. Did she have a gun under the folds of that plain cotton sari?

And A. K. Bhattacharya seemed more jovial now too, as if his troubles were about to come to an end. Yet Mrs Chiplunkar could not, look on her how he might, seem at this moment menacing. She had seated herself near Mr Ramaswamy and was listening, with some impatience, to his riddle about his occupation in life.

'Well, well,' she said briskly when the secret was out, 'I suppose we must have such things as Inspectors of Forms and Stationery in our railway system. But certainly Gandhiji would hardly have understood.'

If she is A. K. Bhattacharya's accomplice, Ghote asked himself, why does she not pull out her gun now instead of talking? She could order me to hand over the door key. The train is still going very slowly. There would be time for the pair of them to drop to the track below without risk of anything worse than a bruising. Why is she not acting?

But instead she was telling Mr Ramaswamy about how the Mahatma had travelled on his tours by rail.

'In third-class always he insisted,' she explained. 'But, of course, we saw to it that air-conditioning was specially installed. People said there was a contradiction there. But of course there was not. Gandhiji knew very well that there was air-conditioning, but he had not asked for it and he never would have done. We saw to all that.'

No, surely she could not be some confederate of the Bengali's. She really sounded too genuine.

But how could he be sure? An idea appeared in his mind, ready-made and gobblingly attractive. With hardly a second for reflection he put it into action.

'Mrs Chiplunkar,' he said. 'No doubt you would like to join us for dinner. I will speak a word to our cook.'

And he marched immediately out of the drawing-room, banging the narrow, heavy door conclusively closed behind him. At once to turn the stainless-steel knob of the handle with quick stealth and to ease the door open again by a fraction of an inch.

If anything was now said in the drawing-room he ought to be able to hear, even above the steady thump-thump of the train as it began to gather speed. And, better than this, it proved to be as he had hoped: pressed close up against the door, he was able to see the picture of a fort-crowned romantic crag that Indian Railways had provided for the pleasure of its most revered passengers. And that picture happily was protected by a sheet of well-polished, highly reflecting glass. His observation of the mysterious Mrs Chiplunkar and of A. K. Bhattacharya was complete.

He directed his whole energy into watching and listening.

Fifteen seconds passed. Half a minute. Three quarters of a minute. A whole minute.

Nobody in the drawing-room had spoken. No one seemed to be taking the least interest in anyone else. Certainly Mrs Chiplunkar had done nothing in the least suspicious. She was sitting splendidly in Ghote's view, and she had closed her eyes and lowered her head, whether in mere tiredness, in meditation or merely in practical thought he did not like to inquire even of himself.

A. K. Bhattacharya's behaviour however was at first less innocent. Ghote could see that he was taking a close interest in the newcomer. Was he waiting till it was undeniably safe to communicate? But no. The longer Mrs Chiplunkar—and with every passing second Ghote felt more and more inclined to bestow on her this name in full title—sat with closed eyes the less grew A. K. Bhattacharya's interest in her.

When at last Ghote was in no doubt that the confidence-trickster had done no more than hope to engage this distinguished visitor in conversation he stood back a pace, rattled the knob of the narrow door in a thoroughly warning way and then re-entered the drawing-room.

It was while this manoeuvre was taking place that A. K. Bhattacharya favoured the desiccated lady in the severe white sari and the plain-lens spectacles with the broadest of winks.

*   *   *

Ghote's return seemed to act as a signal to Mrs Chiplunkar, who had already ended her meditation, or session of hard thought, or pause of mere nothingness. At once she began to lecture, just as the real Mrs Chiplunkar would surely have done. She lectured as the

264

train ate into the flat, just darkened countryside on the essence of the Gandhian spirit in public life today. And Mr Ramaswamy, listening as respectfully as Ghote himself, assented and deplored his own inability to bring those noble concepts into the curious unreality of his own professional life. And then the two hippies joined in since higher and more mystical things were being discussed and they put the world in its place, pausing from time to time to take verbal nips at each other like a pair of puppies. And even A. K. Biswas, sitting cheerfully having a thorough scratch on the floor in the corner, once or twice tried to hurl his way into the discussion and was not at all disconcerted when nobody took any notice of him.

The cook, despite his having received no warning from Ghote, entered in due course and served them all with a copious meal. And again Ghote, though he felt too bone-tired to be at all hungry, was obliged to consume the largest helping in order to keep the cook firmly on his side. It made him yet sleepier.

And the train made steady progress, with no stop now till Jalgaon at about 2 a.m. shortly after the point at which their wide, southern-swinging route would join that other northern swing they had taken on the way to Calcutta. Outside there was little to be seen except the occasional dowsed light that indicated some village sleeping the darkness away or less frequently a town with a station, Pulgaon, Badnera, Murtazapur, when the reflection of lonely lamps would swing by slowly on the dark glass of the window.

At last Ghote thought he must make a positive move. That confession had at all costs to be obtained.

It was getting reasonably late now so he simply offered Mrs Chiplunkar his bed.

'But, Inspector,' Mrs Chiplunkar said, 'I had not understood when I asked for room in your bogie that you had so many people in here already. I had thought there would be a spare bed. I cannot possibly take yours.'

At once Ghote's suspicions returned. So you are waiting your time, are you, he thought. When are you going to do it then? What plan have you got?

'But if you are insisting,' Mrs Chiplunkar went on after the smallest of pauses, 'very well, I will accept.'

She rose and went over to retrieve her battered briefcase. Ghote escorted her to the sleeping compartment and showed her where he had slept the night before. The bunk looked very tempting.

When he got back he found Mr Ramaswamy tactfully also preparing to retire, and, obeying some mysterious internal impulse, the two hippies suddenly wrapped their arms round each other and, to Ghote's dismay, kissed in public. Then they too headed for the sleeping

266

compartment.

Ghote put them out of his mind. His struggle with A. K. Bhattacharya was about to be renewed.

He did not start by addressing the confidence-trickster directly. He had tried that too often, and with such disastrous results.

Instead he got up and went and stood over the tall, sprawly A. K. Biswas sitting cross-legged in his corner working hard at cleaning out his right ear.

'Now,' he said sharply, 'it is time you and I had a talk. We must think what is going to happen to you when we get to Bombay tomorrow.'

A. K. Biswas looked up with a grin.

'Two years R.I. this time, bhai,' he said.

He ought to have been much more despondent. But Ghote persisted.

'There is no reason for it to be two years' rigorous imprisonment,' he said. 'You could be much more lucky.'

'I could be much more unlucky,' A. K. Biswas broke in. 'You get some magistrate had his son met a fellow like me in a train and I would be doing five.'

'Nonsense,' Ghote said sharply. 'Magistrates are not influenced by such considerations.'

A. K. Biswas made a rude gesture, and Ghote reflected that a person of his sort actually preferred to keep his illusions about how sharp and knowing he was than take a chance of getting a shorter sentence. At any other time he would have let the fellow suffer for his fancies. But now his role was to stimulate another criminal's thoughts, and a much bigger one.

'Just you listen to me,' he said. 'Do you think the police are interested in going to court over you? Do you think we want to sit for hours waiting to be called as witnesses just for you?'

'It is sitting,' A. K. Biswas said with an air of reasonableness. 'That is better than running about trying to catch fellows like me.'

'No, it is not,' Ghote snapped. 'We have jobs to do, and we wish to get on with them.'

It was not totally true, he knew. He had heard occasional men in the lower ranks say how much pleasanter it was to be waiting in a cool courtroom than to be out on duty in the hot sun. But some things had to be sacrificed.

'Yes,' he went on less severely, 'we have jobs and we want to do them. And we are stopped by having to give evidence about people like you. Now, just supposing—'

'Wait a moment, my friend, I beg.'

It was A. K. Bhattacharya. Ghote turned and looked at him.

'There is one thing, my dear Inspector, that I fear you have not taken into account in your otherwise excellent arguments,' he said. 'You have considered the time of the police, and you had begun to hint, in a manner admirably subtle, that what you have in mind will give the criminal too his own accretion of time. Well and good. But have you considered our brethren the lawyers? They would hardly welcome no one ever contesting a case.'

Damn the man. Why must he demolish every argument? And why must he talk so much?

'Be silent.'

A. K. Bhattacharya sat back in pained surprise. Ghote turned again to A. K. Biswas and picked up the threads of his plea. And then, as he talked and the stupid card-sharper failed and failed spontaneously to praise the advantages of pleading guilty to a charge, he began to notice something out of the corner of his eye: the silent A. K. Bhattacharya was positively wriggling in his place on the sofa in his desire to join in the talk and take it soaring swiftly up to those windy heights he loved.

That observation gave Ghote his idea. He turned away from A. K. Biswas sharply.

'Do not be a fool, man,' he snarled. 'Plead guilty and give yourself a chance of a shorter sentence. And now go to sleep.'

With an unoffended grin the gangly card-sharper rolled over on to his side and tucked his knees up to his chin. Within a couple of minutes he was, as ordered, asleep. Once again Ghote was alone with A. K. Bhattacharya. But now he had his idea.

CHAPTER SEVEN

Despite the fact that A. K. Bhattacharya was looking up expectantly Inspector Ghote said nothing. Instead he took a chair opposite the Bengali and waited.

Sure enough, after a minute or so the confidence-trickster cleared his throat.

'Silence,' Ghote hissed.

'But, my dear Inspector—'

'I said silence. Do you want to be put in handcuffs?'

'Well, no, that would be, I confess—'

'Silence.'

And silence there was.

Ghote sat in his armchair, endeavouring to keep his back ramrod straight so as to prevent himself falling asleep. A. K. Bhattacharya sat at the far end of the sofa and shifted this way and that like a caged beast in the Victoria Gardens zoo back in Bombay.

After something more than an hour the tall Bengali took a visible decision. He altered his position one more time. But on this occasion he stretched out his long legs in a relaxed way with one ankle over the other, threw back his fleshy face and shut his eyes.

'Pay attention,' Ghote snapped.

A. K. Bhattacharya sat up like a jack-in-a-box. He leant forward prepared to hear,

270

prepared plainly to hear anything to which he could give a reply that would set him off at last on his longed-for ascending mountain-path of talk.

And Ghote said not a thing.

The minutes passed. A. K. Bhattacharya sat still, craning forward to hear. Ghote sat upright looking at him. And at last A. K. Bhattacharya shifted once more, irritably, in his place.

Inwardly Ghote permitted himself a grim smile.

Twice more before they reached Jalgaon just after two a.m. he had to prevent the Bengali sleeping, and each time he did so with the very minimum of words.

Each time too he felt a growing sense of triumph as he jerked the confidence-trickster back into his torture. He began to nurture a feeling that this device—and it was, he acknowledged, the last he had left—was going to work. It was after all in essence only an old and well-tried plan: to prevent your man from sleeping in order to wear him down. Preventing A. K. Bhattacharya from talking was a refinement he had been lucky to hit on.

The hours wore on. Steadily through the night the long train steamed its way across the cotton-fields of Berar. The windows of the drawing-room, over which Ghote had not bothered to draw the long flower-patterned curtains, showed nothing but blackness for hour after hour. Only the reflection of that still

271

scene in the lit drawing-room flickered on to them like badly-reproduced colour photographs.

There Ghote saw his own face and figure, a slight man in white shirt and trousers—the stains and crumpling of the long journey too small to appear in this shifting transparency—with features which could at times be glimpsed as greyly tired, hollow eyes, pinched cheeks, downward-turning mouth.

Beside this dim and worn figure that was himself he could see constantly the side and back of A. K. Bhattacharya's head, projecting well above the top of the angled sofa. There was that fan of hair, black enough in the reflection but obviously dyed now when Ghote turned his eyes on the real man. There was the outline, just, of that prow of a nose, fleshy and disdainful, but beginning to droop now. There was a glimpse of the mouth, not breaking into frequent and devastating white-teeth flashing grins any more, but harshly closed and obstinate.

And, what never appeared in the window-reflections as the train swung and rumbled through the night was the tension in the air of the drawing-room, though so hard and grit-shot was it that Ghote felt he could almost touch it as a palpable substance.

At last there came a break in the routine, a small one but momentously significant in the solidly-built edifice of mutual silence. The train slowed and came to a sighing halt at Jalgaon. The time was exactly three minutes past two. Outside now, instead of the heavy clack-clack of the wheels and the faint but equally steady panting of the engine, there was the long hiss of escaping steam and the sparse and anxious callings-out of middle-of-the-night passengers boarding a long-awaited train.

And then with a faint shrill of the guard's whistle, with long reluctant snorts from their immense locomotive, with a jerk echoing back and forth along the length of the great train, they were off again. Off with an unaccountable but extraordinarily definite change in the atmosphere of the bogie drawing-room.

Ghote was unsure how it had happened. Perhaps with the new start in the journey there had been a tiny lightning-flash of sympathy between him and A. K. Bhattacharya, less than a look, the mere quiver of facial muscles. But, whatever it was, it was clearly there. A sympathy had begun to vibrate between the two of them.

Ghote observed it, as closely as he had observed Mrs Chiplunkar, or the false Mrs Chiplunkar, trying to see if she carried a gun under her workmanlike white sari. It must not, this feeling be allowed to steam itself up into anything properly shared between himself and A. K. Bhattacharya. It must not become a weakness. But, if he could keep a check on it, could keep any boiling-up falseness out of it,

273

could force it to stay as a thread—a real black thread, he saw it as—and not allow it to become high, fluttering streamers of delusion, then it was valuable.

Then it might become the frail path along which, inch by inch, he would haul from the Bengali's mind a willingness to admit.

So he sat and watched. He held his head at an angle now that enabled him, without appearing to be looking for anything in the Bengali's features, to watch them for the least telltale sign they might give.

An hour passed. An hour, or something like it, passed, he judged, while the train steadily went on with its journey climbing now up the inner slope of the Western Ghats ready for its steep final descent to the coast.

Despite the rigidity of his attitude, despite A. K. Biswas's animal snores, he felt he was really succeeding in fighting off sleep, though it never ceased to lurk at the back of his mind like a black formless shape ready to spring. And at the end of this period he felt safe in acknowledging that a definite change had come about in A. K. Bhattacharya's looks. The man was haggard.

If his own cheeks felt pinched in with fatigue, the Bengali's too were now plainly so. And the mouth, that had before been shut in a rat-trap of resentment, was now downturned in sheer depression. Across the thread of sympathy between them, in faint tugs and uneasy twitches, Ghote could sense this black depression invading the Bengali's mind, seeping into its every last corner, as depression often invaded his own head, oily and thick.

And indeed as a guard against that very feeling sliding along the thin cord from the Bengali to him he forced himself to record the difference between the confidence-trickster's present state of mind—he knew it as clearly as if it were his own thoughts he was passing in review—and the cocksureness that had radiated from every long limb and fleshy feature of the fellow when he had been that unpleasant Mr Banerjee, so long ago now it seemed.

More time passed. Not an hour, perhaps forty-five minutes. There was no occasion now for Ghote to bully the Bengali into silence. Silence was embedded in his person, like cement that had hardened.

But a change was taking place. A change marked in tiny, almost imperceptible alterations in the repose of the face muscles, in the tension of the limbs, almost imperceptible, but clear, quite clear, to Ghote's intense watchfulness.

A. K. Bhattacharya was passing from a feeling of wide-spreading depression into a fierce resentment. But it was, Ghote knew, a very different resentment from that which had first afflicted the talk-fixated Bengali when silence had been imposed on him. Then he had fretted and fumed and hated. He had erupted in a series of stifled, pinhead objections. Now he was the subject of a more general and altogether deeper resentment. He was not hating this little inspector of police using arbitrary powers against him: he was hating mankind and the whole wide world. This was a massive resentment, a hard peak thrusting upwards. And such a resentment would be fruitful. It was a force. It would have its effect.

And, Ghote thought, it had presented him with a new A. K. Bhattacharya. He had seen, and writhed under, the self-confident teaser. He had observed on the way to Calcutta the hints of sharpness in this apparently always affable character. There had been the time when he had deliberately delayed telling the two hippies that he himself was from the police just so that he could betray that silent promise when it would cause most pain. Then, worse, there had been the really not at all pleasant incident when the so-called Mr Banerjee simply to protect himself from the faint chance that a photograph in young Red's camera would have presented had stolen his films and with remorseless efficiency had thrown away so much valuable material.

Now there was something new to add to that slowly built-up picture of a man. There was this ability for massive hate.

It fitted in well enough, Ghote noted, with the readiness with which the fellow had once advocated that little Mr Ramaswamy should spend his life submitting false returns, making a mockery of years of quiet and painstaking work. It fitted in with the sharp brutality the man had shown in bribing the one-eyed barber to hold him himself back at Hazaribagh Road with all the adverse effect it was bound to have on an innocent man's career. That too had been an over-fierce move: A. K. Bhattacharya had been under no real threat then.

Here was a dangerous hidden side of the man who might seem to be no more than high-flying, toothless fantasy.

So as the Calcutta Mail wound its way up into the Ghats, going detectably more slowly now, Ghote sat, still as one of the statues the ingenious A. K. Bhattacharya had fabricated to deceive the museum hounds of Europe and America, and completed the portrait of his adversary. At the right moment, he hoped, it might give him what he needed to play his cards in the right way. And all the while the hardly-to-be-seen expression of heavy and solid resentment hardened on the Bengali's fleshy features.

It hardened and at the same time, Ghote saw despite the dark backlog of fatigue he was still fighting, it started to alter once again. Degree by degree the hardness was becoming a blankness.

Ghote added this fact to his store of facts, and hoped that he was right in thinking that it would be from the hard blankness that a breaking-out stream of relief would come in the form of that long-awaited, long-angled-for confession.

But there would be a lengthy time to go yet. He recognised that. Would the time be too long? Would daylight and signs of approaching Bombay come in the end too soon?

In face of the blank visage opposite he was already finding it was even harder to keep awake himself. He was connected to his prey still. He knew, as it were instinctively, what the man was thinking, what he was feeling, or failing to feel. But the icy blankness that he saw stretching away for hours yet perhaps, till it broke, he hoped and hoped, in the flood of confession, gave him nothing to watch over. There would be no more telltale signs from the Bengali's face now. It would be the full flood or nothing.

But he had to wait for it. He had to endure.

And the tiredness began to assume an almost active malice inside him. It fought him and had to be held down at every instant. The fan-haired face of A. K. Bhattacharya swayed in his vision and misted over. Without daring to move and break the spell that now permeated every corner of the bogie drawing-room from the dim lights in the domed ceiling to the huddled snoring out-of-account A. K. Biswas down on the floor, he shook himself. He had to stay awake. Just that.

He pictured to himself what might happen otherwise. Say he succumbed, and A. K. Bhattacharya realised it. The tables would be simply turned then. The aggressor would swing back again into hapless victim and A. K. Bhattacharya would smile.

He pricked himself with that thought to stimulate his clogging mind into another hour, another half-hour, of wakefulness. He succeeded too. He was awake and alert in spite of everything when at precisely one minute before 5a.m. the train pulled into Manmad Station. So strong was his will indeed that in all the outward bustle of this eight-minute halt neither he nor A. K. Bhattacharya moved at all.

But almost as soon as they had set off again into their suffocating calm there came a squealing intrusion. The door leading from the sleeping compartment abruptly opened and Mrs Chiplunkar, severely white in her night sari, stood there.

'There is an unoccupied berth,' she said accusingly. 'I awoke at the station just now—one never sleeps well in trains—and I saw that one of the berths is empty. One or the other of you ought to take it for an hour or two at least.'

In a way Ghote could not but admire her, she was so right for what she was. She had been organizing for perhaps forty years, and here was one more small, practical thing to be put right. So she was putting it right.

But the utter unexpectedness of her entrance had also revived as if from deadened embers all his suspicions of the newcomer that he had considered entirely doused by his manoeuvre with the compartment door. Was he after all admiring the skill of a woman who could so surely do what Mrs Chiplunkar, the real Mrs Chiplunkar, would have done? Was this the first move?

His glance flicked back to A. K. Bhattacharya. So far he had not been transformed in an instant from frozen monolith into tiger crouching for the spring.

But neither had the intrusion, whatever purpose it had, left him unmoved. It had given him a chance to talk, and though his night guarded mind was being unusually slow to take it, he was about to seize the opportunity with all the gratitude that an unexpected rescue earns.

Ghote pushed himself, fighting sheer physical fatigue, to his feet.

'Mrs Chiplunkar, madam,' he said. 'I must request that you return at once to your berth. I am conducting an official interrogation. It is of prime importance that we are not disturbed.'

Mrs Chiplunkar—real or feigned?—looked at him.

'Very well, Inspector,' she said. 'I will do as you request.'

She turned and left them at once, but it was

280

apparent from the wideawake look in her eyes, deprived at this night hour of their severe spectacles, with the plain lenses, that she had seen and understood everything that was going on.

Ghote turned back to A. K. Bhattacharya. To his intense pleasure he saw that the tall Bengali had not quite roused himself from his torpor. He had begun to move, but now he stayed just where he was.

Quietly Ghote sat himself down again in his own chair and forced his face muscles, that cried out to relax in sleep, into a coldly aloof expression.

The wait began once more.

*   *   *

This time he was certain that an hour had passed and five minutes more. Nor was this because he was able to see through the uncurtained windows the first signs of the new day—he was uncertain of the exact time of dawn—but simply that, triumphant now against the dark hordes of sleep, he was at such a pitch of alertness that he felt certain he could keep time accurately in his head.

But what it was that shattered the silence after precisely one hour and five minutes boded no good. It was Mrs Chiplunkar again, and a Mrs Chiplunkar, real or false, enraged. Enraged and from glinting spectacles to the very foot of her newly put-on daytime sari ready for battle.

'Inspector,' she began at once, 'I have been lying awake ever since I was in here last, and I have been thinking.'

'Madam, I am conducting interrogation.'

'Yes, indeed, Inspector, I know that. And I know the method you have chosen. Inspector, you are torturing this poor unfortunate wretch.'

Was this it? Was this A. K. Bhattacharya's plan for his accomplice? No, his own brain was befuddled into stupidity. It could not be. The fellow could not have known he would be interrogated in this way. But what was the woman trying to do? Did she know A. K. Bhattacharya was on the point, the very point, of cracking? She must go.

'Inspector, I have come to insist you allow this man to sleep. No one should be deprived of this natural right.'

'Madam—'

But he was cut short. And by A. K. Bhattacharya, a rapidly reviving A. K. Bhattacharya.

'My dear lady, it is really most kind of you to intervene. I had, of course, intended to lodge an official complaint at the end of our journey. But I had thought it beneath my dignity to voice any plea to the man himself.'

He was reviving. He was pulling himself away from the black plain. It could be seen.

'Madam, leave,' Ghote shouted.

'I have no intention to leave. Not while you are torturing this poor man.'

And he could see in the glance he darted at A. K. Bhattacharya that the work was done. He was his old self again. In two seconds it had been done. His night's long work had been ruined. Yet he persisted in hoping he could save it.

'No,' he snapped, rising and positively trying to push Mrs Chiplunkar out. 'No, he is no poor man. And you know it well. He is A. K. Bhattacharya, wanted on charges of Rupees 72.85 lakhs, and you, you are his accomplice. You are no more Mrs Sulbha Chiplunkar than I am.'

The skinny woman in front of him drew herself up with enormous sharp pride. She was battling it out to the last then.

'I?' she said. 'I am not Mrs Chiplunkar? Then I should like you to tell me who I am.'

'That I do not know. But I do know you are not what you pretend.'

'And how can you know that?'

'Because,' answered Ghote in florid triumph, 'your spectacles have in them plain lenses.'

And Mrs Chiplunkar, the false Mrs Chiplunkar, actually blushed.

You could see the dark colour come up on her years-hardened skin. She blushed for shame like a schoolgirl.

'Well, Inspector,' she said, in a much-chastened voice, 'now I understand much that was not clear to me. You all along suspected I might be this man's accomplice.'

She favoured A. K. Bhattacharya with one quick glance of sheer disapproval.

'That was why,' she went on, 'when you left the drawing-room no doubt with the excellent intention of observing us in secret just as you returned he appeared to wink at me. He wanted you to believe I was a fraud. But although indeed my spectacles have plain lenses, they have them as mere show.'

She looked at him with something like defiance.

'What I have never told,' she said, 'never told a single person is why I wear such spectacles. But the reason is simple. Many years ago, when I was no more than a humble worker for Gandhiji's cause, one day he himself stopped to speak to me as I sat at my spinning-wheel spinning my daily allowance. I must have had for some reason my face very close to the thread because he stopped and said to me "You must wear spectacles, let me see you with some the next time I am here." Well, Inspector, my sight is good and always has been. It is better than average, a great deal. But since that day I have always worn a pair of spectacles. Their plain lenses deceived Gandhiji. They did not deceive you.'

CHAPTER EIGHT

Mrs Chiplunkar, the real Mrs Chiplunkar, disciple of Mahatma Gandhi, practiser over many years of the most innocent of deceptions, person of entrenched influence, practical doer of practical necessities, turned round and scuttled out of the bogie drawing-room like a shamed child seeking its mother's sari.

And Ghote turned implacably to A. K. Bhattacharya.

He hoped, with good reason he felt sure, that this abrupt removal of the figure who had by chance rescued him from his cement bonds of silence and despair might plunge him back again to the position he had been in at the moment when Mrs Chiplunkar, in daytime sari and glinting spectacles, had burst into the drawing-room. It would take, no doubt, a further span of time to get him once more as near to breakdown-point as he had been ten minutes before. But there was still enough perhaps. It was about 6a.m. now. They did not arrive at V.T. Station, Bombay, till 11.30a.m. It could be done.

But what actually happened when he turned back to the Bengali confidence-trickster came as a complete surprise to him.

'Inspector,' A. K. Bhattacharya said in a low, half-strangled voice, 'I am ready to plead

285

guilty at my trial.'

Ghote was almost unable to take it in. It seemed a happening of such unlikeliness that it could not have occurred.

But he had heard the words. And there sat A. K. Bhattacharya, the once gleaming A. K. Bhattacharya, looking up at him now with an expression that it would be correct to describe only as piteous.

A little forced thought, striving to combat the grey sludge of tiredness poised over his mind still, produced an explanation. The spectre of hope having appeared dazzlingly to the Bengali with the unexpected action of Mrs Chiplunkar—all the more unexpected since there plainly never had been any real accomplice ready with help—and that spectre having altogether suddenly been dispelled, the true bleakness of his position must have come rushing in on him at last. Everything then that had been said to him about the advantages of making a full confession and pleading guilty would have suddenly rung true. And, with little more than five hours in which to make a chance escape before the train arrived in Bombay and police by the dozen surrounded him, there must have seemed to be only one course open.

So he had spoken the words 'I am ready to plead guilty' and it was done.

Ghote drove his fatigued brain to produce with all rapidity the right series of responses.

'Excellent,' he heard himself say. 'You have made the only decision. Now what we will do is this. I will take a full note of everything you are ready to say. Produce every fact, I beg you, otherwise there may be charges to which you will appear not to have pleaded and the court would come down on you most severely.'

His brain was almost reeling, but he forced himself on.

'Now I will at once summon our good friend, Mr Ramaswamy, to come in here. I am sure he will assist. He will be witness for your statement. And when I have written it in précis form he will sign.'

'Very good,' said A. K. Bhattacharya, sounding as weary as he felt himself.

Quickly Ghote summoned the Madrasi Inspector of Forms, and within a few minutes he was sitting, in orange-spotted pyjamas and neat green dressing-gown, on one of the flowered arm-chairs, taking in everything that A. K. Bhattacharya was saying.

And he had a great deal to say, though Ghote noted that commendably he never once deviated from the point and he gave all the information he had to impart in a businesslike manner that contrasted strongly with the airy flights of his usual conversation. But then, he reflected, this was the man's business they were hearing all about.

He sat, note-pad on his knee, pencil busily flying in automatic though rusty shorthand, taking it all down, the outline of frauds amounting in all to some fifty-six separate cases. There were technical details of the precise statues forged, there were the curious foreign names of museum experts to be laboriously written down in block capitals (A. K. Bhattacharya never once hesitated over a spelling), there were sums of money to be entered, there were dates, times and places.

When the train made its last station-halt before Bombay, at Nasik Road, Ghote did not even look up to see the familiar sights of this disembarkation point for his old police college. Instead he took advantage of the stillness to make his shorthand outlines even faster and catch up a little on A. K. Bhattacharya's rapid recital. And all too soon they were off again and he was once more falling behind in his scribbling of fact after fact after fact.

They made a truly formidable catalogue. Ghote had hardly energy to spare to reflect on what he was hearing. He was whacking at his already dead-tired brain like a tonga-wallah frenziedly thwacking with his frayed whip at the lean ribs of his horse with an impatient fare making promises. But it did once briefly occur to him with a sense of awe that, when what he was writing was completed, it would almost beyond doubt constitute the greatest record of forgery and fraud in the whole annals of the Indian Police.

And at last it was done.

Ghote looked up.

'I will begin making précis statement version now,' he said leadenly.

A. K. Bhattacharya, dropping back from his position of controlled alertness on the sofa, gave one happy smile of relaxation.

'Good gracious me,' he said, 'there are, I find, quite unexpected pleasures in possessing, perhaps for the first time in my adult life, an easy conscience.'

Mr Ramaswamy giggled in pleasure.

But Ghote knew he could spare no force to join this atmosphere of celebration. Bone-wearily he tugged his pages and pages of shorthand out of his notebook and at the head of the blank sheet that was revealed he inscribed, writing as neatly as the sway of the train would permit, the words 'Statement of A. K. Bhattacharya.'

Then he began writing, the tip of his tongue moving back and forth across his dried lips with the concentration he needed both to fight against the train's motion and against the tiredness which now seemed to leave only his eyes, nose and mouth above the surface of a sucking black ocean.

After a little, though he scarcely noticed it, Mrs Chiplunkar came in. She said a very quiet good morning to Mr Ramaswamy and directed at A. K. Bhattacharya the sort of look she might have given from the top of some well-wooded hill at a village inhabited principally by one of what used to be called the criminal tribes.

Shortly after she had come in the rotund little cook followed and busily took orders for breakfasts, anxious only that the greatest possible quantity of his cooking should be eaten, as if nothing at all out of the ordinary had happened in the bogie on this particular trip. Ghote hardly noticed when he brushed aside all offers of sustenance.

The smell of food brought into the gathering in the drawing-room the two hippies, and Ghote was just aware that Mr Ramaswamy was explaining to them in a low voice what was going on.

Glancing up to seek clarification on some obscure point from A. K. Bhattacharya—every such question was carefully answered, even though the tall Bengali was plainly lightly asleep between whiles—he realised that the news of the confession had had a certain definite effect both on the aggressive Red and on practical, pretty Mary Jane.

Red was looking, Ghote saw, at A. K. Bhattacharya with an expression more than usually hostile. And, without even giving the matter a moment's thought, it was obvious why the Bengali was attracting the full brunt of Red's disapproval. Confessing his crimes was thoroughly unworthy. Till now he had been a master anarchist, the embodiment of the forces breaking up the corrupt ways of a materialist society. By his confession he had simply acknowledged the rules that society laid down.

Ghote went on with his writing, with no energy to spare for considering Red's disillusion. And not even energy enough to resent the fact that A. K. Bhattacharya could sleep. Every ounce of effort he could summon up he was directing like a sharpened knife to pinning the words down on the pages of his note-book. Then at last they could be duly signed and witnessed. And that must be done before A. K. Bhattacharya, refreshed perhaps, could think of changing his mind and withdrawing the whole avowal.

Gradually the pages were filled with the script that Ghote had been taught in distant, distant days as a schoolboy sitting cross-legged with a slate in front of him forming the twirls and twists of the letters, tongue emerging from between taut lips, eyes darting up occasionally to estimate the threat of the old teacher's erratic cane.

The next time Ghote had a question to ask he took in on the side the fact that Mary Jane had begun to shift the centre of her interest. Earlier he had noticed, without noticing, that she had been looking laughably balked of her prey since A. K. Bhattacharya no longer needed tender assistance. Now she had got up from the sofa where she had been eating the delicious breakfast the cook had produced and had perched on the arm of Red's chair. Her hand was on his shoulder. That was all. But Ghote knew what it meant: here after all is the person who really needs looking after.

A. K. Bhattacharya shook his head to clear the doziness out of it and supplied the answer to the particular query Ghote had put. Ghote went back to his endless, endless writing. A. K. Bhattacharya lapsed into a light sleep again. Mary Jane began quietly stroking Red's shoulders.

At last and at last the end of the long document began to approach. A silence quivered in the drawing-room as everybody watched Ghote at his task. An atmosphere of helpful sympathy washed up to him in warm successions, like a torpid sea running up parched sands. Even A. K. Biswas, sitting cross-legged on the floor, wide-eyed with wonder, was moving his tongue along the choppy ridges of his stump teeth in sympathy with the movements of Ghote's pen.

Even the subject of the monumental task himself was, through his doze, radiating sympathy for the carrying out of the work.

Out of the corner of his eye Ghote was aware that young Red had shifted his position on the chair. He was looking up at Mary Jane now. Under the heavy bar of his auburn moustache his mouth had ceased to hold its hard twist. There might be one less inconoclast in the hated materialist world, but there was still compensation.

Ghote went back to writing the very last few pages. He realised that the train had come to a halt and that they were at Igatpuri at the top of the Ghats. The great steam locomotive that had hauled them almost all the way across the subcontinent was being replaced by the diesel that would take them swiftly into V.T. Station, Bombay. With the rhythmic sway temporarily stilled his pen could race all the faster. He buried his head and wrote.

Then, some ten minutes after their departure from Igatpuri and just before he had finished, he was aware of voices.

'That's fine with me,' young Red was saying.

'To the States? Really?' Mary Jane answered.

'Why not?'

'You won't hate leaving India?'

'No,' Red assured her. 'I think I've got all I can out of India.'

Ghote was half-aware that they were kissing. In public again.

A. K. Biswas, that deplorably bad-breathed card-sharper, no doubt to cover his embarrassment at this naked scene, broke in loudly, addressing his fellow-criminal.

'Hey, listen, bhai,' he said. 'I gotta tell you this. Prison not too bad, you know. You get to eat there. You can sleep plenty too. Prison okay.'

But A. K. Bhattacharya was still lightly dozing. Ghote wrote the last words of the whole long statement, ' . . . unfortunately the heat of the professor's cigar-lighter melted the wax beneath the layer of stone-powder, and he lodged a complaint.' Then he got up and lightly shook A. K. Bhattacharya's shoulder.

'Please read over carefully,' he said, 'initial the foot of each page and sign at end.'

It did not take him very long to skim through the sheets, muttering occasionally 'Yes, ah, yes' or even 'Good, very good' and jotting down his initials—those haunting letters A.K.B.—just before flicking over each page. In a short time he looked across at Ghote.

'Inspector,' he said, 'allow me to offer you my sincere congratulations on a most exemplary job. Not a detail has been omitted. Not one is wrong. I sign with pleasure.'

'And now, Mr Ramaswamy, if you would witness?' Ghote asked.

And down went the neat precise words 'M. N. Ramaswamy, Inspector of Forms and Stationery.'

And it was finished, completed, secured.

'My dear e-sir,' Mr Ramaswamy said, looking at Ghote with keen anxiety, 'you are half-killed with fatigue, isn't it? I perceive it. Take my advice, my dear fellow, and retire to sleep.'

'No,' said Ghote, shaking his head dully.

'Prisoner.'

'Prisoner? Prisoner? I am afraid I do not understand—Ah, my dear sir, you are referring of course to this gentleman. But my dear fellow, you should not have any fears on his account. He is already quite a reformed character. Are you not, my dear e-sir?'

'I am, I am,' beamed A. K. Bhattacharya. 'Reformed, and like my good friend, Inspector Ghote here, devilishly tired.'

He yawned.

'Inspector,' Mr Ramaswamy said to Ghote, 'allow me to beg you a personal favour. Put me in charge of this incorrigible rogue until you have slept an hour or two next door. I beg.'

Ghote looked up at him, almost unseeing with fatigue.

And his mind at last yielded. After all what was there to fear? They had stopped for the last time. It was downhill all the way now to Bombay. Escape was not really a possibility, even if his prisoner still wanted to.

He tried to rise to his feet to go to the bedroom compartment, but he was unable even to make the effort. He slumped sideways in his chair.

'Poor fellow, poor fellow,' he dimly heard Mr Ramaswamy say. 'Let us leave him here. I will go next door to the bedroom compartment with, ha, ha, my prisoner.'

Those were the last words Ghote at all registered before total blackness lapped him round.

It was a blackness which, to him, seemed to last however only for two or three seconds.

At the end of that time—or what had seemed to be that time only—a violent shaking dragged him back to reality.

He emerged into the light of day much like the great train that was bearing him towards Bombay had emerged from the tunnels it had encountered on its route. For a long time light was the merest pinprick, far away. Gradually it grew larger, but remained circumscribed by the blackness of the tunnel all round it. Only after a long while did it dispel the blackness altogether.

When it did so Ghote was able to put away the confused and mysterious impressions that had greeted him as he slowly emerged from his sleep, and to realise that Mr Ramaswamy was leaning over him, desperately shaking him by the shoulder, and that Mr Ramaswamy's forehead was gashed wide open in a deep cut.

CHAPTER NINE

Blinking dazedly from the depth of his sleep, Inspector Ghote became aware that drops of blood from the gashed forehead of Mr Ramaswamy, leaning loomingly over him, were actually falling on to his own upturned face, tapping on to his chin and neck.

'Bhattacharya,' Mr Ramaswamy croaked out. 'Gone. Escaped. E-struck me.'

Ghote found he was on his feet. The last swathes of sleep dropped from him as if they had been actually entangling his legs. He looked automatically at his wrist-watch. It was 9.39a.m. He had slept for a whole hour and more. There was less than two hours left of the journey.

The thoughts hardly took any time to flash on to his brain. And then he was asking questions, the right questions, automatically.

Mr Ramaswamy's only just coherent replies told him that his prisoner had bided his time until such minor, almost play-acting vigilance as the Inspector of Forms had shown had been entirely dissipated. And then, without a word or sign of warning, he had risen up and struck him a single knock-out blow with his heavy copy of *The Art Treasures of Bali*.

The blow, however, had not been as crippling as it had been intended to be, because Mr Ramaswamy had begun to come to just as the Bengali was in the act of removing his wallet before disappearing from the bedroom compartment. By a strong effort of will he had managed to drag himself out to Ghote.

Right, Ghote thought, there are only two places Bhattacharya can have gone to: the bathroom cubicles or the kitchen.

He was through the door to the lobby in an

instant. One glance into the open bathrooms was enough to tell him Bhattacharya was not there. He flung open the narrow door that cut off the kitchen.

And sitting on the floor with a stupid, warding-off-trouble grin on his moony face, there was the fat cook. Ghote guessed at once what must have happened: the fellow had resented his brushing aside of breakfast earlier and had become at that moment an adherent of Bhattacharya's again.

The narrow window of the kitchen, the only other exit from the bogie besides the locked door, was still open.

But, Ghote registered, the train was moving and moving at speed on its descent of the steep Ghats. Bhattacharya could not have jumped off. All he could have done was to have clung to the side and moved slowly along till he could find somewhere where he could get in and trust somehow to hide himself.

Slowly.

Bhattacharya could work his way along the train only slowly.

'Help me through that window or you will find your face kicked in,' he snarled at the still hopefully grinning cook.

Then he lunged for the small opening at the top of the window. To his delight at once he felt the cook's soft hands pushing at his body. He heaved hard himself, wriggled and tugged and at last he was through, clutching on to the top of the window with his hands and with his feet sliding about looking for a purchase on the running-board.

They found it, and he looked rapidly one way and then another along the length of the huge train.

Three long carriages down towards the rear he caught one split-second, tantalising glimpse of a brown, sandal-shod leg disappearing in at an open window. The glimpse was so brief it almost might have been a piece of pure wishfulness. But Ghote grimly set off in that direction at once.

Bhattacharya, he reckoned, must aim somehow to disappear while still on the swiftly-moving train. He might try to disguise himself in some way, or he might hope to find some cranny where he could lie undetected until he got a chance, perhaps as they slowed at the approaches to V.T. Station, to drop down on to the tracks. So the important thing was to give him the very least possible time out of sight.

He stretched his left arm to its utmost, grasped a smoke-grimed, dust-encrusted projection and swung himself along. Again he stretched, grasped, swung.

But had he seen what he thought he had? Had it really been a brown, sandal-shod leg there? Could he have imagined it entirely?

Stretch, grasp, swing. Caked dust from the carriage side smeared across his already sweating face. He became conscious of the combined heats of the exhaust fumes of the big diesel engine far ahead and of the already pitiless sun beating down on his back.

No, he must not allow imagination to cloud his inner knowledge that he had really seen what he had seen. He would cling to that.

Stretch, grasp, swing. It was not easy to breathe, but he must hurry. He must not spare himself in the least. Stretch and stretch, grasp and quickly swing.

Had it really been—? No. Not that.

And swing. And swing.

Now, there was an open window just in sight. Was that where that leg and sandal-shod foot had disappeared? They had disappeared. They had been there. And, yes, Bhattacharya was bound to have tried to get in at the first window that offered.

Stretch. Swing. One more. Stretch.

It was a third-class carriage that Ghote found he was looking into. His first impression was of torsos and limbs. They were everywhere, sprawled on top of and beside one another. It must be incredibly airless in there, he thought. No wonder they had tried opening a window. And, of course, that would only make it hotter in all probability and certainly dirtier.

He thrust his head well inside and peered each way to see if he could get a glimpse of Bhattacharya. But in all the multitude of bodies in saris, in dhotis, in shirts, in trousers, in loincloths, there was of course little hope of that.

'Help me in, please,' he demanded sharply.

A man who had been sitting on the floor just beside the window, looking at him with much the same close interest as he himself had looked at the other people in the carriage, pushed himself to his feet bringing a cheerfully grinning face close up to his own.

There was a sharp smell of chewed betel.

'It is a long time since Igatpuri,' the man said. 'You will be glad to get in also.'

He put a hand under Ghote's armpit and heaved. Ghote, thankful for the great freemasonry of travellers without tickets, scrabbled with his feet and in a second or two was safely inside the train again.

He thanked his helper.

'You are welcome,' the man said. 'And not you only. It is not five minutes since I helped the last one in.'

Ghote's heart leapt. So it had not been a vision of hope. Bhattacharya had got in here.

He thrust himself up on to tiptoes and raked the jam-packed carriage from end to end in search of his quarry. He did not spot him. But he knew he would have been lucky to have done so. In all the press of people in the length of the carriage it would be perfectly possible for a man, even a tall man like the Bengali, not to have been visible from his view-point.

But the scent of the hunted was in his nostrils. He flung himself round on the man who had helped him in.

'Not five minutes ago?' he pounced. 'Quick, give me a description of the fellow. He was tall? Wearing a white kurta and dhoti? With sandals? Yes?'

He snapped the questions out. First, be sure you are on the right scent. Then find out what you can of the direction your quarry has taken.

But he had forgotten he was not a hunter. Not in the eyes of the member of the freemasonry of ticketless travellers who had been so glad to help him in. And his mistake cost him dear.

The grin vanished from the betel-wafting mouth. The lips closed in sullen silence.

'Another without ticket . . .' Ghote began, striving hard for the old note of cheerful comradeship.

But he knew that he was not going to be able to wipe the look of sullen watchfulness away, and he did not. He reverted to the policeman.

'Listen to me,' he barked, thrusting his face close to his witness's. 'That man is an escaped prisoner. Which way did he go? Where is he? Answer up or it will be the worse for you.'

'I am not knowing, sahib. I am knowing nothing.'

'Which way did he go?'

Ghote stretched high and darted furious

glances up and down the length of the humanity-packed carriage. But with several hundred people in it, on the floor, perched on the luggage racks, on the hard wooden benches, it was by no means possible to see everywhere. Bhattacharya could be crawling along towards either end of the carriage completely out of sight. And he might too have spotted the fact that he was being chased, and then he would take special precautions to keep well hidden.

He turned in a fury to the sullen betel-chewer. Here was his last link with Bhattacharya.

'Now, speak up and speak quickly,' he shouted. 'Which way did that man go?'

'Sahib, there was no man.'

'All right. But watch out. When we get to Bombay expect to find the railway police on your tail.'

And he left him.

The only thing to do now was to search. To search as quickly as he could, but absolutely thoroughly and with system. He must keep Bhattacharya running if it was at all possible. That way he might force him to betray himself.

It was a toss-up which way to set out first. The window he had come in by, the only one open in the whole length of the crowded, stifling carriage he saw, was almost in the exact middle. Bhattacharya might be sneaking away in either direction.

He turned to his right and started to thrust

his way all along the length of the carriage, shooting glances to either side. He would get him in the end, he thought. He had tracked him to the carriage here, and there was time and time enough before the train started to slow at the approaches to V.T. Station. He would get him.

But he would like to have spotted him all the same.

He reached the far end of the carriage, having thrust past more than a hundred people, he reckoned. There was a long smear of yellow-brown sauce superimposed on the grey dust on his shirt where he had tried to go too quickly past someone busy eating a chapatti dipped into a small brass pot.

Ahead of him was the lavatory compartment. Its door was closed.

He could be in there, he reasoned. It would provide the most secure hiding-place in the carriage, or equally secure with the lavatory at the other end.

He pushed at the door. It opened. He stepped inside. The place smelt appallingly in the brewed-up heat. It needed a bit of looking into to make absolutely sure no one was flattened against a wall inside. He had to make a strong effort to carry out that search conscientiously.

But it was still fruitless. He turned with relief to pull open the door. Outside it had been by no means pleasant to the nostrils.

There had been the odour of a dozen or more different types of food. There had been the scents the women were using. There had been plenty of betel being chewed besides that which the man who had helped Bhattacharya in had been masticating. There had been the concentrated sweat of hundreds of hot bodies. There had been the urine of children, and their vomit.

But he would be glad indeed to be out there. The door resisted him. He pulled at it impatiently. Still it seemed to be being held. He gave it a sharp, furious tug. It swung in on him.

Bhattacharya's helpful ticketless friend was there. Ghote opened his mouth to curse him hard. And then, just in time, he controlled himself.

The fellow must have made his way up the length of the carriage a little behind him. It was not at all easy to move about in the close-packed jam. Why had he done so? Could it be because that threat of bringing the railway police on to him had had some effect? It might be.

'You were wanting me?' he asked the man eagerly.

'Inside there I am wanting to go,' the man answered with a nod of his head towards the lavatory.

So that was all it had been. Angrily Ghote turned away and subjected the carriage to

305

another prolonged scrutiny, hauling himself up on the edge of a wooden bench to do so. A sprawlingly fat woman looked down at his shoe tucking into her voluminous sari and began complaining. He took no notice. Bhattacharya must be here somewhere. Literally under his eyes. He would find him.

But, if he was to find him, it would not be just yet. There was no sign of him anywhere.

Well, he would set about asking people. And at the same time he would not relax his watch over the carriage. He would get him in the end.

He plunged into the mass of people with his questions, and into the vast variety of their baggage with searching eyes and often searching hands. There were tin trunks and wooden chests which he demanded to have opened. There were cloth bundles of every shape, size and colour. And he prodded at each one of them. There were baskets, round and square, water-pots of brass and earthenware, bowls to eat from, bowls to spit into, cages for chickens, cradles for babies. If anywhere a man could be hidden, Ghote looked.

He met argument after argument, screeching and refusals, but he allowed nothing to put him off. Implacably he insisted and battle after battle he won. He ordered in Hindi. He ordered in Marathi. He ordered in crude English. He even ordered in elementary

306

Bengali. And even during the middle of the fiercest altercations he darted looks everywhere, up and down the whole packed and crammed carriage.

Painstakingly he ploughed on. He broke up passionate discussions of marriages and funerals and demanded that one by one each of the participants would answer his questions. He interrupted the many and varied meals that were being continuously eaten to put his questions again and to insist that the trunk that was perhaps serving as a table should be opened and rummaged through, even though it might be hardly big enough to hold a performing dwarf—and there was a group of those in the carriage.

Each time that he moved on from one questioned group to the next unquestioned one he had to heave and push himself past human bodies, close-packed and soft and each issuing its private supply of heat. He had to squirm and wriggle, to contort himself past mothers with babies at the breast, to slide along beside mothers with babies performing their natural functions, to disentangle children from his feet, to unhook his clothing from their toys, their arms and their legs.

And as he got nearer and nearer the far end of the carriage, without getting even one clue to the whereabouts of his quarry from any of the dozens and dozens of people he had questioned, he became convinced that it must be in the lavatory that he was approaching that his man was hiding.

Next to its closed door a beggar sat pushed up against the wall in what was probably the most unpleasant part of the whole far-from-pleasant carriage. The creature was dressed only in a gunny-sack and it was even possible that it was not a man but a woman, with as a sole possession a wooden bowl with a split down its side. As he neared this being Ghote became convinced that he would get his answer at last from between those toothless lips.

There might be trouble taking Bhattacharya again, if he had shut himself in that stinking lavatory knowing the hunt was near. It would make it a little easier to have confirmation that he was certainly there.

And where else could he be now?

One last unlikely wooden box remained to be searched. Should he leave it out and question the beggar at once?

He decided not to. True, the box was surely so small that the tall Bengali could never squeeze into it. But then choosing somewhere as unlikely as this would be his only way of escape.

'Police,' he said tersely to the wide-eyed, crouching mother with three small children clinging to her who appeared to be the owner of the box. 'Police. I must search your box. Open it please.'

Slowly and in totally frightened silence the girl—girl she was despite her three children—took a key from inside her sari and turned it in the lock of the box. She opened the lid. Ghote peered in.

Just as he did so the notion came into his head that the beggar by the lavatory door must be Bhattacharya somehow in disguise. It was nonsense. He knew it. But the conviction was so strong that he lifted his head up and glared hard at the miserable creature.

No, it could not be. The features just were not at all the same. He plunged his hand into the softness of the few poor clothes in the box in front of him, as a last gesture to thoroughness. And then he stood up.

It was the lavatory then.

Not stopping now to bother to get his confirmation from the beggar, he pushed quickly towards the closed door and without hesitation threw it open.

A shock of foul-smellingness worse than even the first lavatory came out at him. He strode forward. But even before crossing the threshold he was almost certain that the evil-reeking area was deserted.

He carried out his search, however, with what he could muster of his old thoroughness, and then he knew that it was indeed over. Bhattacharya was not there.

He even questioned the beggar then. But it was only to stop himself having to think about what he knew.

At last even this final pitiful resource was denied to him. The beggar had not seen anyone at all resembling the tall kurta-clad Bengali.

So at last he had to face the fact squarely that he had lost his man. And when he did so he was able to see at once how it had come about: Bhattacharya had tricked him with the aid of the grinning, betel-smelling fellow who had hauled him into the carriage. He had got out again by the same window that he had come in by, and he had done it in those few moments that he himself had been in the first lavatory. That had been why the door had been held for a second or two as he had tried to leave.

And that was that. He had lost Bhattacharya, completely.

CHAPTER TEN

Pressed up against a wall in the close stink of the third-class carriage as the Calcutta Mail thundered swiftly along the narrow coastal plain that it had now reached on the last stage of its journey to Bombay, only half an hour away, Inspector Ghote thought about the quarry he had let escape. Despite the engulfing misery that washed down on him, he found himself possessed of a hard smooth rock of determination still somehow to get his man. The fellow was still on the train. In an uncertain world that was certain. At this speed he could not get off. But equally unless he was found, and soon, there would come a moment when the train would slow. And then a jump from some point far distant from himself, a quick dash to cover and it would be all over.

Where would he have gone when he got out of that window? What would he have done to hide?

Churningly Ghote pushed every scrap of information he had gathered, every item he had deduced about Bhattacharya into the mill of his mind. There was an answer somewhere. Put a person into a known situation and they would react in a certain way. He knew what Bhattacharya's situation was. Did he know enough of his mind to find what solution he had arrived at?

The great train hurried on. Minute by minute it reduced the distance to V.T. Station and the large police party no doubt waiting to greet him and his valuable prisoner. His failure would at an instant become known to everybody. Already they had crossed the creek at Thana, where on the way out an innocently playful Bengali gentleman had won a wager about guessing his fellow-passenger's occupation.

Beneath, the train-wheels clicked and

clacked in urgent rhythm. Through the clear-glass third-class windows the jungly countryside of the lake district of Vehar rushed by, hurried and meaningless. And somewhere along the train, this length of steel and wood, bolted, riveted and chained together, Bhattacharya too was being rushed along at precisely the same speed.

Desperately Ghote reviewed the facts he had learnt about the man from that moment of meeting—how pleased he must have felt with himself as he leant forward and greeted the idiot inspector he had planned to sit directly opposite—on through his gradual revelation as less and less merely a figure of mischief, more and more an actively evil person, till there had come the culminating moment of the attack on helpful, pleasant, decent, little Mr Ramaswamy.

Was Mr Ramaswamy being looked after now? Yes, Mary Jane could be relied on for that. But he must not allow himself the luxury of such thoughts. Bhattacharya. Bhattacharya. That was who he must think about.

Bhattacharya. Bhattacharya. The drumming wheels of the great train seemed to be repeating the rhythm in his head.

Bhattacharya, Bhattacharya, Bhattacharya.

Repeating and repeating the rhythm, faster and ever faster.

Surely much faster than when they had covered this same stretch of rail on the way out? They would be early into V.T. Station. Early.

He glanced at his watch and did a brief calculation. Yes, he was quite right. At this rate the train would be in before 11.30, decidedly before. It was unfair. His precious ration of time was being wantonly cut down.

Bhattacharya, Bhattacharya. Listen to those wheels.

And then, with a click like a quietly closing door, the facts he had learnt about this man, the suppositions he had made about him, even the scarcely conscious observations made in this very carriage, all came softly together, neatly fitting and true.

For a moment, rigid-faced, Ghote worked out what it was that he would have to do. And then he pushed his way brutally across the crammed carriage to the one open window. Without a word of explanation he hauled it fully down, put his two hands on the bottom edge and heaved himself out.

What he had to do, he knew, was to get on to the roof of the train. If he was to get hold of Bhattacharya he had to do so as quickly as possible. Before very long the first slowing-up or halt might occur. With the train rapidly getting more and more ahead of schedule it could easily be stopped at a signal at any time. And unless he had got to Bhattacharya before then this last slim chance would be gone.

He twisted himself round rapidly, reached

high up and found secure holding-places for his hands on the dust-encrusted edge of the carriage roof. He kicked himself clear of the window and started to heave upwards. His scrabbling right leg encountered some small projection. He did not dare spare the time to look down to see exactly what it was. He braced himself and heaved again. His face came level with the grey expanse of the curving roof. He took his right hand from its hold and sought another one farther into the roof. There was nothing to grip on, but the embedded layer of dust and grime on the rooftop seemed to give some hope of support.

He decided he must risk it. The seconds were ticking by. A vision of his body falling away from the onward-thundering train came into his mind, a slight figure in white shirt and trousers heavily blackened down the front, tumbling floppily. Resolutely he pushed the thought back.

And then he heaved upwards again.

The train did seem at that moment to lean out against him as it took a long gentle curve. But he flung himself scrapingly forward and found his face mercifully kissing the thick encrusted grime of the roof.

He swung his dangling legs up and for a second or two lay just where he was, willing his body to stick limpet-like to the rocking roof under it. But then the small, iron-hard thing that was his will asserted itself. There was no time to be lost. He must hurry along the train roof to his destination. He must get to his feet and walk. He might even have to run.

He took one deep breath, the acid smell of smoke-layered grime sharp in his nostrils, and then he pushed himself upwards with his hands. Even when he was doing no more than kneel he felt the rock and sway of the thundering train embrace him. What would it do to him when he was standing fully upright? How much would it swing him in a rising, unbreakable rhythm till it flung him off when he no longer had toes, knees and clutching hands on the safe roof under him?

He had to find out.

Slowly he straightened his back, keeping his knees wide-spread. But this was not enough. He bent forward again and pushed himself to his feet, turning as he did so to face the front of the onward-rushing train.

With legs wide braced he felt he could do it. The ground below, an orange-brown hurrying blur, looked far, far farther down than he had ever expected. But nevertheless, high and exposed as he was, he thought he could endure it. Only he had to move. He had to go forward. And fast.

He looked ahead. The train was still hurrying through the countryside. There were fields now instead of the jungle there had been earlier. But it could not be long before they would get to the first traffic-checks, signals, points, sidings, on the outermost limits of the Bombay rail complex. And then would come that inevitable, fatal slowing-down.

He took a step forward. He felt as if his body lurched terribly as he did so, and the roof in front of him that, when he had been lying flat on it, had hardly seemed curved at all now looked as if it fell away to either side so steeply that keeping any foothold would be impossible.

But the very centre was flat, or almost so. He knew it must be. He forced himself to give his reason full charge. And he set forward on the narrow path.

By the time he had got to the end of the carriage he had already begun to move at a cautious lope. But then he was confronted with the gap before the next carriage. And again he was astounded at how big it was. Looking at trains off and on all his life it had always seemed that carriages were so close to each other as to be practically touching. Up here, isolated and in the clutch of the train's swaying rhythm, the distance between himself and the curving roof of the carriage ahead seemed enormous. Too far even to jump.

Nonsense, he told himself sharply. Estimate the exact distance. Less than four feet. A jump like that would be nothing down on the ground. Jump.

He found himself, swaying and swinging fantastically it seemed, splay-legged and wide-armed, but well on the next roof. He set off again at once at a low-crouching, loping run. He must put to the test his inspired guess at Bhattacharya's answer at the very first possible moment. In a matter of seconds he was tackling the jump to the next carriage. And then on again.

The train seemed to be going even faster now. Ahead the countryside was wide and open. In the distance the washed blue sky looked grey and heavy. Bombay. That would be the smoke of mill chimneys and the thousand upon thousand of cooking fires. They were getting terribly near.

He increased his pace. Another jump.

And his foot slipped.

He felt his whole body toppling. His left leg was skidding wildly down the curved surface of the roof. Under his down-turned face he saw a dust-humped projection. He grabbed with one hand. His digging fingers found something hard. His sliding fall was checked.

And on again. Up and on again. No time to waste. Do not spare a quarter-second to think how much safer it would feel to progress on hands and knees, to reason out that that might be a better way of getting there because it would be surer. There was no time.

The end of the carriage appeared ahead of his running feet. Another jump. Would it—?

He forced himself to remember that he had jumped twice before without trouble, that a slip was a slip, a mere accident.

He leapt. And landed four-squarely.

On once more, and another jump, and another good landing. And then suddenly he found that the racing train had reached one of the enormous causeways that take the rail line over the low sea marshes to the north of Bombay Island itself. If the ground had been far below before, now the dark, moss-green level stretches seemed infinitely much further away. It was as if he was on, not a train, but an aeroplane. A low-flying aeroplane certainly but going at a height sickeningly greater than anything connected with the firm earth.

His loping feet came involuntarily to a halt. He could think only of flinging himself flat on the comforting surface of the train roof in front of him. Of flinging himself flat and shutting his eyes and letting the whole experience take on the distance of a nightmare.

Bhattacharya. What did Bhattacharya matter? Why should he lose his life for him?

And in half an instant more he would have taken that abnegating plunge forward to cling to safety. But there was something in him that stopped him. Some tiny tenacious claw in his mind that had fastened on to the master confidence-trickster and which would not let go.

He stumbled on again and took with ease the next leap forward on to the last but one carriage before the diesel-engine, even despite the fact that they were still on the causeway.

But the next and last leap came at an even worse time. The ridiculously speeding train had come to a comparatively sharp bend. At its normal rate for this point there would have been no trouble. But it was going a great deal faster than normal and the sway of the enormous weight as it hurled into the bend was all the more powerful. Ghote felt himself flung to the side as if by a great invisible giant. It was a force he could not resist. He felt his feet sucked from the roof.

With all his strength he twisted and hurled his body downwards. It struck the roof, dangerously near the edge. But it did strike the roof, and once again he clung safely to its grime, with hard-digging, scrabbling fingers.

And in a very short time the train came out of that vast, almost catastrophic swing. It righted itself and roared on. Ghote got to his feet again. As he did so heat from the enormous, whirring, square-shouldered diesel just ahead struck at his face like a red-hot blast. But he put his head down and marched forward.

In an instant more he would know whether his guess had been right.

Five more steps. Four. The train seemed to be going even faster than ever. Three steps. Two. One.

Now. Now he was there, standing a little crouchingly looking down into the driver's cab of the heavy, powerful diesel. And as he had known it would be from the moment he had recalled the statement made, it seemed, in a distant, distant past by one Mr Banerjee that if he had to travel by lowly, earth-bound train he would do so in the driver's cab, there was Bhattacharya.

He was standing at the controls with his hand nonchalantly resting on a lever, looking even from the set of his shoulders superbly sure of himself. No wonder the train had been going at that fantastic, telltale speed.

For a second or two Ghote watched. And then, judging his moment, he launched himself slitheringly downwards into the open-backed cab.

He landed, easily and on the balls of his feet, right behind Bhattacharya and between him and the white-vested, strongly-muscled Anglo-Indian driver and his equally tough-looking younger mate.

'A. K. Bhattacharya,' he said sharply, 'you are again in custody.'

The Bengali swept round. His face was a painting of fury. Ghote looked him directly in the eyes.

'No,' Bhattacharya shouted. 'No, I will not be pinioned. You will not do it.'

'It is too late,' Ghote said. 'I have found you, and we are nearly there.'

Without turning round he spoke to the driver.

'Take the controls again, please,' he said.

'And come into V.T. Station at proper speed.'

The driver came cautiously round Bhattacharya's side and grasped the control lever. Ghote felt through the soles of his vibrating feet that the huge train was at once slackening its pace.

Bhattacharya leant towards the driver.

'Listen,' he said, taking Mr Ramaswamy's wallet from his pocket, 'I have money. It is yours, all of it for the two of you, if you help me throw this fellow out on to the rails.'

'They will not do it,' Ghote said, without moving.

'Money, money,' Bhattacharya said to the driver. 'There is a hell of a lot of money in this wallet. More than you earn in a year.'

'Yes, it may be a lot,' Ghote said. 'But he has more than one year to live. He is a family man, no doubt. He has his responsibilities in the world. You and your like cannot offer him enough.'

'Money, money,' Bhattacharya repeated, thrusting the open wallet in front of the driver's face.

In reply the man said something, but what it was they none of them could hear since at that moment the great train smoothly passed on an adjoining line a little busy tank-engine, squirting steam and making so much racket that nothing round it for yards was at all audible. But at last the driver's voice emerged again from the noise-blanket.

'Keep back, if you please. Keep back. Pushing that thing in my face: I can't see where the hell I'm going.'

Ghote permitted himself the hint of a smile as from his back pocket he drew out the handcuffs that he had brought all the way from Calcutta unused.

'Hold out your hands,' he said to Bhattacharya.

And, as he clicked the steel bracelets round the wrists of the Bengali's long-fingered hands, he made a last comment.

'You will find these are something no amount of talking will get you out of.'

The train clattered and rattled on, superbly unconscious of the petty drama that had just been completed along its length. It slowed, it almost ground to a halt, it clicked at points from one line to another, it passed perilously close to an old woman picking up pieces of coal from between the tracks, it slotted into a place in the complicated schedules of Bombay suburban traffic.

And Ghote stood beside his handcuffed prisoner and allowed his thoughts to play a little. Could, for instance, he asked himself, A. K. Bhattacharya, that wizard, perhaps dematerialise and thus escape the steel bands on his wrists? Could he turn himself to liquid silver perhaps and just flow away into the nearby waiting sea? Could he by the power of thought turn himself into a bird, twig-legged and twig-wristed, and fly high, high up into the great arch of the sky?

'Inspector Ghote.'

'Ghote.'

'Wake up, man. Wake up.'

He jerked his head round, looking wildly this way and that.

D.S.P. Samant was standing just below him. He was on the platform at V.T. Station. They were back.